"**D**on't worry," Logan said to Zoe. "I'm sure Scratch had nothing to do with what happened to Pelly."

I hope you're right, Logan, Zoe thought. But she could see the looks on the SNAPA agents' faces, and it was hard to disagree with their skepticism. There was the broken anklet right there. There was Scratch's shifty, strange behavior and the blood on his teeth. And there was his history with Pelly, which the agents didn't even know about.

All signs point to guilty. And if this was all our fault and we lose the trial, that means the end of Scratch . . . and the end of this Menagerie.

THE MENACE

DRAGON

E
GERIE
n TRIAL

TUI T. SUTHERLAND
KARI SUTHERLAND

HARPER
An Imprint of HarperCollins Publishers

The Menagerie: Dragon on Trial

Copyright © 2014 by Tui T. Sutherland and Kari Sutherland

Map and glossary art by Ali Solomon

Library of Congress Cataloging-in-Publication Data

Sutherland, Tui.

Dragon on trial / Tui T. Sutherland. — First Edition.

pages   cm

Summary: "Someone or something has murdered the goose who laid the golden eggs, and the evidence points to a dragon named Scratch. But this mystery won't be that easy to solve. Zoe and Logan are back on the case in another exciting fantasy adventure"— Provided by publisher.

ISBN 978-0-06-085145-3 (pbk.)

[1. Dragons—Juvenile fiction. 2. Animals, Mythical—Juvenile fiction. 3. Zoos—Juvenile fiction. 4. Crime—Juvenile fiction. 5. Dragons—Fiction. 6. Imaginary creatures—Fiction. 7. Zoos—Fiction. 8. Crime—Fiction. 9. Fantasy. Animals, Mythical. 10. Crime. 11. Dragons. 12. Zoos.] I. Title.

PZ7.S96694 Dp 2014   2014378277

[Fic]—dc23   CIP

                                                        AC

Typography by Torborg Davern

18 19 BVG 10 9 8 7 6 5

❖

First paperback edition, 2015

For Mum and Dad, who are brave
enough to wake sleeping dragons,
even without a fireproof suit.

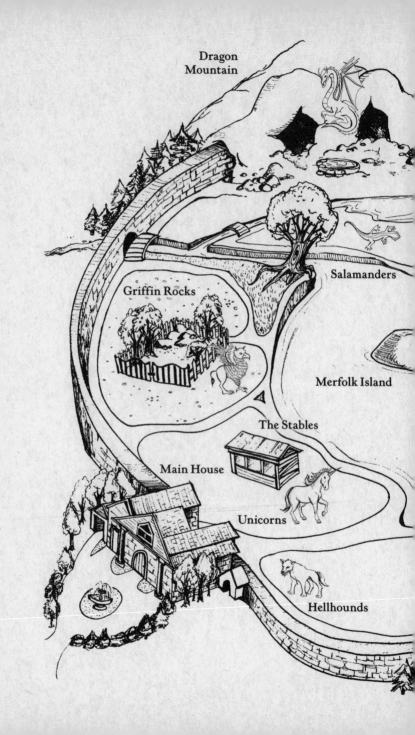

Dragon
Mountain

Salamanders

Griffin Rocks

Merfolk Island

The Stables

Main House

Unicorns

Hellhounds

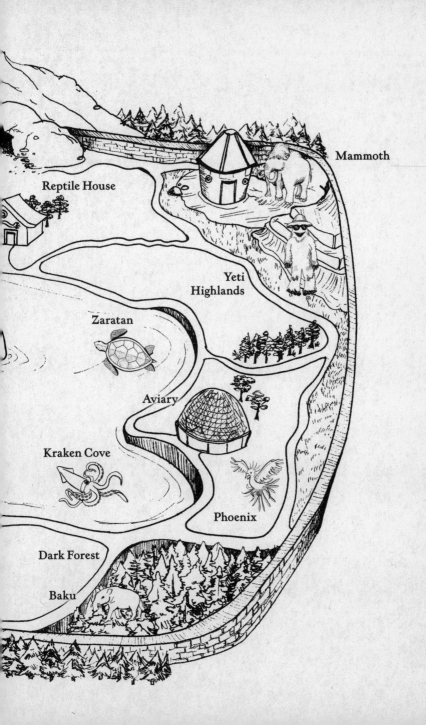

Reptile House

Mammoth

Yeti
Highlands

Zaratan

Aviary

Kraken Cove

Phoenix

Dark Forest

Baku

THE
MENAGERIE
DRAGON
on
TRIAL

ONE

Sunlight reflected off the tails of the mermaids gathered at the edge of the lake. The two unicorns bent their heads gracefully to sip the water, pretending they weren't eavesdropping. In the distance, Logan Wilde could hear the yips and squawks of the griffin cubs playing in their enclosure, happy to be home.

It seemed like a peaceful Sunday morning in the Menagerie . . . except for the bloodstained feather lying on the wet grass between him and Zoe.

Feathers. Again.

It had been only two days since Logan Wilde woke up to find giant feathers on his bedroom floor. Those feathers had belonged to a griffin cub hiding under his bed, who had led him here, to the Menagerie—a secret home for mythical animals run by the family of Logan's classmate Zoe Kahn.

But this feather was white, bigger than the griffin feathers, and part of a murder scene.

Logan crouched to pick it up and Zoe grabbed his shoulder.

"Don't touch it," she said. "It could be evidence." She shuddered. "Also, it's horrible." She rubbed her wrist anxiously and shook her chin-length red-brown hair out of her face. Her eyes were fixed on the door of the Aviary. No one had emerged in half an hour, not since Zoe's dad had sent the two of them away from the crime scene.

Logan studied the feather for a moment, then used his phone to take a picture of it with the Aviary in the background. There had been feathers all *over* the place in there, not to mention the blood splatters on the pillows and silks of Pelly's nest. At least there wasn't a body—the goose herself was nowhere to be found. Logan was pretty sure he wouldn't want to see whatever was left of her.

"What do you think happened?" he asked Zoe. "That poor goose." He'd spent only five minutes with Pelly, but it was horrifying to think that someone who had been alive two days ago was now gone.

"I have no idea," said Zoe. "There's never been an attack in the Menagerie before. It feels impossible."

Logan wanted to agree, but in the past couple days he'd learned to be careful of using that word. After all, there were lots of things that Logan had thought were impossible that turned out to be not just possible but living only a few miles from his house.

The yeti currently zipping toward them on a golf cart, for instance.

"What's happening?" Zoe called as Mooncrusher jumped off the cart and bounded toward the Aviary, brandishing a walkie-talkie in his paws.

"BLAAAAAARGH!" the yeti answered before disappearing inside.

"Hmm," Zoe said. "Okay. I guess I asked for that." She narrowed her eyes at the mermaids, who were whispering and snickering behind their hands.

"At least the birds have stopped screaming," Logan said. A muted bellow came from the white dome of the Aviary. "Apart from whatever that is."

"The roc," Zoe said. "We have this tranquillity mist Dad must have released to calm down the other birds, but she's too big for it to work on her. Poor Aliya, she sounds totally traumatized." She pulled out her phone and checked it again. "Come *on*, Blue, where are you? I've texted him like forty times."

"He's trapped inside Jasmin's house," Logan reminded her. "Where we left him." They'd called their friend Blue to distract Jasmin while they snuck out of her house with the last missing griffin cub. But given her crush on Blue, Logan wasn't entirely sure Jasmin would ever let him leave. "We might have to mount a follow-up rescue mission," he tried to joke, but Zoe looked too devastated to smile.

Logan shifted uncertainly—he was no good at comforting people—then glanced up at the house. A large, furry shape was lumbering down the hill toward them. "Here comes someone who might cheer you up," he said.

"No one can cheer me up right now," Zoe said. "Nothing and no one and—" She let out a little shriek as the mammoth came up behind her, wrapped its trunk around her waist, and lifted her off the ground.

"Well, Captain Fuzzbutt is willing to try," said Logan.

Zoe patted the Captain's trunk until he put her down, and then she turned and hugged him. "All right. Maybe you," she said. "I can't believe Pelly's really gone. Do you think it's our fault? We should have protected her better—but from *what*? I can't even imagine. . . . It doesn't seem real."

She leaned into the mammoth's thick brown fur. "What if SNAPA decides we're terrible caretakers and shuts down the Menagerie? Fuzzbutt, if they revoke our license and relocate all the creatures, I might never see you again."

Her pet mammoth gently wrapped his trunk around her again and patted her on the back.

"They wouldn't do that," Logan said, almost more to

reassure himself than her. Not that he knew anything, really, about the SuperNatural Animal Protection Agency. He'd learned about it only in the last two days, despite the fact that apparently his mother had worked for them as a mythical creature Tracker her whole life. Or at least she had up until six months ago, when she disappeared into thin air.

"They definitely would," Zoe said. "They closed that Amazon menagerie not too long ago. SNAPA's whole job is to make sure we keep the animals safe, and obviously we just failed. This, on top of the jackalope my sister's boyfriend nearly ran off with and the Chinese dragon that went missing on its way here . . ." She trailed off.

"The one they think my mom stole," he finished for her.

"I know she didn't," Zoe said. "We'll prove them wrong. But the point is, SNAPA has a lot of reasons not to like us. I bet they'd love to shut us down."

Logan didn't know what he would do if he lost the Menagerie now. Zoe Kahn and Blue Merevy were the only friends he'd met since moving to Xanadu, Wyoming, and helping them find the griffin cubs had made him feel happy for the first time in months. The fact that he was the only one who could hear Squorp and the other griffin cubs also made him feel like working with these creatures was his destiny—like he was born to be a Tracker or a Menagerie caretaker.

Most important, if Zoe's theory was right, this place might be his only chance to find his mom.

"I need you to sign these," said a voice behind him.

Logan turned and saw that Melissa Merevy, Blue's mom, had followed Fuzzbutt down from the house. She was holding out a silver pen and a clipboard full of papers. Her blond hair was as smooth as shiny metal and in her pressed suit, she looked, as usual, ready for a business meeting, never mind that it was breakfast time on a Sunday morning.

"Um," Logan said. "Me?"

"Of course you," said Melissa. "Unless there's someone else I'm supposed to conjure up an entire set of papers for out of nowhere."

Earlier that morning, Zoe's dad had told the SNAPA agents that Logan was a new hire, which was probably one of the coolest things that had ever happened to Logan. The agents had asked to see his paperwork before they left—but in the chaos of Pelly's murder, surely they'd forget, wouldn't they?

Then again, it probably wasn't a good idea to argue, given the look on Melissa's face.

He took the pen and flipped through the papers, signing at each of the little sticky tabs without reading any of it. There was an awful lot of small print.

"Did you hear about Pelly?" Zoe asked Melissa.

"Yes, your father radioed us. Your mom's on the phone with SNAPA headquarters right now," Melissa said. "It's awful. A complete disaster. To make matters worse, I have no idea how we're supposed to run this place without a weekly golden egg to keep us solvent. Dragons don't exactly eat dandelions, you know. And don't get me started on how expensive certain fish people are." Melissa raised an eyebrow at the gathered mermaids, all of whom were loyal to her ex-husband, King Cobalt.

"Here comes Blue," Zoe said, sounding relieved. Logan found that he also felt a bit calmer at the sight of their part-merman friend strolling down from the house with a garment bag slung over his shoulder. Blue never seemed to get stressed about anything. Even the six griffin cubs escaping from the Menagerie hadn't rattled him.

"That should do it." Melissa scooped the clipboard out of Logan's hands as he signed the last form. She headed straight back to the house, patting Blue's shoulder briefly as she went by. Logan rubbed his head, hoping his forms weren't going to cause more trouble for the Menagerie. They had enough to deal with.

"You owe me big-time," Blue said, pointing at Zoe and Logan. "Thanks to you, I'm now going to Jasmin's Halloween party as a knight. In a suit of armor." He tossed the garment bag down and it clanked as it hit the ground.

Captain Fuzzbutt jumped, then cautiously circled the bag.

Blue turned to Logan. "And you are coming with me, whether you like it or not. Also, I get to choose your costume, and heads up, it is probably going to involve bunny ears or fairy wings or whatever is the most embarrassing thing I can think of."

"But your great sacrifice was worth it," Logan pointed out. "We got the cub back here, and SNAPA never knew any of them were gone."

Blue poked the garment bag with his toe. "Oh, good. From all of Zoe's frantic texts, I thought they'd figured it out. So if everything's fine with the cubs, then what's wrong? Why did I have to HURRY BACK OMG 911 END OF THE WORLD?"

"Blue . . ." Zoe's voice wavered and she stopped.

"What's going on?" Blue looked back and forth between Zoe and Logan, his annoyance fading as he noticed their expressions.

Zoe took a deep breath. "It's Pelly. She's dead—or, or missing, or—no, she's probably dead."

Logan thought of how the nest had looked and had to agree.

"What?" Blue exclaimed. "How?"

"We don't know. Dad and the SNAPA agents are inside looking for clues."

"Wow, that's just . . ." Blue shook his head, unable to finish the thought. "What do we know?"

"Not much." Zoe filled him in on what they'd seen. She

rubbed her eyes and sighed. "I just can't imagine who would want to kill Pelly."

"You mean, apart from anyone who's ever met her?" Blue said.

"Blue!" Zoe cried.

"Well, it's true. I mean, it's still sad and awful, but you have to admit she was not the nicest bird. Always demanding stuff and going on about how important she is to the Menagerie. Didn't she once make you spend two hours fluffing up the pillows on her nest only to decide they were the wrong color?"

Pelly had seemed like kind of a diva to Logan. But still, she was a mythical creature. A talking goose who could lay actual golden eggs . . . who would destroy something that rare?

"I can't handle just standing here," Zoe said. "We have to do something. Maybe we could look for witnesses. Or check the security footage. Or—"

"We have to let SNAPA do their job," Blue interrupted gently. "This is the kind of thing they investigate all the time."

"Is there another way into the Aviary?" Logan asked. "Could we at least go check on the roc and make sure she's okay?"

Zoe smacked her forehead. "That is *absolutely what we should do.* We're doing that right now. Blue, go get my iPod and meet us in the Aviary."

Blue nodded and took off toward the house. The mermaids called his name and whistled as he went past, but he ignored them.

Logan followed Zoe around to the back of the Aviary, where a narrow metal ladder went straight up the side of the dome. Zoe looked at it for a moment, then kicked off her shoes and climbed in her socks. Logan did the same, guessing this way the adults inside the Aviary wouldn't hear them.

"Maybe Pelly's not dead," Logan said, trying to distract himself from how high they were about to climb. "Maybe someone took her for the golden eggs."

"Then where did all the blood and feathers come from?" Zoe asked. "Those aren't ordinary goose feathers. They were definitely hers. I *wish* I could think of an explanation where she might still be alive, but I can't."

Zoe stepped off the top of the ladder onto a rusted platform that seemed entirely too small, considering how high in the air it was. She reached up to a large crank on a wheel right over her head and then paused.

"That's weird," she whispered to Logan, pointing.

He peered awkwardly over her shoulder without relaxing his death grip on the ladder. Now he could see there was a large panel of the dome that could roll open, like a garage door. It was big enough for a small house to fit through. A house the size of Logan's, for example.

"What's weird?" he whispered back. "What is that door for?"

"This is how we get the roc in and out if we ever need to," Zoe said. "We installed it when she was brought here." She pointed at the door again. "But look. It's already a little bit open."

Logan saw what she meant. A gap at the bottom of the door was just wide enough for them to slip through.

"Maybe this is where whoever it was got Pelly's body out," Zoe said. She crouched and studied the door. "I don't see any blood, though."

"We shouldn't touch it," Logan said. "There could be evidence here."

Zoe hesitated, and they both heard another tragic gigantic-bird noise from inside the Aviary.

"I really want to check on Aliya," she said. "We'll squeeze through—just try not to disturb anything."

She crouched and ducked through the gap, disappearing inside before Logan could argue. He glanced around at the Menagerie. From up this high he could see almost the entire place. He could see the distant shapes of the griffins, now sprawled on their boulders sunning themselves. He could see the house and a couple of black hellhounds playing chase around it. He could even see the dark shape of the kraken coiled below the lake's surface, and what he guessed were the dragons' caves in the cliff at the back of the Menagerie. No sign of any dragons themselves, though.

"Come on," Zoe's voice whispered from inside.

Logan ducked and stepped cautiously through the gap in the rolling door. His socks touched smooth, dark brown wood. He nearly slipped, caught his balance, and looked up—and found himself face-to-face with a wickedly hooked beak the size of a school bus.

"Don't move," Zoe said. "She's hungry."

TWO

Logan froze in place, half-crouched just inside the rolling door. He was on a ledge high up in the Aviary, surrounded by treetops and greenery. Next to him was a huge, messy nest built from piles of scattered branches.

But mostly what he noticed were the sharp black eyes pinning him to the ledge, the giant talons only a few feet away, and the sleek white feathers of the world's most enormous bird of prey.

"It's okay, Aliya," Zoe said soothingly. "This is Logan. He's a friend. He works here now."

Aliya clacked her beak, once, with a loud snap that reverberated off the dome overhead. Then she stepped back and settled into her nest, although her gaze stayed fixed on Logan.

"She's just rattled today," Zoe said. "Normally she's really calm, but the strangers and all the noise around Pelly's nest must have freaked her out. And we usually bring her breakfast at sunrise, so she's hungry and confused, too."

Logan peered over the edge, but he couldn't see Pelly's nest from up here—there were too many trees in the way. A spiral staircase wound down from the roc's ledge into the greenery below. Zoe's dad and the two SNAPA agents had stopped shouting, but their voices were still loud and angry. He spotted several birds perched in the branches with their eyes closed, so the tranquillity mist must have worked.

"It's all right, Aliya," Zoe said. She reached into the tangled nest and pulled out a small set of speakers. "There was a—um, an accident of some kind. Something's happened to Pelly."

The roc let out a kind of "*awk*" sound and made a face that to Logan looked hilariously like *Well, that bird had it coming.*

"How much does she understand?" he asked Zoe.

"It's hard to tell," said Zoe, "but I think she's very intelligent."

"Me, too," Logan said. The roc blinked slowly, as if she were trying to look wiser. "Did my mom bring her in?"

He knew his mom had found Zoe's mammoth. He kind of liked picturing his mom flying an enormous bird into the Menagerie. At the same time, it made him pretty mad that she'd never told him the truth about her amazingly cool job, when Zoe got to know everything about it. But then whenever he thought about what might have happened to her, he started to worry, and then he felt guilty about how angry he'd been after the last postcard she'd sent . . . but he still wasn't sure he'd forgiven her for that, and anyway he had no idea what the truth was, so maybe it was better not to think about Mom too much for now.

Zoe shook her head. "No, that was a different Tracker. Your mom brought the alicanto, though; you should meet it sometime. With earplugs."

Blue's feet appeared through the gap in the door, followed closely by the rest of Blue, and then almost immediately by Keiko. Now that he'd seen her as a fox, Logan wasn't sure whether he was more or less intimidated by the sixth grader Zoe's family had adopted from Japan.

Keiko had changed out of her shape-shifting white kimono into a pair of sleek black pants and a fitted sapphire-blue T-shirt that spelled out FOXY in little rhinestones.

"Oh," Logan said, pointing at her shirt. "Foxy! Ha-ha! I get it!"

Keiko gave him a golden-brown glare.

"Because you're a . . . kittensy . . . kiztoony . . . um, the thing where you turn into a fox sometimes . . ."

"Kitsune," Keiko snapped. "And I do not *turn into a fox*. I *am* a fox, but right now I'm choosing to be a girl."

Logan blinked in confusion, but no one seemed to think that required any more explanation.

"Why is she here?" Zoe asked, plucking her iPod out of Blue's hand. "She'll just make Aliya worse."

Keiko tossed her braids over her shoulders, put her hands on her hips, and sniffed the air. The roc shifted on its nest, rumbling unhappily. Logan realized that it didn't like having Keiko around—like most of the animals in the Menagerie, now that he thought about it. The unicorns hated her, too. Perhaps they could all smell or sense her foxiness.

"She saw me taking your iPod," Blue said, "and she wanted to know what was going on."

Zoe rolled her eyes and crouched beside the speakers, scrolling through songs on her iPod. A moment later, the faint sound of Bollywood music echoed tinnily through the air, and the roc visibly relaxed, flopping her head down on her nest.

"Someone murdered Pelly," Logan said to Keiko. "It's a huge mess down there."

"Oh, I highly doubt she was murdered," said Keiko.

"Really?" Zoe said, lifting her head with a hopeful expression. "Like, you can't smell enough blood or something?"

"Right," said Keiko. "More likely she was eaten."

"Oh, VERY COMFORTING," Zoe yelled.

"I wasn't trying to be comforting!" Keiko yelled back.

"Shhhh," Blue said. They all fell silent, and Logan realized that the adult voices below had stopped.

"Oops," said Zoe.

The spiral staircase began to shake, and then Mr. Kahn emerged from the trees, climbing toward them. His reddish-brown hair was standing up in wild tufts and he looked exhausted.

"Zoe!" he said in a shocked voice. "What—"

"We were checking on Aliya!" Zoe said quickly. "Didn't you hear how upset she was? We were just making sure she was all right." She patted the nest of branches, and the roc clacked her beak in a self-righteous way.

"You should be back at the house," he said sternly.

"All right, I know," said Zoe, "but come up here and look at this door first. It was a little bit open when we got here. Maybe someone came in and out this way last night."

The two SNAPA agents did not look pleased when they followed Mr. Kahn up to the ledge and found not only Zoe but also Logan, Blue, and Keiko gathered around the roc's nest.

"Dad, is Pelly really dead?" Zoe asked.

Logan could guess what she was thinking, because he was hoping the same thing. *Maybe it was a mistake. Maybe it was some kind of stunt Pelly set up to scare us all into appreciating her more.*

"I'm afraid so, dear," Agent Dantes said softly, and Mr. Kahn nodded, his shoulders slumping.

"Although it's impossible to know for sure with no body,"

Agent Runcible said in a voice that sounded like it had its edges ironed flat. "Robert, I must insist we lock down the entire Aviary. This is no place for children right now."

Logan tried not to stare at him. So far it seemed like the SNAPA agent hadn't recognized him, and Logan wasn't sure how Agent Runcible would react once he realized where they'd first met.

It had been six months ago, when Logan and his dad still lived in Chicago. They'd gotten the postcard from Logan's mom only two days before Runcible showed up. The postcard that said basically, *Hello hello, sorry to say, just got a great new job opportunity, love you heaps but I won't be home again anytime soon, have a nice life, etc.*

Dad had asked if Logan wanted to take a couple days off from school "to process," which had sounded kind of dopey to Logan. Lying on the couch watching TV wasn't going to make him feel any better about Mom being gone, so he might as well take his math test. Even failing couldn't make him feel worse, he'd figured.

So he'd heard Runcible before seeing him—that clipped, severe voice on the other side of the apartment door when Logan got home from school.

"You're telling me you have no idea where she is."

Logan had stopped with his keys halfway out of his pocket, leaned into the door, and listened.

"Sorry," said Logan's dad. "We haven't heard from her since she left."

No mention of the postcard, Logan thought. *Okay. So Dad doesn't trust this guy.*

"No packages?" said the stranger's voice. "Does she have a security deposit box anywhere? Or a storage unit?"

"Nope," said Logan's dad, sounding slightly less friendly. "What is this about?"

"Your wife didn't just disappear," said the other man. "She disappeared with something quite important to us. If you're helping her hide it, there will be serious consequences, Mr. Wilde."

There was a pause. "I think you'd better go," said Logan's dad.

Footsteps on the other side of the door. Logan had scrambled back to the stairs and pretended like he was just reaching the top of them as the apartment door opened.

Runcible had given him a severe look as he went by, but they had seen each other for only about ten seconds in passing. Maybe that was why he didn't remember Logan now. Or maybe he made so many kids feel bad about their parents that he couldn't keep them straight.

The other agent, Delia Dantes, seemed much nicer than Runcible. She smiled more, and according to Zoe, she kept telling the kids to call her Delia. Logan couldn't imagine doing that; it was strange enough when Zoe did it.

But even Agent Dantes was frowning as she inspected the roll-up door. She pushed a strand of dark hair out of her face and pointed at a few scratches on the paintwork with her pen.

"Something big could have come through here last night," she said. "Judging from these claw marks, perhaps a griffin, a taniwha, or a mapinguari."

Logan felt a shiver run down his spine. He didn't know what two of those were, but he knew plenty about the Menagerie's griffins. And the tone of the agent's voice didn't bode well for his new friends.

"Our griffins would never attack another mythical creature," Zoe protested.

"That's true," said Logan. "Besides, the cubs are afraid of the goose—Squorp told me they once tried to play with her and she snapped at them."

"Ah," said Agent Dantes, making a note. "That could be a motive for one of the parents to kill her."

"No!" Logan said. "They're not like that. Nira wants them to learn to fend for themselves and Riff—well, Riff can be kind of overprotective, but—"

"Logan, stop helping," Keiko said snidely.

Logan subsided, feeling awful. Zoe was fidgeting anxiously with her fingernails and didn't meet his eyes.

"These griffins are bred for intelligence rather than

ferocity," Mr. Kahn interjected calmly. "And our mapinguari is well contained, so he's a vegetarian these days."

Keiko snorted and muttered, "Eating carrots. Might as well be a cow."

"And we don't even have a taniwha," Zoe said. "Besides, we'd be able to see its tunnel outside if a taniwha came this way."

"Well then," said Agent Dantes. "Perhaps a dragon."

"No way," said Zoe, nearly dropping her iPod. "Not our dragons!"

"We have strict security measures in place on our three," said Mr. Kahn. "I can't imagine any of our dragons would do this even if they could get past their restraints. Given the claw marks, the probable use of the tranquillity mist during the attack, and the advance planning that must have been involved—could it have been a werewolf?"

Logan wasn't sure why he was surprised. After meeting griffins and unicorns and mermaids, finding out that werewolves were real should have been quite normal. But it still sounded so weird. He imagined that guy from the *Twilight* movies trying to eat a giant goose. Somehow he thought Pelly would be a match for him.

"You keep werewolves here?" he whispered to Blue.

"No," Blue whispered back. "Werewolves are classified as Mostly Human, so they don't usually end up in places like the Menagerie unless they choose to—like my dad's merfolk.

There's a different agency that monitors us Mostly Human guys."

"There are no registered werecreatures in this part of Wyoming," Runcible said with a scowl.

"Perhaps an unregistered one—" Mr. Kahn started.

"Very unlikely," Runcible said forcefully. "And before you go pointing fingers at hypothetical creatures outside your Menagerie, I suggest we investigate the predators within these walls." He drew a tablet computer out of his briefcase and started tapping on it vigorously.

"Dad," Zoe said, "why don't we just check the security camera footage? Wouldn't that show us exactly . . ." Her voice trailed off at the look on her dad's face, and the roc made a sympathetically dismal noise.

"Your mom already checked," said Mr. Kahn, holding up his walkie-talkie. "And there's a . . . problem."

"Yes," said Runcible icily. "I'd call the loss of all your camera feeds a problem, indeed."

"Nothing but static on all the recordings from last night," Agent Dantes said grimly.

Logan and Zoe exchanged shocked looks. *That can't be a coincidence*, Logan thought. *Someone wanted to make sure nobody saw what happened to Pelly. But what kind of creature can both hack into a computer and eat a goose?*

"This is why we insisted on the upgrade for the surveillance equipment," Agent Runcible said, his stern tone sending a shiver up Logan's spine.

"But we did that!" Zoe cried. "We did everything you asked. Matthew spent all day yesterday installing the update you gave us."

"It's okay, Zoe," her father said. "I've told them the upgrade was in place. Something must have severed the connection, or perhaps the software patch had a problem—"

"It hasn't malfunctioned at any of the other locations where it's been installed," Agent Runcible pointed out.

"What about Nero?" Logan asked. The roc couldn't talk, but Logan knew the melodramatic phoenix could. "We could ask him if he saw anything last night."

Mr. Kahn sighed. "I had the same thought. So I asked Mooncrusher to find him, but Nero burst into flames the minute he saw the yeti." The phoenix tended to spontaneously combust any time he felt stressed or unappreciated, or whenever he just wanted to make a point about how nobody paid any attention to him. "He's a very unhelpful pile of ashes now. We'll have to try again later."

"Regardless, we have to launch a full investigation at once into the death of the goose," said Agent Dantes. "Do you have any predators with a grudge against her?"

"The goose was not a particularly beloved bird," said Mr. Kahn evenly, "but she had no specific enemies that I can think of."

Logan spotted the expression on Zoe's face before she

could hide it. *Hmm.* Did that mean there was someone who had it out for Pelly?

"Then let's start with the dragons," Agent Dantes murmured. "They are, after all, the most dangerous."

Despite the tension, despite the murder scene, despite the threat to the Menagerie, Logan felt prickles of excitement scramble along his skin.

He was about to meet a dragon.

THREE

"Okay, these things looked cool on the wall, but I feel ridiculous."

Logan shifted uncomfortably in the fireproof suit. His whole body was encased; only his face was visible through a clear pane in the helmet. The heavy fabric of the suit insulated him a little *too* well. He could feel sweat collecting on his back and behind his knees. Who even knew you could sweat behind your knees?

Ahead of him, Zoe pivoted around in her own suit so he could see her face.

"I know, it's an annoying rule, right? SNAPA worries a lot about dragonfire accidents." She turned to keep climbing.

Blue held out his gloved hand to help Logan up the rocky slope. "As they should," he said. "Dragons aren't known for their impulse control. It's safer this way."

Mr. Kahn and the two SNAPA agents were way ahead of them. Logan wasn't sure how they could move so fast in their bulky suits. Keiko had gone back to the house; apparently the dragons *really* couldn't stand being around her, which she said was "totally mutual" and fine by her.

Logan clambered up the final stretch with Blue's help and paused at the top of the embankment. In front of him lay a shelf of rock the size of a soccer field, surrounded on two sides by steep cliffs, each with a large, dark cave in it. On the third side was a jagged low wall of boulders and then the craggy hillside stretching down to the Menagerie lake. The path they'd taken through the rocks continued along the side of one of the cliffs to another cave higher on the mountain.

Outside one of the caves, sprawled in the sunshine, was the most magnificent creature Logan had ever seen.

The dragon's scales shone, moving from a pure silver over most of its body to an opalescent sheen on its underbelly. Massive wings that looked like beaten silver leather stretched out on either side of its torso. If Logan had to guess, he'd say that the dragon was sunning itself, like a cat.

"Stay back here," Zoe said, stopping Logan at the edge of the path. Mr. Kahn had let them come only if they promised to keep out of the way.

"Technically, SNAPA says nobody under sixteen is allowed to work with dragons," Blue explained.

"But that's one of those bendy rules," Zoe said with a shrug.

Blue shook his head at Logan. "It's really not. And Zoe wonders why this Menagerie keeps getting in trouble with the agency."

"Clawdius," Mr. Kahn said, so quietly that Logan almost couldn't hear him. "We request a moment of your time."

The silver dragon's eyes slowly slid open into narrow slits. Gleams of dark red glinted in their black depths. His head, which was as big as an SUV, lifted as the humans approached.

"You remember Agent Runcible and Agent Dantes," said Mr. Kahn.

Logan noticed that Agent Dantes had stopped a fair distance from Clawdius, allowing her partner to get closer while she scanned the rocks around them. She kept glancing at the other two caves as if waiting for another dragon to leap out, teeth bared. But only a faint line of smoke from the upper cave indicated that either of the other dragons was home.

"SSSSSSSSSNAPA," hissed the large silver dragon, eyeing the agents.

"That's right," said Zoe's dad. "We'd like to question whoever was on intruder alert duty last night."

The dragon closed his eyes and sat still, as if he was thinking.

"Intruder alert?" Logan whispered to his friends. He remembered the alarm that had blared when he first snuck into the Menagerie with Squorp. It had sounded like someone bellowing "INTRUDER!" at the approximate volume of four hundred roaring jet engines. "Wait, the dragons are your alert system?"

"Yeah, they're perfect for it," Zoe said. "All dragons have a kind of sixth sense that keeps track of everyone around them. They know exactly who should and shouldn't be in the Menagerie, and they can tell when a stranger gets inside our walls. They're also, as you may have noticed, really freaking loud."

"And untrustworthy," Blue added, sitting down on a boulder.

"Blue's not a fan of our system, but we think it works great," said Zoe. "We were the first Menagerie to figure out dragons could be used this way, and now everyone's doing it."

"The only reason dragons have that skill is to protect their treasure and hunt their prey," Blue said. "They don't care about human problems." He shrugged. "It wouldn't be hard to figure out a way around it, is all I'm saying."

"It's worked fine so far," Zoe said. "They let us know when Jonathan tried to steal the jackalope, and they warned us about Logan sneaking in."

"But aren't you hoping it didn't work last night?" Logan said. Zoe gave him a confused look. "I mean, because if the system was working fine, then whatever happened to Pelly was done by someone inside the Menagerie. Right?"

Zoe went pale and turned back to the dragon without answering.

Clawdius opened his eyes again, slowly.

"Last time of darkness," he said in a deep voice. "Turn of Scratch."

"It was Scratch's turn to guard the Menagerie last night," Zoe translated, glancing up at the higher cave. Logan saw her reach for her wrist, but with the suit in the way, she couldn't twist her hand around it in her usual nervous gesture. She tugged on the sleeves and gloves instead.

"So you detected nothing," Agent Runcible pressed. "No intruders, nothing unusual? Do you know what happened?"

The dragon turned his silver head so the morning sun glinted off his scales, shining right into the SNAPA agents' eyes. His tongue flicked in and out like he was tasting the air.

"Gone the fat honk-bird now," he intoned. "Quiet the birdcage." His claws curled, scraping the rock underneath him. "Sad is nobody."

Logan glanced at Zoe. "Is he saying nobody is sad that Pelly's dead? Can dragons sense that kind of thing, too?" *Because he's wrong*, he thought. *Zoe looks like she's lost someone's favorite puppy.*

"No. He's just guessing," she answered.

"Or projecting," Blue said.

"We need to figure out what happened to her," Mr. Kahn said to Clawdius.

"Asleep was Clawdius," said the dragon. "Also not caring is Clawdius." A small puff of smoke snorted from his nose. "Now asleep is Clawdius." The dragon turned, majestically presenting his back to the SNAPA agents, and lay down in the sun again.

"Let's go talk to Scratch," Mr. Kahn suggested.

"We need to inspect all the dragons' chains first," said Agent Dantes, putting her hands on her hips.

Mr. Kahn winced. "We don't call them chains," he said. "We call them 'assisted restraints.'"

Her look was not amused.

Logan crouched, feeling the sweat roll down his back, and watched Zoe's dad lead the agents to Clawdius's back legs. One of the dragon's ankles had an iron clamp around it, connected to a large, solid-looking chain that led back into the darkness of the cave.

Clawdius shifted and Agent Dantes took a quick step back. Agent Runcible crouched and poked at the clamp, then carefully inspected each link in the chain. He went into the cave for a while, then emerged shaking his head.

"Looks fine," he said to Dantes. "Let's check the next one."

"You checked their restraints last Sunday," Mr. Kahn pointed out. "Is it really necessary to check them again?"

"I think you know the answer to that," Runcible said witheringly.

Clawdius turned his head to peer at them as the three adults approached the second cave. "Asleep is Firebella," the silver dragon warned. "*Extremely* displeased to be woken shall be Firebella."

Dantes hesitated, and Runcible strode forward with a snort. "I'll do it," he said, vanishing into the cave.

"Uh-oh," Zoe muttered.

A moment later, a blast of flames shot out of the cave entrance. Logan jumped up and stumbled back from the searing heat.

"She was just startled," Zoe said quickly. "She doesn't normally breathe fire at people. Not unless you wake her up."

"Or talk too loud," Blue offered. "Or bring her the wrong food. Or ask her to do something. Or criticize her singing. Or—"

"Okay, but she's a dragon!" Zoe protested. "That's how they're supposed to be!"

"Exactly." Blue leaned against one of the twisted boulders.

Logan decided he agreed with Zoe. Of course dragons breathed fire and got a little grumpy when humans tried to boss them around. They wouldn't be nearly as cool if they had the personalities of sheep.

Runcible stormed out of the cave with smoke trailing

from his suit. Without speaking to the others, he headed for the path up to the third cave.

Zoe let out a quiet sigh of relief. "I guess Firebella's restraints were fine, too." She chased after the adults, and Logan and Blue hurried along behind.

"So the dragons each have just the one chain?" Logan asked as they climbed. "Dragons don't require something . . . more than that?"

"It's a special kind of dragonfire-resistant metal," Zoe said. "And of course there's the fence."

"What fence?" Logan glanced around, but there wasn't a fence in sight.

"The invisible fence." Blue waved a hand at the air above them. "The dragons are chipped so a shock knocks them out when they try to go too far from their caves."

"So it *couldn't* have been a dragon in the Aviary," Zoe said. "They can't go that far."

Logan wondered why it sounded like she was trying to convince herself.

They reached the top of the path, opposite the last cave.

Flopped across the entrance was a sleeping dragon about a third smaller than Clawdius. Its reddish-orange-yellow skin morphed into a rusty brown along its belly, and when it exhaled, its scales clanked together like steel against armor. Two wings protruded from its back, and barbs ran along the length of its tail.

"Scratch," Mr. Kahn said soothingly, edging toward him. "Don't be alarmed. I'm here with the two SNAPA agents you met last week—"

The dragon's eyes flew open. He surged upright, let out a panicked roar . . . and disappeared into thin air.

FOUR

Zoe's heart sank. She'd really hoped Scratch would keep his new trick hidden. The SNAPA agents hadn't found out about it during their inspection the previous week. But there was no hiding it now.

"Where did he go?" shouted Agent Runcible. Agent Dantes pressed her back against a boulder and glanced around wildly.

"It's all right," said her dad, jumping in front of the agents. "He's still here. It's just a glamour. Look." He stepped over to where Scratch had been and knocked on the air. *Clang clang.* A small burst of fire popped into the sky above his head.

"Wow," Logan breathed. "Dragons can be invisible?"

"Not all of them," Zoe said. "Some of them can cast, like, illusions, or what we call 'glamours.' Most of them try to make themselves look bigger or scarier. I have no idea why Scratch decided to go for invisible instead."

"Childhood trauma," Logan guessed, and Blue snorted a half laugh.

"Yeah," he said. "Maybe he was bullied at dragon school."

Logan's eyes nearly popped out of his head. *"There's dragon sch—"*

"No," said Zoe, rolling her eyes.

"Oh," Logan said, sounding disappointed. "You have to admit that would be cool. But seriously, maybe something happened to him that made him want to hide."

"You're thinking as if dragons are anything like people," Blue said. "It's more likely that he's planning something sinister and being invisible is how he'll get away with it."

Zoe winced, remembering why they were there. Had Scratch learned to make himself invisible just so he could sneak in and eat Pelly? That was . . . crazy, wasn't it?

Besides, there were the restraints and the fence. Invisibility wouldn't get him past those.

Her dad had been murmuring at Scratch for a while, and now the dragon's red-brown-gold scales were shimmering back into view. Scratch still looked very uncomfortable. Zoe didn't like the way he kept glancing guiltily at the SNAPA agents.

Should she have told them about Scratch's feud with Pelly?

No. It wasn't serious. They're suspicious enough.

"All right, Scratch," said her dad. "Everything is okay. We just need to ask you about the intruder watch last night."

"Watching was Scratch," said the dragon. His voice was as deep as Clawdius's, but with a waver to it that always made him sound a bit anxious. "Most dark was time of darkness. Most quiet under the star-time." He avoided Mr. Kahn's eyes, scratching his claws along the rock below him.

Zoe thought of her to-do list and how "check on Scratch" had been on there because he'd been refusing his food lately. She'd been worried he was sick—but he looked healthier than ever. Too healthy. *Too well fed.*

She didn't want to think about what he might just have eaten.

"Really?" said Zoe's dad. "There were no intruders at all?"

"Intruders none," said Scratch. He rolled his eyes up and squinted at the sky. "Full zero of intruders were there."

He's lying, Zoe thought. She could see the shimmer of the invisibility glamour starting around his tail, as if he desperately wanted to disappear. *But why?*

"Think carefully, Scratch," said her dad. "It's very important."

Scratch hunched his shoulders and muttered, "None intruders none."

Mr. Kahn reached toward his helmet as if he wanted to rub his temples, then sighed and lowered his hands again. "Then what happened in the Aviary, Scratch? While you were on duty, something got in and killed Pelly."

The dragon blinked several times, and Zoe felt a glimmer of hope. *He looks genuinely surprised*, she thought. *At least, I think he does. I don't think he's that good an actor.*

Scratch closed his eyes, evidently using his sixth sense to feel the presences in the Menagerie. A startled, pleased expression flickered over his face. "Gone the fat selfish mean herself-full honk-bird!" he cried, opening them again. "Magnificent the day!"

"Oh, dear," said Zoe.

"I'm guessing that's not going to help his cause," said Logan.

"Scratch," said Mr. Kahn with a hint of impatience. "If you were on duty, how could you not know that?"

Scratch looked canny and guilty and miserable all at once.

Oh, Zoe thought. *Maybe he fell asleep. Maybe he wasn't paying attention. Maybe that's all he's lying about . . . in which case, that's not the end of the world. He'd get in a little trouble, but not too much, and they wouldn't shut us down just for having a lazy dragon. I don't think.*

Agent Runcible growled something under his breath and stalked over to Scratch's restraints. He crouched beside the anklet, picked up a stick, and poked at the metal band.

With a horrible, ominous *clank*, the anklet fell right off Scratch's leg.

Scratch and Runcible both stared down at the anklet for a long, awful moment. Zoe wondered if this was what having a heart attack felt like.

"Uh-oh," said Blue.

SNAPA is going to kill him, Zoe thought, starting to panic. *Literally. And then they're going to shut us down.*

Faster than Zoe could blink, Agent Runcible reached into his suit jacket and whipped out a fat silver weapon that looked like a short, futuristic crossbow. He pointed it at Scratch and yelled, "Stay exactly where you are!"

Scratch roared with dismay and promptly vanished again.

"He's not being disrespectful!" Zoe yelled. "He's just scared! He does that when he's nervous!"

"Don't hurt him!" Logan shouted.

But the agents weren't paying any attention to them. Dantes had thrown herself behind the nearest boulder with her arms over her head. Runcible hit a button on the crossbow and fired at the empty space where Scratch had been.

Another panicked roar filled the air, and a moment later, Scratch thudded to the ground, visible once more. His head flopped onto the rocks and he let out a little wheeze, closing his eyes.

"Oh, no," Logan said, starting forward.

Blue and Zoe jumped to grab him and pull him back.

"It's just a tranq dart," Zoe said. "I think. I mean, I'm sure." She studied the dragon anxiously until she saw his side going up and down. Unconscious, not dead. At least for now.

With the dragon out of commission, the SNAPA agents removed their helmets. Dantes looked red and flustered as she crept out from behind the boulder. Runcible strode up to Scratch's head and whipped out a camera the size of a playing card. He snapped a few pictures of Scratch's snout and then prodded open his lips to examine his teeth.

"Aha," he said. "Blood. And it's fresh."

Zoe had to sit down. Her heart was pounding. Scratch hadn't eaten his food in days. *How did he get blood on his snout?*

"*Blood?*" Agent Dantes cried. "Are you sure?" She whirled to face Mr. Kahn. "Haven't you been brushing his teeth like we told you to?"

"I—we—" Mr. Kahn stammered, clearly as shocked as Zoe was. "Sometimes?"

"Delia, is that really the most important question right now?" Runcible asked Dantes sternly.

"Only because they might have noticed blood sooner if they were using the toothbrushes," she said. "What if he's killed someone else this week?" She pulled out her phone. "I'm calling the Exterminators."

Icicles froze and snapped throughout Zoe's veins. She'd grown up thinking that Exterminators were a myth. And even now that she knew they were as real as unicorns, she'd hoped never to meet one.

"Wait," said Mr. Kahn. "There must be an explanation."

"Indeed," said Runcible. "Here's one: you were careless about containing your dragons, and one escaped to kill another priceless mythical creature, whom you failed to protect. Not only should this dragon be terminated but this whole Menagerie should be shut down. I might even recommend kraken ink for all employees and associates."

That was worse than Zoe could ever have imagined. Shutting down the Menagerie, taking away her memories of her whole life, killing Scratch—even her most terrifying nightmares were never this awful.

"You don't know for sure that he ate Pelly," Logan blurted. "Maybe it was someone else. Maybe it wasn't the Menagerie's fault at all."

"I'm sorry, kid," Agent Dantes said. "That looks like pretty compelling evidence to me." She pointed at the broken anklet.

"But you can't just kill him!" Logan said.

"We have to," she said. "This is how we deal with creatures who are that dangerous, for the safety of humans."

"And the protection of all other supernatural animals," said Zoe's dad, looking stricken.

"No, it isn't," Zoe said, suddenly remembering something. She'd read about a case like this in a SNAPA history guide—well, not exactly like this, but close enough.

"I beg your pardon?" said Dantes.

"Dragons are higher-order, sentient beings," said Zoe. "Not like basilisks or kelpies—more like griffins or phoenixes. That means when they're accused of something, especially something with a death penalty, they're entitled to a fair trial. It's a SNAPA rule."

Agent Dantes snapped her phone shut and pushed her hair behind her ears, frowning. With a snort, Runcible pulled out his tablet again and started tapping. After a moment, he sighed.

"She's right," he said. "We'll need a SNAPA authority to be the judge. And lawyers. And—" He paused as if it pained him to say the next bit. "And a jury of his peers."

"*What?*" Dantes and Mr. Kahn said simultaneously.

"Like, twelve other dragons?" Logan asked. Zoe couldn't imagine where they would put twelve dragons in the Menagerie, let alone how they would feed them, even for a day.

"No, no," said Runcible. "No more than six mythical creatures, and they don't all have to be dragons—even Mostly Humans can serve as jurors. And we'll need a caladrius or a qilin."

"A caladrius is a truth bird," Zoe whispered, seeing

Logan's puzzled expression. "A qilin is kind of like a Chinese unicorn."

"That doesn't really clear things up," he whispered back.

"Camp Underpaw lost their qilin this summer," said Dantes. "And even if we could get the caladrius from the Oregon menagerie, who would want to represent this miserable creature?" She waved her hand at Scratch.

"We will," Mr. Kahn said, and the agents both turned to frown at him. "Give us two weeks to investigate internally. Please."

"You have until Thursday," said Runcible, shoving his tablet back into his bag. "And we will be staying to oversee this 'investigation.' Meanwhile, I will be writing my report on all the reasons this place should be shut down, which will go straight to my superiors once the dragon is found guilty."

"I understand," said Mr. Kahn.

"But if he's not guilty—" Logan interjected. "I mean, if we prove that Scratch is innocent, then you'll reconsider. Right?"

The agents exchanged glances. "We'll see," said Agent Dantes.

"Don't worry," Logan said to Zoe. "I'm sure Scratch had nothing to do with what happened to Pelly."

I hope you're right, Logan, Zoe thought. But she could see the looks on the SNAPA agents' faces, and it was hard to disagree with their skepticism. There was the broken anklet right there. There was Scratch's shifty, strange behavior and the blood on his teeth. And there was his history with Pelly, which the agents didn't even know about.

   All signs point to guilty. And if this was all our fault and we lose the trial, that means the end of Scratch . . . and the end of this Menagerie.

FIVE

"So what do we do first?" Logan asked, pulling off his fire-proof helmet as he caught up with Zoe at the base of the cliff. He would have been happy to stay and watch the dragons all day, but the SNAPA agents had declared Scratch a Potential Class X Threat, whatever that meant, and sent everyone away.

"*You* should go home," Zoe said. She tugged off her gloves and dug a small notebook out of an inside pocket of the suit. Logan recognized it as the one where she wrote her to-do list in code. "You haven't been home in forever."

That was true. Friday night, Logan had stayed in Blue's

room so the Kahns could keep an eye on him. That was before they decided to trust him and promised not to use kraken ink to erase his memories of the mythical creatures. And Saturday night he'd been stuck in a secret staircase in Jasmin's house with Zoe and the last missing griffin cub, hiding until it was safe to sneak out.

Now it was Sunday morning, and his dad would definitely think it was weird if Logan didn't get home soon, no matter how pleased he was that Logan had finally found a friend. (Meaning Blue. Logan hadn't said anything about Zoe to his dad. Being friends with a girl was too complicated for parents to understand.)

"I don't have to rush home," Logan said, checking his phone. There weren't any messages from his dad yet. "We should make a list of suspects, witnesses, and possible alibis for Scratch. Hey, maybe the other dragons could testify that he was in his cave all night."

"Not if they were sleeping," Blue said. He'd already pulled off the whole suit and had it bundled under one arm, except for the giant boots, which looked pretty silly with his jeans. Logan started to do the same, unzipping his own fireproof jacket as Blue continued. "Dragons sleep pretty soundly. And they're unreliable witnesses because they'll lie just for fun. Most courts won't hear their testimony."

"Oh, *no!*" Zoe yelped with dismay, dropping her helmet.

She took off running down the path toward the lake, stuffing her notebook back inside her suit.

"What?" Logan called after her. "What is it?"

"It was my turn today!" Zoe called back. "According to the chore chart! I bet nobody else thought to do it!"

Logan gave Blue a quizzical look as he bent to pick up Zoe's helmet. "Really suddenly urgent chores?" Blue shrugged and they both hurried after her, although in the boots it was less like running and more like stomping on the moon.

Zoe turned to follow a path that wound around the giant lake. Ahead of her was a squat structure with a sloped roof. Snakes were carved all along the outside as if they were crawling out of the woodwork.

As she reached the building's front door, Blue stopped abruptly. Logan turned and saw a weird look on Blue's face.

"What?" Logan asked.

"Um," said Blue. "You know, actually, maybe I should—uh—go . . . investigate . . . something . . . somewhere else."

"Oh, come *on*, Blue," Zoe called. "We have to feed them *right now* or else they'll turn on each other and probably burn down the Reptile House. I promise they won't bite. They literally don't even have teeth."

"I know," Blue said, shoving one hand in his pocket and shaking his hair out of his eyes. "I mean, that's not even why. I just think I could do something more useful—uh, elsewhere."

"Whoa," Logan said. "Something in there really freaks you out. What is it? Some kind of man-eating monster? Like a giant mythical flying crocodile?"

"Basically," Blue said.

"Except for how it's the opposite of that," Zoe said, rolling her eyes. "Blue, if you don't get in here, I'll steal your phone and text Jasmin about what a great time you had this morning."

Blue pointed at her. "Low."

He shook out his fireproof suit and started putting it back on.

"Should I do that, too?" Logan asked, alarmed.

"Totally not necessary," Zoe said. "The gloves can be helpful, but they're really harmless, as long as you feed them on time every morning. Blue, seriously, of all the things in here to worry about—"

"I'm not worried," Blue said, muffled through the giant fireproof mask. "Carry on."

Zoe shook her head and pulled out her phone. She tapped a few buttons and stood looking at it for a moment, muttering, "Come on, come on."

"Are you . . . calling the giant flying crocodile?" Logan asked.

"No, this is for the basilisk," Zoe said. She tapped one more button, and her phone started crowing like a rooster.

"There." She hit the button again, opened the snake-covered door, threw her crowing phone inside, and slammed the door behind it.

There was a pause.

"Do I want to know what just happened?" Logan asked.

"That should be long enough," Zoe said. She opened the door again cautiously, waited a minute, and then stuck her head inside. "Yup." She glanced back at Logan. "Do you know what a basilisk is?"

"Some kind of lizard?" Logan guessed. "Wasn't there one in *Harry Potter*?"

"Right," Zoe said. "Come on, I'll show you what they really look like."

Logan glanced at Blue one more time and followed Zoe into the building. It was really dim inside, like a zoo or aquarium where the only light came from inside the animal cages. It took Logan's eyes a moment to adjust.

To his left, taking up most of one wall, was a glass enclosure that radiated heat. Its floor was covered in sand and a few large gray rocks. Conked out on the sand was a perfectly hideous giant lizard who was almost as long as Logan was tall. A spiky crest fanned out around the top of its head like a small crown, and its stumpy legs ended in thick claws. Its scales were grayish-green with white spots as if someone had splattered it with milk. Its eyes were closed and a weak snoring sound came from its snout, which lay on the sand in a puddle of drool.

"You're scared of that?" Logan said to Blue. "It looks like some kind of ancient grandpa lizard."

"That's not what he's afraid of," Zoe said as Blue made a muffled grumbly noise. "Although Basil is probably the most dangerous animal in the Menagerie." She picked up her phone and crouched to peer at the lizard through the glass. "If you look a basilisk in the eye, it kills you instantly. If you hear a basilisk hiss, it kills you instantly. If you smell a wide-awake basilisk—"

"It kills you instantly?" Logan guessed.

"No, but you'll regret it for days," Zoe said. "Trust me, I know. I couldn't eat for a week the first time I got a whiff of one." She pulled a lever on the side of the cage and a small door opened in the enclosure wall. A pile of fruit—kiwis, apples, and figs—tumbled onto the sand by the basilisk's head, but it didn't even stir.

"So, the phone thing . . . ," Logan said.

"The sound of a rooster crowing knocks them unconscious," Zoe said. "So we all got rooster ringtones. You should get one, too."

Logan liked the way she said that, as if she was sure he'd be sticking around.

"Once we check that Basil is still breathing—he's

ridiculously old, like four hundred or something—and send his food in, we hit this button," Zoe said. A panel slid down to cover the glass and hid the basilisk from sight. "It's sound-proof, too, so we can work in here without worrying about him waking up. Although he usually doesn't, and even when he does he kind of wanders around bumping into the walls for a while before he finds the fruit."

Blue was leaning against the wall in a way that looked sort of casual and nonchalant, but also like he might suddenly bolt out the door any minute. Logan turned and scanned the rest of the room, but the other two walls were lined with long tables that only had small cages on them, not much bigger than the terrarium Logan had at home for his mice.

"Where's the man-eating crocodile?" Logan asked Blue.

"Here," Zoe said, lifting the top off one of the cages and sticking her hand in. A thin red lizard, about as long as a pen-cil and the same color as a tomato, emerged from the pile of pebbles inside and climbed up onto Zoe's glove. Its small red tongue flickered in and out and it tilted its head at Logan, studying him with bright black eyes.

Logan raised his eyebrows at Blue.

"I never said man-eating," Blue pointed out.

"You never said adorable, either," said Logan. "Are you afraid of all incredibly cute things, or only the ones smaller than your average banana?"

"Oh, sure, it's funny now," Blue said as Zoe started laughing. "Pyrosalamanders are going to kill us all in our sleep one day. Look at that face. It's got an evil plan."

The tiny lizard smiled serenely.

"Pyrosalamanders?" Logan asked.

"That's what we call the fire-eating kind of salamander," Zoe said. "The kind that counts as supernatural and has to be protected from the rest of the world."

"It's the rest of the world that needs protecting from them," Blue muttered, eyeing the lizard suspiciously.

"They can be slightly bad tempered," Zoe admitted. "Especially if they're not fed regularly. Sorry we're a bit late, little guy." The salamander flicked its tail and stared at her. "But so far no menagerie in history has ever reported a salamander-related casualty."

"That's because they're biding their time," Blue said. "Can we hurry up and get out of here?"

Zoe nudged the pyrosalamander back into its rock pile. She unlocked a box on the table and took out a lighter, then picked up a twig from a pile of branches next to it, set it on fire, and dropped it into the cage. As she set the lid back on top, the salamander darted over to the fire and flung itself into the flames. Wriggling contentedly, it opened its mouth and started gobbling at the fiery air.

"Whoa," Logan said.

"So creepy," Blue said. "And sinister. Maybe they're the ones who killed Pelly." Zoe shot him a look. "Okay, probably not."

"I'm worried that it really might have been Scratch," Zoe said. She moved to the next cage and lit another twig on fire. "How did he open his anklet? And how did he get past the electric fence?"

"And how did he deactivate the security cameras?" Logan asked.

She paused, watching the next salamander eat. "You think that's connected? I thought maybe the update had a glitch in it."

"Wouldn't Matthew have noticed that when he installed it?" Logan pointed out. "It's too weird that the cameras stopped working on the same night that the goose was murdered, or eaten or whatever. So is there a creature that can hack computers and also likes to eat oversized birds?"

Zoe and Blue exchanged glances.

"Something Mostly Human," Blue said.

"You heard my dad," said Zoe. "He guessed it might be a werewolf."

"Could also be a werecougar," said Blue. "Or a werebear. Weretiger. WERESALAMANDER."

"Blue, good grief," said Zoe.

Logan closed his eyes and thought about what he'd seen

out the window the night before. "It was a full moon last night," he said.

"Well, a werecreature like a werewolf can become his wolf self anytime he wants to," Zoe said. "But it's true that during the three days around the full moon he has no choice—that's when they all turn into wolves or whatever whether they want to or not, so they always lock themselves up for the night to be safe."

"Unless they're new," Blue said. "Or unregistered. Or both."

Logan picked up a twig and held it for Zoe to light, then dropped it in the next cage. "Could a new werewolf have found the Menagerie?"

"Yeah, maybe by smell," Zoe said. "Our deflector works best on humans, less well on other animals."

"Your what?" Logan said. He blinked. He couldn't remember what he was asking about.

"I think it's safe to say the intruder alert failed," Blue said. "Sorry, Zoe."

"I know," she said with a sigh. "Scratch definitely wasn't on watch like he was supposed to be. Maybe he fell asleep." She brightened. "On the other hand, that means there's a good chance it was someone outside the Menagerie instead of someone we know. If a werecreature snuck in here, then Pelly's death wasn't our fault. If we can prove that, maybe

SNAPA won't shut us down."

"Tonight is the third night of the full moon," Blue pointed out. "If there is a werewolf wandering the area, this is the last night he or she will have to change."

"Then I know what we're doing tonight," Zoe said. The firelight reflected in her eyes like dancing sprites as she looked at Logan. "We're going to hunt a werewolf."

SIX

Logan's dad was nowhere to be seen when Logan got home around one o'clock, after helping Zoe groom the griffin cubs. Logan fed his pets, took a shower, made himself a sandwich, and sat down at his desk to try to concentrate on homework. The Bill of Rights had a hard time competing against a dragon accused of eating a golden goose, though.

And the death stare he was getting from the cat wasn't much help, either.

"Purrsimmon, I said I was sorry," Logan offered. "I know I was gone for a long time, but I was doing something important."

She twitched her gray-and-white tail with an expression

that said, *Oh, I'm SURE YOU WERE.*

Logan gave up and opened his notebook to a blank page. He wrote *Questions* at the top and then:

How did Scratch get out of his anklet?

Did any of the birds in the Aviary see what happened? He still hoped Nero could tell them something, whenever he wasn't in the middle of a meltdown.

The unicorns would have been galloping around the Menagerie at night—did they see anyone go in or out of the Aviary?

If it was a werewolf, how did he or she get access to the computer system?

And why specifically go to the trouble of shutting down the cameras, sneaking into the Aviary, and eating just one very important bird?

Logan tapped his pencil against the edge of his desk. Next to his computer, his Siamese fighting fish swished grandly around in circles, which was sort of how Logan's brain felt.

There was also still the mystery of how the griffin cubs had escaped the Menagerie on Thursday night. The unicorns had unlocked the griffin door and encouraged the cubs to run away. But that didn't explain why there was a hole in the river grate big enough for the cubs to squeeze through. Maybe someone had done that to help the griffins slip out, but who, and why? And was it connected to Pelly's murder?

Is someone trying to get the Menagerie in trouble?

He studied his list of questions. After a moment, he wrote:

Where is Mom?

He stared at the paper. That was the most important question—and the most impossible to answer.

The front door clicked open. Logan scrambled to hide his notebook under the other books on his desk right before his dad popped his head into the room.

Jackson Wilde was tall—over six feet tall, just like Logan's mom—with a shaved head and a huge smile, and he often joked that people in Wyoming kept mistaking him for Michael Jordan. He was about as laid-back as a person could be without being asleep. He never yelled at Logan; he never even got mad at slow traffic or shouted at the TV when their Chicago teams were losing.

He liked to tell people he was raising Logan free-range-style, like a chicken who was allowed to roam around the farm and do whatever it wanted, right up until the farmer decided to eat it. Dad thought that last part was particularly funny and occasionally poked Logan to see if he was ready to be Christmas dinner.

The postcard from Mom had seemed to confuse Dad more than upset him. Although they'd never talked about it, Logan was pretty sure Dad had uprooted the two of them from Chicago and moved out here to Wyoming so he could look for her.

It suddenly occurred to Logan that his dad might know a lot more than he'd ever let on. Maybe he even knew about

Mom's real job—tracking and capturing mythical creatures for SNAPA. Logan had always thought his dad would never lie to him, but maybe he'd been lying to Logan as much as Mom had.

"Hey there," Dad said. "You finally made it home. I was beginning to think Blue's parents must be cooler than I am, but then I realized, well, *that's* impossible." He grinned.

"Where were you?" Logan asked.

"Running." Dad checked the pedometer on his wrist. "Yup. Farther than last week. Let's not admit it's because I got lost again." He paused and squinted at Logan.

"What?" Logan asked.

"You okay? Usually I say *running* and you immediately tell me how much more fun it would be with a dog."

"Well," said Logan. "It would be." Before Friday, getting a dog had been his main goal in life. Now he felt like there were several bigger things to worry about.

His dad waited for a minute, as if expecting more, then said, "Okay. How about I shower and then we make nachos for the Bears game?"

"Sure." Logan turned to his computer and then swiveled back. "Um. I kind of ate all the hamburger meat, though." Or rather, he had fed it to a couple of hungry griffin cubs.

"There's more in the back of the freezer," said Dad.

Logan rubbed the back of his head. "No . . . I ate that, too."

Dad raised his eyebrows. "When did you have time to eat fourteen hamburgers if you were with Blue all weekend? No, don't even explain. I was always starving when I was your age, too. We'll just use beans." He laughed and headed off to his room.

Logan waited until he heard the shower running. Out in the living room, his dad had left his phone and wallet on the coffee table. Logan hesitated, looking at them for a moment. He didn't want to spy on his dad, but if Dad knew something about Logan's mom and wasn't telling him . . . how else would Logan be able to help find her?

He picked up the phone and scrolled through the call history, but the only numbers he recognized were his own and his grandparents' in Arizona. A couple of names appeared over and over, including Mr. Sterling, Jasmin's dad. But that wasn't a surprise—Logan had heard them talking to each other the night before, in Mr. Sterling's library, about something to do with Dad's work.

He was about to put the phone down when it suddenly started ringing. Startled, he dropped the phone on the floor, snatched it up, flung it on the table, and bolted back into his room.

The phone stopped ringing. Logan could hear his dad singing Adele over the sound of the shower.

He snuck back into the living room and quickly flipped through the business cards in the wallet. His dad worked for the wildlife department, so most of them were other government people.

Then his eye caught on a name he'd seen in the phone history.

Mark Zembolobel. Private Investigator.

Hmm. Logan saved the number from the card in his own phone and put everything back the way he'd found it. As he turned to go, he noticed the town newsletter on the floor, folded up, as if it had fallen out of his dad's pocket. The *Xanadu Bee* was a pretty goofy weekly notice printed up by the town hall and distributed in places like the library. The font made it look like an old-fashioned WANTED poster and the "news" usually involved a production of *The Unsinkable Molly Brown* at the high school or an old lady winning a rose-growing prize.

But today one of the headlines jumped out at Logan.

COYOTES?! bellowed the bold font.

Logan scooped up the newsletter and took it to his room.

Two minutes later, he dialed Blue's number.

"I know where we should start looking tonight," he said as soon as Blue answered. "The town thinks there's a coyote loose in Teddy Roosevelt Park. The *Bee* says they've found half-eaten rabbits all along the hiking trails. Could be a werewolf, right?"

"Or it could be a coyote," Blue pointed out in his sensible voice.

Logan's dad's phone started ringing again.

"Hang on," Logan said to Blue. This time the shower stopped, and Logan heard his dad hustle into the living room.

"Wilde," said his dad. A pause. "Seriously? That's the fourth one this week. We gotta catch this thing. Give me the address, I'll check it out." Another pause. "Okay, see you there."

"I'll call you back," Logan whispered. He strolled into the living room as if he was on his way to the kitchen for a drink. His dad was typing a note into his phone, wearing a towel around his waist.

"Hey, Logan, I need to go out for a bit. Sorry about that." He went into his room and Logan heard him open the closet door. "Rain check on the nachos? I should be back in an hour or so."

"Can I come with you?" Logan asked.

Dad emerged in jeans, buttoning up a light brown shirt. "Really? I'm just going to one of the ranches—some kind of animal attacked one of their sheep."

Logan shrugged, trying to hide the surge of curiosity that swept over him. "Sounds like more fun than algebra."

"I can't guarantee that." Dad smiled and scooped his things off the coffee table. "Let's go."

Outside, gold-tipped clouds swooshed across the enormous blue Wyoming sky. As they drove along the bumpy dirt path that led around the ranch, Logan fiddled with the GPS until he could see a bigger map of the area. The back of his neck prickled as he realized that the ranch was right next to Teddy Roosevelt Park, where the half-eaten rabbits had been found.

This is his hunting ground, he thought. *If there is a werewolf on the loose, this is where we'll find him. And then we can show SNAPA that Pelly was attacked by an outsider and it wasn't the Menagerie's fault. So there'd be no reason to shut them down or exterminate Scratch.*

He had a feeling it wouldn't be that simple, but he had to hope.

Logan's dad pulled over behind the sheriff's jeep. Sheriff Baxter and a man in a cowboy hat were leaning on the wooden rail fence. Behind them, in the paddock, Logan could see something lying on the ground, part dirty white wool and part bloodstained lumps.

"Do me a favor, stay in the car," said Logan's dad. "This could be pretty gruesome."

"What kind of animal attacked it?" Logan asked.

His dad rubbed his head. "Well, if it's like the last three, it seems like something bigger than a coyote, and it doesn't leave clear prints behind. The ranchers are also complaining that several sheep have disappeared completely, but that sounds like a thieving problem, not a wild animal problem. Not my department." He made a wry face. "Except I'm the only wildlife guy here in Xanadu, so everything's my department. I'll be right back, okay?"

Logan nodded and watched as his dad climbed out and went over to the sheriff and the rancher. He was just as happy not to get a closer look at the dead sheep.

But this had to be the right area to look for the werewolf. He could see the pine trees on the edge of Teddy Roosevelt Park from here.

He pulled out his phone and texted Blue and Zoe.

Meet me @ TR Park tonight. Dad should be asleep by 10.

He'd never snuck out of the house before, but this was a real case of life or death—Scratch's life, and possibly the Menagerie's. Logan looked up at the trees again and thought for another minute. The park was one of the smaller reserves in Wyoming, according to Dad, but it was still a pretty big area for three kids to cover in one night.

Unless they had a secret weapon, of course.

He looked back down at his phone and sent one more text.

VERY IMPORTANT: BRING KEIKO.

SEVEN

"Why," said Keiko, "would *I* do *anything* to help a dragon?"

"Forget about Scratch, then," Zoe said. She fired the tennis ball launcher three times in rapid succession. The hellhounds lunged to their feet and bolted across the grass, chasing the balls downhill toward the lake. Their black pelts disappeared into the darkness outside the house's circle of lights. "Think of it as stopping a dangerous werewolf."

Keiko crossed her arms. "If there even *is* a werewolf, why shouldn't it eat whatever it wants?"

"Don't overidentify," Blue said from his perch on the low wall around the hellhounds' Doghouse. "Kitsune and

werewolves are totally different. You're much more sophisticated and in control than they are."

"True." Keiko tossed her long, dark braids back over her
shoulders. "But we're more sophisticated than everyone."

Zoe understood why Logan wanted them to bring Keiko
tonight. Her sense of smell was naturally much better than
any of theirs—perhaps good enough to find a werewolf in a
big park. But he wasn't the one here trying to convince Keiko,
of all people, to be a glorified bloodhound. She'd refused to
help with tracking the griffin cubs. This wouldn't be any different.

It had already been a horribly frustrating day. The agents
had cordoned off the dragons and the Aviary while they gathered evidence, so the Kahns couldn't do any investigating of
their own. Zoe wanted to look at that broken anklet, and
she wanted to compare the marks on the Aviary's back door
to Scratch's claws, and she wanted to test his electric fence
implant, but she couldn't do any of those things. Her parents
had made her focus on regular Menagerie chores all day, and
now she felt like kicking something. It was too late to save
Pelly, but Zoe refused to lose Scratch, too.

The trial was set for Thursday. Four days—how could
they clear Scratch's name in just a few days unless they were
allowed access to everything?

Well, step one: find another suspect.

Jaws, Killer, and Ripper came barreling back into the

light and flung slobbery tennis balls at Zoe's feet. It was a little late to be exercising the hellhounds, but there hadn't been any time before dinner, and if they didn't burn off some energy they might literally burn up something else. Zoe fired the machine again and the dogs all sprinted away. Except for Sheldon, who was flopped in front of Keiko, presenting his belly in a hilariously optimistic way. Sheldon the Misfit Hellhound was just about the only animal in the Menagerie—or person, for that matter—who didn't have a healthy fear of Keiko.

"Why isn't Logan here, again?" Blue asked Zoe.

She wrinkled her nose. "Something to do with bears. He said he had to watch bears with his dad. I guess it's on the Nature Channel? I have no idea."

A figure moved, out in the darkness, and Zoe held up her hand to shield her eyes from the light. Someone was heading up from the lake to the garage on the other side of the house. From the shape, she guessed it was her brother.

Matthew had been to Tracker camp this past summer. Maybe they'd learned about tracking werewolves. Maybe he'd have some ideas she could use.

"Be right back," she said to Blue.

The garage had two back doors: one leading directly into the Kahns' kitchen, and the other leading out to the Menagerie. This last one was swinging shut as Zoe ran up to it.

She pushed through into the garage and found the lights were off.

"Matthew?" she said, flicking them on.

Her brother leaped away from the van as if a chupacabra had bitten his toes.

"Zoe!" he yelped, nearly tripping over a pile of chains on the floor. "Give me a heart attack, why don't you?"

"What were you doing in the dark?" she asked, puzzled.

"Um . . . checking for holes in the fireproof suits." He pulled a black flashlight out of his hip holster. "I shine this at them and see if any light comes through on the walls."

"Wow," Zoe said. "That is so far down on our list of things to do. Are you kidding? If you need some real work, come to me. I could keep you busy for weeks."

"Why are you creeping around after me?" Matthew asked.

"I wasn't CREEPING," Zoe objected. "I wanted to ask you something. Hypothetically, if you needed to track a werewolf, what would you do?"

Matthew frowned. "Well," he said, "for starters, I would *not* be twelve years old, and I would *not* be planning to sneak out of the house and go wandering around the woods in the middle of the night. Even with my special amazing friend and his natural Tracker instincts."

For a moment Zoe thought he meant Keiko, and then she

realized he was talking about Logan. She'd been bothered by how easily Logan got along with all the animals, too, until he spent the whole weekend helping to save the Menagerie and also turned out to be generally pretty cool.

But Matthew had dreamed of becoming a Tracker his whole life. He'd been studying and practicing for as long as Zoe could remember, long before he finally qualified for Tracker camp. It must be extra-weird for him to have Logan come in and instinctively be good at everything Tracker related.

"I didn't say anything about sneaking out," she said. "I was just *wondering* what you would do if you thought there might be a werewolf around."

"I would call SNAMHP," Matthew said firmly. "Catching werecreatures is their problem." The SuperNatural Agency for Mostly Human Protection was SNAPA's sister department; they showed up occasionally to bustle around and check on the mermaids. Zoe figured the Menagerie had enough problems with SNAPA. Besides, she wasn't even sure yet there *was* a werewolf.

"Well, you're a fountain of helpfulness," Zoe said. "Thanks anyway."

"Zoe, you'd better not be planning something stupid," Matthew said. "Mom and Dad let you do lots of crazy things, but I'm pretty sure looking for a werewolf during the full moon isn't one of them."

"You should talk," Zoe said. She darted past him and pulled open the van door. A loaded tranquilizer gun was leaning against the passenger seat.

"Aha!" she cried. "I knew you weren't checking the fire-proof suits! Where do you think you're going with this?"

Matthew flushed bright red, making the scar next to his eyebrow stand out even whiter. "I have important Tracker business to do." He reached around Zoe and slammed the door shut again.

"You aren't a Tracker," Zoe said. "You're still in high school. Is this about Pelly? Are you looking for whatever killed her, too?"

"Ye-es," Matthew admitted reluctantly. Relief swept through Zoe. That meant they could all work together. She'd feel much safer about their werewolf escapade if Matthew—and all his Tracker training—was with them.

She was about to invite him to join their hunting party when he cut her off. "But no, you can't come."

Zoe's mouth snapped shut and she decided to keep Logan's theory about Teddy Roosevelt Park to herself. If Matthew didn't want help, then fine, she'd catch the were-wolf herself.

"All right," she said. "I won't tell Mom and Dad on you if you don't tell them on me."

Matthew sighed huffily. "Fine," he said. "Don't you dare get eaten."

"Same to you." Zoe lifted her chin and marched back outside.

Okay, she thought. *Potentially I haven't completely thought this through.* Like, if they *did* find a werewolf, she didn't exactly have a plan for catching it. *A tranq gun would be pretty useful. Not to mention chains or a net or something.*

But she couldn't really imagine they would catch a full-grown werewolf by themselves. *No, what we're looking for is information*, she told herself. *We just need to know there is a werewolf, and if possible what his human face looks like. Then we tell SNAPA and they'll see there's a better suspect than Scratch for them to investigate—one that wouldn't result in shutting down the Menagerie.*

She knew, deep down inside, that even if they found a werewolf, Scratch might still be guilty. There was a lot of upsetting evidence stacked against him. But the jury needed reasonable doubt in order to find him innocent, which meant they needed another believable suspect. Plus investigating a werewolf would keep SNAPA busy and might buy the Menagerie a little more time to clear Scratch. If he hadn't done it. *Surely he couldn't have done it.*

When she got back to the Doghouse, Blue was still trying to convince Keiko to go with them.

"Well," he was saying as Zoe came up. "What if Zoe did all your homework for a month?"

"Blue!" Zoe protested. As if she had time for another set of homework!

"Oooh. I do hate homework," Keiko said thoughtfully.

"You keep saying foxes don't need math," Blue observed.

"Or history," Keiko said. "Or shove-a-spike-in-my-ears stupid SPANISH."

"Wait, wait," Zoe said. "How about something else? Half my lunch money for a week?"

"Lame," said Keiko. She gave Blue an appraising look. "Did I hear that you're going to Jasmin's Halloween party on Friday?"

Blue's sigh was epic and long-suffering. Zoe felt a stab of irritation. She'd give almost anything to be invited to Jasmin's party—not because she cared about the party itself, but because it would mean being friends with Jasmin again.

Last Halloween they'd dressed up as Anne of Green Gables and her best friend Diana. Almost nobody knew who they were supposed to be, but they didn't care. Jasmin had insisted that Zoe be Anne because of her red hair, even though Zoe thought Jasmin was a lot more Anne-like than she was. They'd trick-or-treated at the fancy houses near Jasmin's and then had a sleepover where they tried to scare themselves with the spookiest-sounding movie in Jonathan's collection, except it turned out *Ghost* was some kind of mushy love story and not that scary at all and then Jasmin yelled at the movie for making them cry, which made Zoe laugh until she fell off the bed and broke Jasmin's tiger lamp, and then they both got in trouble. It was the best Halloween ever.

This Halloween she would be at home, alone, most likely trying to distract Captain Fuzzbutt with *It's the Great Pumpkin, Charlie Brown* while combing out the knots in his fur. So when Blue acted like seeing Jasmin was such dreadful torture, it made her want to smack him.

"All right," Keiko said. "I'll come to the woods with you tonight *if* you promise to get me invited to the party. Don't give me that face. I know you can make it happen."

"Why would you want to go?" Zoe asked. "Isn't it terribly boring and human to care about popular kids' parties?"

Keiko narrowed her eyes at Zoe. "Then again, my Spanish homework has been particularly awful lately . . ."

"Okay, okay," Blue said, waving his hands. "I'm sure I can bring you, too. Jasmin won't care who's there."

Except me, Zoe thought sadly. She remembered the day her parents had made her slip kraken ink to Jasmin. Its magic erased any supernatural memories, so if Jasmin knew anything about the Menagerie—if her brother, Jonathan, had told the rest of the Sterlings—then it would all disappear from her mind.

But of course she hadn't known anything. Most of all,

Jasmin hadn't known that would be the last day she and Zoe could hang out, since the Kahns couldn't risk Zoe's presence triggering any memories in the Sterlings. Jasmin hadn't understood why Zoe kept bursting into tears. Instead Jasmin had hugged her and made her sit on the counter while Jasmin made banana bread and told her whatever it was would be okay.

Which it hadn't been, and still wasn't.

That was the same day Zoe's sister, Ruby, dosed Jonathan and his parents, so the scene at home was All About Ruby and the Epic Tragedy of her Failed Romance, featuring lots of wailing on the couch about how Ruby would have sacrificed ten jackalopes for her one true love and now he wouldn't remember *anything* about their time together (her sister's own fault, Zoe thought savagely, for telling him about the Menagerie and letting his memories of Ruby get all wound up with supernatural secrets in the first place). Zoe's mom and dad had been too busy comforting Ruby to notice Zoe going up to her room and crying into Captain Fuzzbutt's fur for the next two weeks.

Keiko had noticed, but Keiko's reaction to human emotions usually involved disgust and/or hiding, which was fine by Zoe. Sympathy from Keiko would only have made things worse.

"Fine," Keiko said. "But if we get caught, I am so letting them ship me back to Japan."

"Sounds awesome," Zoe muttered.

Three hours later, they were pacing in the parking lot near the picnic area of the reserve—the same part of the park where they'd caught a griffin cub on Saturday. According to Logan, Yump still hadn't forgiven them for the cheeseburgers trick, although his new fish-and-vegetables diet probably wasn't helping his mood.

Streaks of clouds gathered overhead, blocking most of the moon and making all the shadows jump and seethe. The wind whipped fiercely through their jackets. Blue and Keiko seemed to have some kind of Mostly Human immunity to cold, but Zoe shivered and stamped her feet, wishing she'd worn boots instead of sneakers.

The lot was mostly deserted, apart from one empty car and one minivan, which made Zoe a bit nervous. Was someone camping out here, in late October on a Sunday night? Or did one of the cars belong to the werewolf? The minivan seemed familiar; Zoe had the weird feeling she'd seen it in this exact parking lot before, but she hadn't been here that often—and she wasn't really into cars, so most likely she was imagining things.

"Why are we waiting for your boyfriend?" Keiko demanded. "He isn't essential to finding this thing; *I* am." She twisted her braids up onto her head and clipped them in place, so the ends stood up like little fox ears.

"He's not my boyfriend!" Zoe said. "And from what we've

seen of him so far, he probably *is* essential. Besides, this was his idea."

The coughing rumble of an engine reached their ears. Something was approaching from the main road, but it wasn't Logan's bike.

Zoe, Blue, and Keiko darted into the shadows behind the restroom building, where they'd hidden their bikes. They crouched and peered out as a rickety van shambled into the lot and wheezed to a stop not far away.

"Isn't that our van?" Blue whispered.

"Shh," said Zoe. The Menagerie's old blue-gray van had been battered enough before a griffin cub had gone nuts in it on Friday. Now there were dents and long scratches on the roof, where Clink had landed, and the back door she'd knocked off had been reattached by Matthew and Dad in a makeshift way that Zoe was pretty sure involved duct tape. So yes, that was definitely their van.

Matthew climbed out of the driver's seat, lifted a clanking duffel bag out of the back, picked up the tranq gun, and strode into the forest. In two minutes, he'd vanished into the trees.

"Huh," said Blue.

"I guess he had the same idea we did," Zoe said. *What does he know?* she wondered. *Why is he here, too?*

She realized a small part of her felt like, *Oh, Matthew's on the case, now we can go home.* But there was also a part of her that wanted to find the werewolf before he did. And there was a third, not so small part that was starting to loudly point out that maybe they were both crazy to be doing this.

Is Pelly's murderer out here right now?

And are we heading straight toward him?

EIGHT

Logan flew along the dark streets of Xanadu on his bike, glancing up at the round silver moon overhead. It was much later than he'd hoped. He kept imagining Zoe and Blue alone in the woods with a werewolf, where he had sent them. He was trying very hard not to think about the sheep or Pelly.

Not that my being there will be much help . . . but still, I would rather be there.

Keiko could just turn into a fox and escape if she needed to. Logan wondered if she'd stay to help if the others were attacked. He found that a bit hard to imagine.

Finally the trees of the reserve loomed up ahead, and he skidded into the parking lot on his bike. Zoe waved him over to where she, Blue, and Keiko were crouched in the shadows behind the restroom building.

"Sorry," he whispered as he joined them. "My dad was up typing on his computer for an hour longer than I expected. I finally stuffed pillows in my bed and went out the same window Squorp came in, except it turns out that's a lot easier with wings, because there are these dumb hedges right out there that tried to eat me alive." He brushed leaf debris out of the short, dark fuzz of his hair.

"Well, I'm glad you're finally here," Zoe said. She plucked a twig off the shoulder of his jacket.

"Me, too," said Blue.

Logan tried to squash his grin. He shrugged. "I'm not a hundred percent sure I can get back inside in one piece, but I guess we worry about that after we catch a werewolf."

"I'm not going to worry about it at all," Keiko said. "Let's go already." She took a few steps into the field where the grills were, stopped, and took a deep breath.

"What do you smell?" Zoe asked.

"Parking lot," Keiko said. "And burned charcoal. Blech." She took off running toward the nearest hiking trail, and the others ran after her.

"Hey," Logan said to Zoe, panting as he ran. "Anything new about Pelly or Scratch?"

Zoe shook her head. "Just that we have to pick a jury on Tuesday. And Mom and Dad are arguing about whether we can afford a fancy SNAPA lawyer to defend Scratch, which we clearly can't, because Pelly's golden eggs were pretty much our entire income."

Keiko stopped again after about twenty minutes of running. She wasn't even breathing heavily. Logan and Blue collapsed on a boulder while Zoe crouched and gasped for air.

"You are being unreasonably loud," Keiko said crossly.

"*You're* being unreasonably nonhuman," Zoe said.

Logan shivered, cold again despite how much he was sweating. Beside him, Blue's blond hair shone like silver in the darts of moonlight that made it through the trees. Branches creaked in the wind, and little paws seemed to be skittering all around them.

"What do you smell now?" Logan asked Keiko.

She wrinkled her nose. "It's really strange out here." She tilted her head, turning slowly as she inhaled. "The forest is busy tonight."

"You mean with people?" Zoe asked. "Can you tell the difference between people, werewolves, and regular wolves?"

Even in the dark, Keiko's glare was icy. "Of course I can. Werewolves smell like both, no matter what form they're in. But there's more than one werecreature out here."

Goose bumps raced across Logan's skin.

"More than one?" Zoe whispered.

Blue touched the button that lit up his watch. "It's almost midnight. If they haven't changed already, that's when it happens whether they want to or not."

"Most of the ones out here have changed already," Keiko said, closing her eyes and reaching her arms out to either side. In the moonlit shadows, she looked like a horror-movie scarecrow.

"How many do you smell?" Logan asked.

Keiko shook her head. "I think there are . . . eight."

Zoe inhaled sharply. "Eight unregistered werecreatures? That could be a pack—a whole pack of werewolves in Xanadu! Hunting sheep and sneaking into our Menagerie!"

"They're not all werewolves," Keiko went on. She glanced up at the trees. "As far as I can smell, perhaps only one werewolf, and then a whole variety of other things. Like, there's a weresquirrel about ten minutes that way."

A weresquirrel? How does that even happen? "We're looking for something a bit bigger than that," Logan said.

"Although maybe if we catch one of the werecreatures, he or she can lead us to the others," Zoe suggested.

"One is still in human form, not far from here," Keiko said, sniffing the air. "So he'll be slower and easier to catch, if we hurry."

"Let's go," Logan said, jumping off the boulder.

They followed Keiko, diving off the trail into the snapping arms of the trees, fallen leaves crunching under their shoes, wind tugging at their clothes. Logan ducked under a branch and tried not to think about who—or what—they might find out here in the dark.

"Here!" Keiko held up her hand and stopped suddenly. Logan tripped over a tree root and sprawled into a pile of leaves. The ground was still wet from the previous night's rainstorm, and his knees slid through mud. Damp leaves stuck to his hands as he climbed to his feet, trying to brush them off.

He had never been out in the woods at night like this. Late-night activities in Chicago usually involved a lot more streetlights and taxicabs. *And Dad.* Dad had taken Logan to a couple of jazz club shows that went until midnight, but that was nothing like this. This was millions of stars. This was eerie whispering trees. This was *oh, we might get eaten by a werewolf at any moment.*

A twig cracked not far away, and they all whirled toward the sound. Logan peered into the dark. Was that—someone moving?

At the same moment, Keiko flung up her arm and pointed. A shape broke from the shadows and bolted into the forest.

"He's seen us," Blue said, but Logan and Zoe were already running after the mystery figure.

And what do we do now? Logan had a moment to think. *Catch the werewolf right before he turns into a wolf? No flaws in that plan . . .*

A bramble bush clawed painfully at his arm as he ran by. And then, up ahead, the fleeing stranger ran smack into a tree branch and keeled over like a cartoon character.

"OWWW," moaned a vaguely familiar-sounding voice.

Logan slowed down and scrambled his flashlight out of his jacket pocket. Flicking it on, he approached cautiously. He could sense Zoe at his elbow, and he was pretty sure Blue and Keiko were close behind.

"Who are you?" Logan called.

"Oh, *no*," the person groaned. The flashlight beam played across the back of a red sweater as he sat up and glanced at the sky. "No, no, no. Please go away. Don't come near me right now. Please, I'm really serious."

"Why?" said Logan. "What do you turn into?"

The stranger froze, then whipped around abruptly to stare into the light.

Logan and Zoe both gasped, and Logan dropped the flashlight.

"*Marco?*" Zoe said as Logan scrambled for the flashlight through the leaves.

Marco Jimenez, Logan thought. *From our class at school.* He suddenly remembered seeing Marco and his family in the reserve on Saturday, climbing into their minivan, while Logan and Zoe were out trying to lure a griffin.

The class clown is a werewolf?

"Who is that?" said the boy in the red sweater, shielding

his eyes. "Do I know you?"

"Only since kindergarten," Zoe said, stepping forward as Logan shone his light up again. "Marco, what are you doing out here?"

Marco looked at the sky again and shrank back, waving his hands. "You have to get out of here. I can't explain, but—"

"You'll become something dangerous?" Zoe guessed. "How did this happen to you? Who else is out here? Anyone who really likes to eat geese?"

Marco blinked at her like she was crazy.

"Uh, Zoe," said Logan. "Maybe now isn't the best—"

"Aaaagh," Marco yelped, clutching his stomach.

"Too late," Blue said from behind them. "He's changing."

Logan and Zoe both took a step back, but neither one ran. Logan imagined that Zoe felt the same way he did—he wanted to know the truth, and he wanted to see what happened.

But as Marco doubled over with a yell, and his skin began to writhe as if snakes were going to explode out of him, and his head changed shape and his whole body shrank, Logan felt his legs shaking. He wasn't sure he could run now even if he wanted to.

And then, suddenly, Marco seemed to vanish right in front of them. All that was left was his red sweater, which lay in a strange heap on the ground on top of Marco's jeans and sneakers.

The sweater moved.

"Too small to be a wolf," Zoe whispered, relief flooding her voice.

"Maybe a raccoon," Logan guessed. "Or a badger? Are there werebadgers? Okay, actually, I have no idea how big a badger is."

"Nothing quite so impressive," Keiko said, strolling past them. She walked over to the pile of clothes and lifted up the sweater with a flourish.

A pair of beady black eyes blinked in the light. Black and white feathers floated around knobbly clawed feet.

"AWK," said Marco.

"Oh, didn't I mention that part?" Keiko said. "Marco Jimenez is a wererooster."

NINE

"So, just to clarify," said Zoe. "You have literally known that Marco Jimenez was a wererooster since the first day of school, but at no point did that seem like a useful thing to tell the Menagerie."

"Why?" Keiko said. "So you could do what? Lock him up? Because he's such a menace to society?" She arched her eyebrows at the rooster Logan was chasing around the clearing.

Catching a rooster hadn't sounded quite so difficult in Logan's head. After all, Logan was a lot bigger than the bird. Advantage: Logan.

"Don't let him peck you," Blue said for the fifth time. "Not all forms of lycanthropy are spread by biting, but we don't know what kind he has."

Advantage: rooster.

Logan jumped back as Marco flapped his wings at him. He really, really did not want to be turned into a werechicken.

"Why can't we leave him here?" Keiko asked. "You realize you can interrogate him at school in about eight hours."

Zoe flinched, and Logan guessed she was thinking of how little sleep she'd get tonight.

"We can't abandon him," he said. "This forest is crawling with dangerous things; you said so yourself."

"Well, I said werecreatures," Keiko said with a shrug. "I didn't actually say they were dangerous."

"Keiko, could you try to be just a *little* helpful, for once?" Zoe asked. "Are they all squirrels and roosters? Is there anything that could have eaten Pelly?"

"I think I have been *extremely* helpful," Keiko said frostily. "But if you would like to sniff out your own werecreatures, be my guest." She turned and flounced away through the trees.

"Keiko!" Blue called, hurrying after her.

"You know, I blame your mom for this," Zoe said to Logan. "It was her idea for us to adopt Keiko in the first place, and why? Because she'd been kicked out of both Japanese menageries. Which apparently didn't set off any warning bells for my parents, oh no."

"Gotcha!" Logan flung his jacket over the rooster and tackled it. A hurricane of frenzied flapping went off under his arms, but he buried his head in the jacket fabric and waited, and finally Marco went quiet. Logan was able to scoop up the whole bird, keeping it carefully wrapped.

"Now what do we do?" he asked.

"We take him to your house," said Zoe. She gathered up Marco's clothes and shoes and set off in the same direction as Blue and Keiko. "And when he turns back into Marco, we ask him what he knows about the rest of the pack out here, and hopefully one of them was the werewolf who ate Pelly, and then we can prove Scratch is innocent and save both him and the Menagerie." She nodded, as if convincing herself. "Yes. That could all definitely happen."

Logan shivered. It was freezing without his jacket. He was glad to be heading indoors, but—"Wait, my house?" he said. "That's a terrible idea."

"Listen, Marco might have a reason for being unregistered," Zoe said. "I don't like it, but if we want his cooperation, we should at least listen to his side of the story first. But if we take him to my place he could get spotted by anyone—my parents, Matthew, Blue's mom, the SNAPA agents—"

"Whereas if I take him home, the only person who might see him is my dad," Logan said with a sigh. "Okay, fine. I get it." *Not sure how I'll explain a new pet rooster to Dad, though.*

Soon they found a trail to follow, but it was a long, cold walk back to the parking lot. Blue was waiting by their bikes, leaning casually against the wall as if he were posing for a movie poster.

"I'm sure you'll be shocked to hear this," he said, "but Keiko has stormed off in great outrage and may never speak to us again."

"I only asked a reasonable question!" Zoe protested. "Mythical creatures are so touchy."

"I'm not," Blue said with a grin.

"Guys, how am I supposed to carry a rooster home on my bike?" Logan asked. His jacket had been making sleepy chicken clucks for a while, but he didn't want to let go of it even for a minute, just in case a beak escaped and pecked him.

Blue scratched his head. "Here," he said, taking off his own jacket. Using Marco's sweater as well, the three of them tied the rooster bundle into an awkward sling around Logan's chest. He still had to hold on to it with one hand, but the other was free to steer. The rest of Marco's clothes went in a plastic bag that Logan could hang from the handlebars.

"We'll ride back with you," Zoe said. "To make sure you get home okay."

"I'll be fine," Logan said. "Go get some sleep."

Zoe hesitated. Even in the half-shadowed moonlight, he could see the rings of exhaustion under her eyes. They hadn't exactly slept well the night before, trapped in the Sterling mansion's secret staircase.

"Seriously, I'll be fine. Come over in the morning," he offered. "What time will Marco turn back?"

"Dawn," said Blue.

"Awesome." Explaining a rooster in his room would be one problem; explaining a whole seventh grader would be another. Logan really hoped tomorrow morning would be one of the ones where his dad left early and their only communication was a note on the kitchen counter.

He rode home slowly, wobbling and off balance with the weight on his chest, but at least the wererooster didn't wake up. By the time he made it back, he thought it had to be at least two o'clock in the morning. His dad's window was dark. Logan leaned his bike against the garage and looked at the hedges around his own window for a minute before deciding that wasn't going to happen. There was no way he could climb through them without accidentally poking Marco, and he could just imagine how loud that reaction would be.

So he slipped in the front door instead and tiptoed to his room. The glow from Warrior's fish tank cast blue light on his bedroom ceiling. On his bed, Purrsimmon's eyes glinted green as she glowered at him.

"You're not going to like this much, either," Logan said to her. He carefully unwrapped the sling and carried the rooster, still in his jacket, over to his closet.

Purrsimmon hissed and arched her back, her hindquarters waggling back and forth, ready to pounce. Chasing birds was one of her specialties.

"No," Logan said firmly. "You leave this one alone." He kicked all his shoes and sports stuff out of the way and gently put the rooster down on his closet floor. No movement from under his jacket. Quickly he bundled up Marco's clothes and left them next to the rooster.

It was going to be a really, really weird morning. Logan felt bad for Marco, waking up in a strange guy's cramped closet. The two of them had barely ever spoken before. He hesitated, glancing around his room, and grabbed a Post-it note from his desk.

Don't panic! We're friendly. We just want to talk.

He stuck that to the inside of his closet door and left his flashlight on, propped up on Marco's shoes and pointing at the note.

He couldn't think of anything else to do, so he closed the door on the rooster and went to bed.

"COCK A DOOOOODLE DOOOOOOOOOOOO!"

Logan struggled awake through a fog of confusion.

"*COCK A DOOOOODLE DOOOOOOOOOOOOOOOOOOOOO!*"

Logan squinted at the window, where the dim gray light still had that presunrise feel. *What evil neighbor decided to get a rooster?*

His bedroom door flew open. His dad stood in the doorway, blinking wildly.

"Did you hear that?" Dad asked.

"Hear what?" Logan rubbed his eyes.

"A *rooster*," his dad said. "It sounded like it was coming from *in here*."

That woke Logan up in a hurry. He forced himself not to look at his closet.

"Oh, uh, sorry," he said. "It's my new . . . alarm clock."

"Good lord, Logan," said his dad. "I know you sleep like the dead, but we'll be run out of town if you let that thing go off again. I'm pretty sure it woke all of Xanadu." He peered around the room. "Wait, what new alarm clock?"

"Blue loaned it to me," Logan said quickly. "He warned me it was loud, so I put it in the closet." *Aaargh, why did I say that? Don't look in the closet. Don't look in the closet.*

"Well, please give it back." Dad yawned hugely. "If you're still having trouble getting up, I'll rearrange my meetings so I can always wake you. Deal?"

"Don't worry, Dad," said Logan. "I can get up. I'll return the rooster today. Uh, the rooster clock."

"The things they think of," Dad muttered, starting

to close the door behind him.

There was a giant thump from inside Logan's closet.

Dad swung the door back open. "What was that?"

"Nothing!" Logan said quickly. "Must have been Purrsimmon."

The cat chose that moment to saunter delicately around the corner of the bed, sit down on the floor, and lick her paws. She gave Logan an arch look that said, *Don't you drag me into this. Especially after you deprived me of rooster chasing and made me spend the whole night with a bird just out of reach, you monster.*

Dad stared at the cat for a moment. Then, shaking his head, he finally closed the door and went back down the hall to his own room.

Logan flung his covers off. His clock said 6:50 a.m.

There was another muffled thump from inside his closet. It sounded like someone trying to get dressed in a cramped space in the dark.

"Marco?" Logan said. "Hey. I don't know if you know my name, but it's Logan, from school. We were worried that something in the woods might eat you, so I brought you back to my house."

His closet door creaked open and Marco's disheveled head poked out. His dark hair stuck up in tufts like wild feathers.

They stared at each other for a minute.

"That's what *I* always say," Marco blurted. "I mean, who would take a defenseless rooster to the woods, right? I keep saying, what if Carlos eats me, and Mom is all, but he would never, and then I'm like, *you* don't know, you're, like, a *porcupine*, and he's, like, a *bear*, and he doesn't like me when we're *people*, so why risk your kids eating each other, like, can't I just stay in my room and be a rooster in there? What's the worst I could do? Poop on my sheets? Guess what, Elena already did that, and she wasn't even a squirrel at the time, she was just potty training and mad at me, which by the way, is the worst, don't ever live with a three-year-old."

He took a deep breath. "Oh my God, I'm starving. I'm missing the pancake breakfast right now. Do you think they're worried? I don't; I bet they're eating bacon and laughing about how I'm probably lost in the woods because roosters have no sense of direction, like, we shouldn't *need* a sense of direction, guys, because we don't *belong in the woods*, hello, and none of them are thinking, hey, maybe something ate Marco, even though that is obviously what happened. I'm *starving*. Can we have pancakes? It's like the only good part of the whole thing, so I should at least get pancakes. With a side order of corn, if you have any, please."

"I—um, I don't know," Logan said. "But we should stay in here until my dad leaves. I have no idea how to explain you."

Marco toppled out of the closet and lay on his back on the

carpet, groaning at the ceiling. "Okay. But you might have to explain my corpse instead, just to warn you. When will he be gone?"

"Soon, I think," Logan said. He could hear his dad clattering around in the kitchen, which usually meant he'd be out the door before Logan. "Did you say something about your mom? And a bear?"

"Not fair," Marco moaned. "I'm too weak from hunger to keep secrets."

"I think the rooster's out of the bag," Logan joked.

"Ha-ha!" Marco chortled. "I get it."

"Logan!" his dad called.

"Back in the closet!" Logan whispered. "Quick!"

Marco flopped sideways like it was too hard to move.

"Hey," Dad called again, his voice coming closer. "If you're ready to leave in five minutes, I can drive you to school."

Logan stepped over Marco and stuck his head into the hallway. "No thanks," he called back. "I'll take my bike. I might go hang out with Blue again after school."

His dad laughed. "All right, but if his parents get sick of you, you can bring him back here anytime. I'll be home for dinner tonight, if you want to invite him over."

"Um," Logan said. "Okay, maybe."

"If I promise not to cook?"

"I'll ask. Bye, Dad." Logan was about to duck back into his room when the doorbell rang.

He ran, but Dad got there first.

Zoe and Blue were standing on the front steps. Logan reached the door just in time to see his dad's eyes widen when he spotted Zoe.

"Oh, hey, guys," Logan said. "Dad, this is Blue and—"

"Zoe," said his dad. "Zoe Kahn."

TEN

There was a really unsettling pause. Zoe stared back at Mr. Wilde, sure she'd never seen him before. How did he know her name?

"You, uh—you've met Zoe?" Logan said.

"I've seen your parents around town," said Mr. Wilde. Zoe noticed that although his face was calm, his hand was gripping the door tightly.

"We were just going to bike to school together," said Logan, shifting from foot to foot.

"Right," said Mr. Wilde. "Come on in. Logan, can I talk to you for a minute?"

Zoe followed Blue into the living room and perched

awkwardly on the edge of the couch.

"I knew we should have waited till his car was gone," Blue said, flopping into one of the easy chairs.

"Well, you could have *said so*," Zoe pointed out. It hadn't occurred to her that Mr. Wilde might recognize her. Or that he'd act so weird if he did. Maybe she was being paranoid, though. Maybe he'd just met her parents somewhere.

The front door opened and closed, and Logan came back into the living room with faint worry lines creasing his forehead.

"Is he gone?" Zoe asked. "Is everything okay?"

"I think so," Logan said. "He wanted to know how I met you."

"What did you say?" If Mr. Wilde knew about Logan's mom's job, maybe she'd told him about the Kahns and their Menagerie, even though it was strictly against SNAPA policy to talk to outsiders about any of the locations.

"I acted like a guy," Logan said. "You know—'Daaaaad! She's just a friend! Don't be WEEEEEIRD about it!'"

Zoe felt herself blushing. Sure, it was a good idea for Logan to act as if his dad thought they were dating, but it still made her feel kind of funny inside.

"And when he asked again, I just said we met because of Blue."

"Freaky," offered Blue. "He definitely knows something is up with you, Zoe."

"Well, when he feels like telling me the truth about Mom, I'll tell him the truth about you," said Logan. "I mean, if you're okay with that—I'll check with you first, I promise. Marco!" he called. "You can come out now."

There was no answer.

Logan bolted into his room, so Zoe jumped up and followed him.

Marco was hanging halfway out the window with his foot tangled in the hedges outside. Purrsimmon sat on Logan's desk chair, hissing.

"What are you *doing*?" Zoe asked.

"I'm escaping!" Marco yelled. He flung himself out the window, hollering in pain as he thrashed through the hedge and sprawled onto the lawn.

Zoe and Logan ran back through the house, startling Blue into following them out the front door and around to where Marco was still lying on the grass, almost nose to nose with a gray squirrel. The squirrel put its paws on its squirrelly hips and chattered angrily at him.

"Hey, I tried," said Marco. "You saw me try. Now go tell Mom and Dad I'm fine."

The squirrel glared at him. Zoe was used to seeing human expressions on mythical creatures, but on an ordinary-looking squirrel, it was pretty unsettling.

Marco sat up and gestured at the squirrel. "Zoe, Logan, Blue, this is my sister Elena."

"*EEEEEEEEEEEEEEKEEKEEEEK*," the squirrel shrilled in outrage.

"And since she's here, that probably means my brother Carlos is, too." Marco squinted around at the neighboring houses. "Anyone see a bear?"

"*AARRBAKAKABAKRRABAK!*" the squirrel shouted.

"If you want to yell at me properly, you'll have to turn back into a person first," Marco hollered back. "I know what you're yapping about, but they knew before they even found me, so don't blame me."

"*ECKECK ECKECK ARRK!*"

"I have no idea how! Now I'm going to school, so go away!"

The squirrel stamped off as huffily as a squirrel could. Zoe saw it dart behind the next house, and then a small black bear shambled out and ran toward town with the squirrel on its head, clinging to its ears.

"I am so confused," said Logan.

"A whole family of werecreatures," Zoe guessed. "I've read about those. It's genetic, right? One werecreature married another?"

"Yeah," said Marco. "It's your classic story of raccoon meets porcupine, raccoon marries porcupine, followed by a white picket fence and lots of cool werechildren, plus one not-so-cool wererooster." He stood up and bowed, brushing leaves off his sweater. "So, wait, how *did* you know I was going to turn into something?"

Zoe and Blue exchanged glances. This was the tricky part—getting answers out of Marco without giving too much away.

"We're kind of . . . related to some mythical-creature Trackers," Zoe tried.

"I didn't know those were real," Marco said. "Not the kind that might throw me in a cage, though, right? Man, Mom and Dad would be so mad, and at the same time, they'd be like, well, of course it was Marco who got caught; that's so typical of him."

"You're safe with us, don't worry," said Logan.

"Yeah, you guys don't have an 'evil government facility' vibe." Marco grinned. "Hey, so, if I'm walking to school from here, I gotta start now. If I'm late again, Coach said I'd have to miss the next game."

"We'll walk with you," Zoe said. "We've got some more questions." *Like: Does anyone in your family have a taste for geese? And: Care to come exonerate a dragon?*

"We can stop at the bakery on the way," Marco suggested, his face brightening. He patted his pockets. "And someone can buy me a doughnut. I think that's a fair price for rooster-napping me."

Logan ran inside to change and get his backpack. The others waited in awkward silence. Marco reached up and tried to flatten his hair, unsuccessfully.

"Hey," Blue said to Marco. "Did you finish the science homework?"

"I tried, but I fell asleep. Being a rooster three nights in a row—being a *terrified* rooster stuck in the *woods* all night long—is surprisingly tiring."

"Why were you in the woods?" Zoe asked as Logan rolled his bike up to them. She and Blue got their bikes and they all set off walking toward the center of town.

"It's my parents' idea." Marco shrugged. "They figure we're less likely to get caught if we're all in the woods when we shift. And they think it's good practice for us to be animals in our natural environment instead of locking ourselves in cages for the full moon nights. Of course, the woods is the right place for my brothers and sisters, but not so much for me. If Carlos doesn't accidentally eat me one of these days, I'm sure something else will."

"Are you going to get in trouble for telling us all this?" Zoe asked anxiously. She knew how her parents would react if she spilled all the Menagerie's secrets to a bunch of random kids at school.

"It's a relief to talk to someone about it," said Marco. "Besides, I figure you'll tell me all your dark secrets in return, right?" He grinned and punched Blue's shoulder.

"Sure," said Blue. "I'm a merman."

"Blue!" Zoe yelled. "Not approved!"

Marco stopped and goggled at Blue. "You're serious," he said. "Like, if I throw water on you, suddenly a fish tail will appear?"

Zoe knew that myth was one of the few things that could irritate Blue. The blond boy frowned.

"Come on, think about that for a minute," he said. "Could we have survived in secret for hundreds of years if you could just spill a glass of water on me and suddenly OMG A FISH TAIL IN THE CAFETERIA? Good grief. No, we control whether we have tails or legs at any given moment."

"Yeah, I thought I remembered you at a pool party once," Marco said. "Guess that explains it. It's like us werefolk; most of the time we can pick if we're human or animal. Except from midnight to dawn during the full moon, which is just awful. I mean, why would anyone ever *choose* to be a rooster, right? So unfair. Victor's an owl and Nina's a freaking *moose*, but no, I got stuck with rooster."

"So you were born that way," said Zoe. "You can't turn other people by biting them, right? Not like some were-wolves."

"Right. What are you?" Marco asked. "Wait, let me guess. Vampire?"

Blue laughed and Zoe smacked him.

"No, I'm human, and so is Logan. We're just . . . involved with mythical creatures. So why aren't you guys registered with SNAMHP?"

"Snamp?" Marco echoed in bewilderment.

"SNAMHP," Zoe said again. "Don't you know there's a government agency for Mostly Human Protection?"

"Called Snamp?" said Marco. "Huh. No. Mom and Dad think the government would lock us up if they caught us."

"Not at all," Blue said. "I mean, as long as you go through the right channels, they're pretty flexible about Mostly Human arrangements."

"They just like to know you're out here," said Zoe. "All werecreatures are supposed to be registered, and in exchange there are benefits, like supernatural health care, since you can't go to a regular hospital, and discounts at were-run clothing stores. Also dental, I think."

"Crazy," Marco said. "A whole secret agency for that stuff? How cool would that job be? Like, dealing with werewolves and vampires and mermaids all the time?"

"I think there's a lot of paperwork involved," Zoe said. "And I have to tell you, mermaids can be a huge pain in the tail."

"Hey," Blue objected mildly. "Well, okay."

"We're looking for an unregistered werewolf," Logan explained to Marco. "We think there might be one eating some of the sheep around here."

Some sheep . . . and one very valuable and annoying goose, Zoe thought. *Oh, I hope Marco can lead us to Pelly's murderer.* She had to admit to herself that he didn't exactly seem like the kind of guy who hung out with devious, creature-eating werewolves. Nor could she imagine him as the savior of the Menagerie.

"Not in my family," Marco said with a grand wave of his arms. "No wolves. Sorry. And Carlos isn't a big enough bear to eat sheep yet, plus he'd be totally grounded for a year if he did."

"Wait," Logan said, counting on his fingers. "Marco the rooster. Elena the squirrel. The bear, the owl, the moose, and your parents. That's seven."

"That's all of us," said Marco.

Logan looked at Zoe, and she felt a shiver down her spine as she realized what he'd remembered.

"Last night . . . ," Logan said. "Keiko said there were *eight* werecreatures in the forest."

ELEVEN

Logan knew there were more important things to think about—catching Pelly's murderer, defending Scratch, figuring out where Mom went—but he couldn't help stopping for a moment as they walked through the school doors to think, *Hey. I just walked to school with people. I have someone to sit with at lunch. I have* friends. Logan half expected someone to come up and say, "Oh, there's been a mistake. These friends aren't for you," and take them all away.

"Gah," said Marco, poking through his books in his locker. "My homework and stuff is in Dad's car. Does anyone have a phone I could borrow?"

Logan handed over his cell phone.

"MOM!" Marco yelled into it over the noise of kids shouting and banging through the halls. "I NEED MY BACKPACK!" He paused. "NO! NOBODY'S DOING EXPERIMENTS ON ME!" Pause. "I'M NOT TRAPPED IN A GOVERNMENT LAB, MA! I'M IN SCHOOL!" Pause. "MAAAAAA! CAN I PLEASE JUST HAVE MY MATH HOMEWORK?" Pause. "Okay, thanks. See you soon." He hung up and tossed the phone back to Logan. "Thanks, Logan. Gotta meet my mom outside. So I should tell her to look up *Snarp*?" he asked Zoe.

"S-N-A-M-H-P," she spelled out. "Here, I'll give you their website and the password to get in." She tore a sheet of paper out of her notebook, scribbled on it for a moment, and passed it to him. "Guard that with your *life*, Marco. It would be *very bad* if the wrong people found out about the agency, although I'm sure they have ways of convincing people it's a joke."

"No worries," said Marco. "I only lose critically important pieces of paper, like, once a week or so, so odds are good I'll make it to the parking lot with this."

Blue shook his head. "I'll go with you."

"Hi, Blue!" Jasmin trilled as she sauntered by.

Blue turned a bright, interesting shade of red, waved vaguely at the ceiling, and hurried after Marco.

"Oh, no," Zoe said, leaning against Logan's locker. "Now he's going to be all weird around her. I can't believe you told him she likes him."

"I thought he knew," Logan protested. He glanced up the hall and saw the school librarian, Sameera Lahiri, wrestling with a poster outside the library. "Hey," he said, lowering his voice. "Did you tell your dad about Miss Sameera?" He and Zoe and Blue had seen her with a griffin feather on Saturday and then overheard her having a disturbing conversation, but they hadn't had a moment to talk about it since.

"No," Zoe said. "I thought I'd deal with her myself."

As usual, Miss Sameera was wearing several bright colors: a long orange skirt with silver paisley embroidery swirls on it, plus a vibrant blue-and-purple top with bell sleeves. Her wispy dark hair was pulled back in a low ponytail. She wrestled with the tape as if it had deeply insulted her ancestors, and Logan wondered why she looked so stressed.

Was it anything to do with the phone call they'd overheard?

He tried to remember exactly what she'd said. She'd been trying to convince someone that she'd seen griffin cubs here in Xanadu. He remembered her saying "I was right" and "this town is crawling with mythical creatures."

"Wait," he said. "What do you mean, 'deal with her'?"

"I was thinking about it last night," Zoe said. She touched the side pocket of her backpack as if checking that something was still there. "She has a cup of tea on her desk every day after school. You can distract her while I slip the kraken ink into it."

"No!" Logan said, a bit louder than he'd meant to. A couple of eighth graders turned to stare at him, and he buried his head in his locker, pretending to be searching for a pencil.

"I won't get caught," Zoe whispered. "I'll be careful."

"That's not the problem," Logan said, keeping his voice as low as he could. "You can't go around wiping people's memories without knowing what you're erasing."

Zoe looked down and fiddled with her backpack straps. "Logan, I already said I was sorry for trying to give it to you. But Miss Sameera is different—we know she saw two of the griffins *and* she's trying to tell people about it. Matthew and his Tracker camp friends would call her a 'clear and present threat.' This is exactly why we have the kraken ink—and why we're always shipping cartons of it out to the other menageries."

"*No*," Logan said again, shaking his head. He'd come way too close to losing his memories of Squorp and the Menagerie, along with his chance to become friends with Zoe and Blue. It made his stomach hurt when he thought that he might never have known about his mother's secret Tracker work. "Promise me you won't use that stuff until we find out exactly what she knows."

"How are we supposed to do that?" Zoe demanded.

Luckily the bell rang before Logan had to admit he had no idea. He glanced down the hall at the library before following

Zoe into Mr. Christopher's homeroom.

Miss Sameera was watching them with bright, curious eyes.

It was torture trying to stay awake for the rest of the morning. Logan drew dragons in all his notebooks, thinking about how to find the eighth werecreature and whether that might be Pelly's attacker, and missed every question the teachers threw at him. He could see Zoe's eyes drooping, too, all through English and science and history. Marco actually fell asleep and clonked his forehead onto his desk, which was hugely amusing to the rest of the class and not so much to Ms. McCaffrey.

At lunchtime, Logan hesitated in the doorway of the cafeteria. It smelled like overboiled pasta and burned meat sauce. His feet instinctively wanted to take him over to his usual table, with the band geeks who talked about *South Park* and ignored him. It was lonely and boring, but it was familiar, and he knew they wouldn't chase him away or give him weird *what are you doing here?* looks.

He scanned the room for Blue and Zoe, realizing he wasn't sure where they normally sat or if they'd want him to join them. Maybe chasing griffins all weekend was one thing, but hanging out at school was another.

There weren't a lot of tables where girls sat with boys;

mostly it was one or the other. He saw Keiko at a table of sixth graders, examining a circle of their lunches and deciding which one she wanted while they all waited with somewhat worshipful expressions. *Maybe I should look up what a kitsune can do before she tries any fox tricks on me*, he noted.

Marco sat at the table with all the football and soccer guys from both seventh and eighth grade. They were the loudest group in the room. Marco was already mixing some kind of horrible "I dare you to drink this" concoction into one of the cafeteria glasses, while the rest of the soccer team hooted and offered suggestions.

"Ketchup!"

"Orange juice!"

"Chocolate syrup! GROOOOOOOSS!"

Logan couldn't see Zoe or Blue anywhere. He scrunched the top of his brown paper bag in his fist. Having no friends during class wasn't so bad, but the cafeteria always made him feel especially lame. It was the only part of Xanadu that made him wish they'd stayed in Chicago.

"Hey." Blue appeared at Logan's side and nudged his elbow. "This way."

Logan tried not to be obvious about the wave of relief that swept over him. He followed Blue through a side door to a shaded courtyard with two small trees in it. Their leaves were turning bright gold and purplish red. Three stone tables with attached benches were spread around the edges. Zoe was the only other person there, sitting at the table under the tree with red leaves. Her lunch was shoved to one side and she was writing furiously in her notebook.

"We're allowed to eat out here?" Logan asked.

"Yeah," Blue said. "Usually it's full of eighth graders, but they all go inside once it gets cold, so we wait until they're gone to use it." He slid onto the bench opposite Zoe and unpacked a tuna fish sandwich and a small bag of dried seaweed.

"Weird," Logan said, pointing at Blue's seaweed as he sat down next to him.

"You mean awesome," Blue said with a grin.

"So I'm afraid the next step is to talk to Keiko again," Zoe said without looking up from her notebook. "I know she's mad, but if we apologize enough, maybe she can tell us more about the other werecreature and if she knows who it was." She sighed. "It'd be really nice if we could figure it out without her, though."

"Get ready to do a lot of sixth-grade math," Blue said.

"Why don't *you* do her math homework?" Zoe asked. "You're just as good at it as I am."

"I think the word you're looking for is *better*," Blue said, flapping his seaweed at her. "But that sounds an awful lot like work, and I'm sure my dad wouldn't approve." He grinned at her frown.

"Oh, *here* you are, Blue!"

They all froze as Jasmin sauntered into the courtyard.

She looked perfectly put together, as always, in a white turtleneck and fake-fur-trimmed candy-pink vest with a black skirt, black leggings, and pink boots. Her long, dark hair was clipped back into a low ponytail. Ignoring Zoe and Logan, she slid onto the tiny edge of the bench on the other side of Blue and leaned one of her elbows on the table.

"Um," Blue stammered. "Hi, Jasmin."

Logan glanced across at Zoe. She was twisting her hand around her wrist, the way she always did when she was nervous, and he suddenly remembered the friendship bracelet the last griffin cub had buried. The one that reminded Zoe of Jasmin—the one she probably used to wear every day, until they couldn't be friends anymore.

"So I was thinking," Jasmin said to Blue, "maybe a knight isn't such a good idea after all. It's like cooping you up in a big tin can, even though my matching warrior princess costume is pretty awesome. How about we go as superheroes instead? I could be the Black Widow and you could be Aquaman."

Blue choked on his sandwich and Logan had to thump him on the back.

"I'm just kidding." Jasmin giggled. "I wouldn't make you wear Aquaman tights, don't worry. Maybe Hawkeye? He's the one with the bow and arrow, right? That guy was pretty cute in the *Avengers* movie. And he's probably got the best costume, as long as nobody thinks you're Robin Hood."

"Um," said Blue.

"Great! I'll see what I can find." Jasmin gave him a sweet smile and let her hand rest briefly on his shoulder, then got up and sailed back into the cafeteria.

"Oh my gosh," said Zoe.

"This is your fault," Blue said to Logan.

"Oh, no," said Logan. "I'm so sorry a pretty, popular girl is paying attention to you." He did actually feel a bit guilty, but not for Blue. He felt bad for Jasmin, who seemed to think something had changed when Blue showed up at her front door on Sunday.

"You have to be nice to her," Zoe said fiercely, poking Blue's tuna sandwich with one of her carrot sticks.

"In what universe can you imagine me not being nice?" Blue demanded.

Zoe shook her head. "This is going to end badly," she muttered. She flipped to a new page in her notebook. "We should come up with other ways to prove Scratch's innocence, in case we don't find the werewolf by Thursday. Mom and Dad checked the width of the claw marks on the door and said it's inconclusive—they could be from a dragon Scratch's size, or they could be something Aliya did a while ago that we never noticed, or it could be something else altogether. So that doesn't help us."

"Wouldn't the other birds have freaked out if a dragon opened the roc door, came flapping in, ate one of them, and flapped out again?" Logan asked. "Wouldn't they have made the kind of noise they did when we found the crime scene? And wouldn't someone have heard that?"

"Good point," Zoe said. "I asked the same thing, and Dad says it looks like someone used the tranquillity mist on them that night."

"One of the switches to turn on the mist is up by Aliya's door," Blue pointed out. "But I don't know. A dragon on a hunting mission? Not usually that stealthy."

"Seriously," Logan said. "Between that and hacking the security system, it seems like it *had* to be someone Mostly Human. The agents have to see that."

"Or maybe someone was helping Scratch," Zoe said, rubbing her eyes.

"What about Nero?" Logan asked. "Did you talk to him? Did he see anything?"

"Nero is being an annoying *basket case*," Zoe said. "I mean, way, way worse than usual. If any of us go anywhere *near* him, he shrieks something like, 'No one is safe! They'll come for me next!' and poof—flames, smoke, pile of ashes with an egg in it."

"I bet he's outraged that everyone is so upset about Pelly," Blue observed. "Typical Nero, he'd like a little more attention back on himself."

"Or maybe he really did see something," Logan said. "Maybe he's afraid of what might happen to him if he talks."

"You haven't been putting up with his hysterics for years,"

Blue said. "This kind of attention seeking is really pretty normal for Nero."

"We'll calm him down eventually," Zoe said. "But he would have been knocked out by the tranquillity mist when it happened anyway, so I doubt he'll be much use."

"AHA!"

Logan jumped and nearly fell off the bench as Marco came bounding into the courtyard.

"You guys are hard to find! Man, it is cold out here! Is that seaweed? Can I have some?" Marco plunked himself down next to Zoe and took a piece of Blue's seaweed. "Whose lunch is this?" He opened Zoe's lunch bag and started poking through the Tupperware containers. "Sometimes it seems like Mom thinks I can live on corn, which, don't get me wrong, I love it, but come on, even a wererooster needs real food sometimes, like—what's this? Vegetable lasagna? Can I have it?"

"Um . . . sure," Zoe said, pushing her hair behind her ears.

"Awesome, thanks." Marco stuffed half the lasagna in his mouth while the others stared at him. After a minute he paused and pulled an apple juice out of his backpack. "So I told my mom about that thing," he said to Zoe as if their conversation in the hallway that morning had just taken a brief break. "And she was all, what did you tell them! And I was like, nothing they didn't already know! Except maybe about our pancake breakfast tradition. And she was like, come home right away after school! We thought something had eaten you! And I was like, well, nice of you to finally worry about *that* for once, and she was like, no, I mean a specific thing, because we saw it running through the woods, and I was like, ooo, if it's a werewolf, I totally know some folks who are looking for him, and she said, what do we know about these friends of yours and how do you know none of them eat roosters and I was like OBVIOUSLY THEY DO NOT EAT ROOSTERS, MA, GIVEN THAT I'M STILL TOTALLY NOT EATEN OVER HERE, NO THANKS TO YOU, plus I pointed out that you completely rescued me, basically, and so, long story short, want to come over after school? Mom wants to meet you guys."

Logan couldn't believe Marco hadn't spilled the beans on his family to someone before now. He reminded Logan of the time the water heater in their Chicago apartment bathroom got a hole in it—his dad had been trying to "fix" it—and there was an instant geyser that sprayed all over the tiles and ceiling and it was practically impossible to turn it off. The way Marco talked was kind of like that, in that it was both unstoppable and hilarious.

Mom was home when that happened, Logan thought. *Not off on a "business trip" hunting mythical animals.* He remembered her laughing and laughing, her hair dripping wet as she tried to plug the hole, while Dad kept insisting it wasn't funny.

"Wait," Zoe said, grabbing Marco's arm. "They saw a

werewolf? Did you say they saw a werewolf?"

"She was kind of yelling," said Marco, "so I'm not sure, but she saw something, so maybe? Come on over and you can ask. I promise they don't bite." He burst out laughing. "I mean, except when they do, of course, but usually they don't when they're people. Okay, maybe Elena, but she's pretty slow, so I think you could get away from her."

"If they saw the eighth werecreature," Logan said, "maybe this is our way to find out who it is without Zoe having to do a bunch of extra homework." He slid his oatmeal raisin cookies across the table and grinned as Marco wolfed them down.

Zoe got up, pulling out her phone. "Let me check with my parents."

Logan guessed she was going to ask how much she could reveal about the Menagerie. He figured a werefamily had to know a thing or two about keeping secrets, even—or maybe especially—with a loudmouth like Marco in the mix.

He just hoped for Scratch's sake that they really had seen a werewolf . . . and that they could lead the Menagerie right to it.

TWELVE

Marco's house was set off by itself, far back from the road. It was tall and painted dark red, with a wide porch across the front and along one side. Toys littered the porch and the yard. Logan stepped carefully over a space blaster, a Barbie with teeth marks all over her arms, a punctured basketball, and several discarded costume hats, including a princess tiara, a cowboy hat, and a purple beret.

On the path leading up to the door was a chalk outline of hopscotch, decorated around the edges with what appeared to be vampire bats and drooling zombies, which were themselves embellished with flower headdresses in a different color of chalk, which were then scribbled out. Little word bubbles came out of the zombies with notes like: *STOP DRAWING FLOWERS ON ME OR I WILL EAT YOUR BRAINS!* and *NINA'S BRAINS ARE MY LUNCH!* and *NINA, STOOOOOP!* and *AAAAAARGH!*

Logan, Zoe, and Blue followed Marco up the steps. Marco kicked aside a couple of newspapers and a toy trumpet and reached for the doorknob.

The front door flew open.

A black bear stood in the frame, up on its hind legs, baring its teeth at them.

"ROAR!" it bellowed.

Even though it was no bigger than Logan, and even though he immediately knew this must be Marco's brother Carlos, Logan still felt his heart thump in his throat for a moment.

Marco picked up one of the newspapers and flung it at the bear, bonking it on the nose. "Carlos, go away! Nobody here is scared of you!"

The bear dropped to all fours and shambled back into the house, grumbling.

"MA!" Marco hollered, leading the way inside, into a cluttered living room that was twice as crowded with stuff as the yard and the porch. Taylor Swift music thumped from a room down the hall and a vacuum cleaner droned upstairs. "Carlos is answering the door as a bear again!"

The vacuum cleaner stopped and a short, plump, dark-haired woman wearing bright parrot green came clattering down the stairs. "Marco!" She grabbed Marco's shoulders and smushed him into her for a giant hug.

"Mooooooom, you already hugged me this morning when you dropped off my bag," Marco complained.

"I will hug you as many times as I want to," Mrs. Jimenez said sternly. "I am the mother. It is one of my privileges." She gave Logan and the other two a suspicious look.

"MAMI!" shrieked a female voice from the room down the hall. "Carlos is poking his nose in my garbage can! Gross! Stop that!" There was a series of thumps.

"Nina, stop throwing shoes at your brother!" Marco's mom shouted. "And don't you dare—"

There was an even louder thump and the sound of furniture overturning.

"Oh, you *did not!*" hollered Marco's mom, letting go of Marco and storming down the hall.

"MOOOM! MOOOM! MOOOM!" screamed a different female voice. "She's stepping on my clothes! MOOOOOOOOM, SHE SQUISHED MY LADYBUG BOOTS AAAAAAAAAAAAAAAAAHHHHH!" The voice escalated into a full-blown wail.

Marco chased after his mom. "You'll want to see this," he called back to the others.

When Logan reached the doorway of what turned out to be a small back bedroom, he nearly ran straight into the long, serious face of a giant moose. Behind the moose, a bookshelf had been knocked over and books were scattered across the Minnie Mouse rug. The moose had one antler caught on the top rail of a bunk bed, where a little girl, maybe three or four years old, was sitting up close to the ceiling, hugging a *Dora the Explorer* pillow and bawling. The edge of a red rain boot stuck out from under one of the moose's giant feet. The black bear was backed into a corner beside a tipped-over trash can and a pink karaoke machine, growling at the moose.

"ENOUGH!" bellowed Marco's mom. "We do not fight as animals in this house! We use our words! Everyone back to human *right now*."

The moose gave Logan a pointed look. He'd never seen a moose up close before; he couldn't even remember seeing one in a zoo or anything. It was absolutely gigantic.

Marco's mom eyeballed the moose. "What are you waiting for, young lady?"

"She can't change back in front of boy-oy-oys," sobbed the girl on the top bunk. She pointed to a ripped pile of clothes under the moose's feet.

"Oh, right," Marco said. He shepherded Logan and Zoe and Blue down the hall to the living room. "Sit, sit," he said, waving at the sagging couch, which was shrouded in a sheet that was so covered in fur that Logan couldn't tell at first whether it was gray, black, or brown, and then he figured out that it was actually green under all that. Marco whisked the sheet away, revealing a slightly less fur-covered mustard-yellow couch, and bounded off to the kitchen. A few clanging noises suggested he was stuffing the cover into a washing machine.

"Who wants lemonade?" he asked, sticking his head back into the room.

"Me," said Blue, so Logan raised his hand, too. Zoe didn't answer; she was busy studying a wall of black-and-white family portraits over the fireplace.

"I'll have some, too," called a voice from over their heads.

Logan peered up and saw a skinny guy who looked about fourteen lounging on one of the rafters with a book, wearing khaki shorts and nothing else.

"I wasn't offering *you* any," Marco called back.

"That is not how we talk to each other in this house," said the older boy in a singsong voice eerily similar to their mother's.

As they argued, Logan saw Zoe take out her phone, snap a picture of one of the wall photos, and then tap a few buttons as if she were emailing it to someone. He went to stand next to her.

"What's up?" he asked.

"My mom has a theory," she said with a shrug. "We'll see in a minute."

"About Pelly's killer? Did you tell her Marco's family may have seen a werewolf? Does she agree a werewolf would make a better suspect than Scratch?"

"Maybe, but no, it's about—"

"Please forgive our chaos," Mrs. Jimenez said as she came back into the room, carrying the little girl in her arms. A slightly older girl, maybe seven years old, trailed behind them, wearing a long-sleeved purple wool dress and a crestfallen expression that still looked sort of moose-y to Logan. She was clutching a ripped shirt in her hands. Marco's mom pointed to one of the armchairs, and the older girl sat down, opened a small basket labeled NINA by her feet, and pulled out a needle and a few rolls of thread.

"It's not fair," she said, poking at the needle with the end of the thread. "I was only trying to stop Carlos from making a mess."

"And a fine job you did of that," said her mother.

"Why doesn't *he* have to sew his clothes back together?" demanded Nina. "I read about this for my biography report on Susan B. Anthony! You are making me sew things because I'm a girl! Carlos doesn't have to do anything!"

"*Carlos* had the good sense to take all his clothes *off* before he turned into a bear," her mother pointed out. "He will still, however, be doing laundry tonight as punishment for being an animal indoors and answering the door to strangers that way."

"What?" hollered Carlos. He marched out of the girls' room with a *Dora* sheet wrapped around him like a toga. Now that he was in human form and not shambling about on four paws, Logan guessed he was around ten years old. "Marco said they knew all about us! I was just having fun! Although I thought they'd be more scared. Lame."

"It's your puny roar," offered the boy in the rafters. "It's so obvious you don't really mean it. It sounds like: 'roar, hey, what's up,' not 'ROAR, I'M A REAL BEAR AND I'M GOING TO EAT YOU NOW.' You should work on that."

"Oh, thank you, great and mighty bird of wisdom," Carlos said sarcastically. "You don't know anything about bears! I should eat you for insubordination!"

"That is *not* how we talk to each other in this house!" their mother barked. "Carlos, go get your brothers' hampers. And for goodness' sakes, put on some clothes. Marco's friends will think we are a house full of barbarians."

Actually, Logan was thinking it must be fun to live in a house this noisy. On the other hand, he was glad he didn't have to compete with four brothers and sisters for his dad's attention; it had always been hard enough competing with his mom's work. And he'd ended up losing that battle—or so her last postcard had made him think.

"You must be Zoe," said Mrs. Jimenez, coming over to the fireplace. She shifted the little girl to one hip and held out her hand for Zoe to shake. "And are you Blue or Logan?"

"Logan," he said, shaking her hand, too. The little girl's dark eyes watched through a curtain of hair, and he recognized the outraged expression from the squirrel that morning.

"Can I ask you who this is?" Zoe asked, pointing at the oldest-looking photo on the wall. All in sepia tones, a man in a cowboy hat stood on a rock with his hands on his hips. Behind him, the land sloped down into a valley with a lake in it. The man looked a bit like Marco, but the landscape looked even more familiar. Logan squinted at it.

"That's the view from the—" he blurted, but managed to stop himself right before he said "dragon caves." None of the Menagerie buildings were there—no Aviary, no Reptile House, no unicorn stable—but the lake was the same shape, only missing one of the islands. And a log cabin filled the space where Zoe's house stood now.

Marco's mom stared at Logan. "You know this place?" she said.

Zoe's phone buzzed. "'Horace Winterton,'" she read off her screen.

"That's right!" Mrs. Jimenez waved at the photo. "Our ancestor. The family legend is that he woke up in the woods around these parts one day with total amnesia—he couldn't remember where he'd come from, who his family was, or how he'd gotten there. All he had were the clothes on his back and this photo, but he could never find the place it was taken, although he searched the surrounding area for years before he met a weresparrow and got married and settled down. It was like his life started over that day."

"He worked with my great-great-great-grandparents,"

Zoe said. She slid her finger across the screen and showed a picture to Marco's mom. Logan leaned in and saw Horace standing with a smiling couple. "He was their dragon tamer, and a werejackrabbit. He's a legend to us, too, because he just disappeared one day. Mom thinks one of the dragons slipped him some kraken ink, trying to get rid of him."

"Jerks," muttered Blue. "Almost as bad as salamanders."

Are dragons really that devious? Logan wondered. *If they could do that . . . what if Scratch did figure out how to disable the cameras and set off the mist so no one would see him eat Pelly? But if he is that smart, why didn't he clean the blood off his teeth or come up with a story about what happened on his watch?*

"I'm glad Horace turned out okay," said Zoe.

"How did you guess they were related?" Logan asked.

"Well, my mom thought it was a little weird that a whole family of unregistered werecreatures were living down the road from us, most likely for generations. The good news is that means I can tell you and Marco all about us. Nobody else, though." Zoe glanced around at the little girls and the boy in the rafters.

"Victor, take your sisters out to play," ordered Mrs. Jimenez, setting Elena down.

"Yay!" cried Nina, flinging down her sewing.

"PIRATE BARBIES!" Elena shrieked, scooping dolls off the floor. "Pirate Barbies on the owl ship in the sky with lollipop treasure!"

"*Mom*, I'm *reading*," Victor objected. "And Elena's lollipops make my *wings* all sticky. And if I have to make *one more Barbie* walk the plank, I will literally die of boredom."

"I will literally worry about that when it literally happens," said Marco's mom. "Go. Now."

Victor huffed and sighed and slammed his book shut. He tucked the book into the corner of the rafter and closed his eyes. A moment later, feathers shimmered across his skin, his face flattened and shrank, and his legs sprouted sharp talons. Soon a large owl sat on the rafter, pinning the shorts to the wood with its claws. Using its beak, the owl rearranged the shorts neatly where they were, and then flew down and out the door. Nina and Elena shrieked happily and chased after him.

"What about Carlos?" Marco asked as he set two glasses of lemonade on the coffee table.

Marco's mom pointed up the stairs just as the sound of a TV popped on, loudly clashing with the Taylor Swift still playing from the bedroom. "Asking your brother to do chores always involves at least half an hour of stomping around in front of the TV first. So we have a moment. Tell me about the place Horace came from."

Zoe explained the Menagerie, SNAPA, and the rules about Mostly Humans. Logan loved feeling like an insider—like someone who knew what was going on and how to help. Although he wished he had more ideas for Scratch's trial.

Thursday was way too soon.

"Well, perhaps it would be nice to join an official community," said Marco's mom. "I'll talk to my husband about it. Thank you for being so honest with us."

"We need to ask you about something, too," said Zoe. "Marco said you saw some kind of predator in the woods last night."

"Was it a werewolf?" Logan asked.

"Absolutely," said Mrs. Jimenez with a shudder. "Carlos has the best sense of smell of any of us, and he confirmed it—it looked like a wolf, but it smelled half-man. Marco, when he told us that, I was so worried for you. I've heard that werewolves are much nastier than other werecreatures. He might eat you even if he could tell you were part human. But don't worry, your dad has a wonderful idea." She got up, went to the sideboard, and started rummaging through a pile of plastic shopping bags.

"I have a wonderful idea, too," said Marco. "DON'T MAKE ME TURN INTO A ROOSTER IN THE FLIPPING WOODS IN THE MIDDLE OF THE NIGHT."

"Oh, no, this is a much better plan," said his mother. "That werewolf will be in for a surprise if he comes after my little rooster."

Marco snorted.

"So it was male?" Zoe asked.

Marco's mom nodded. "Carlos and Elena and I all saw

the wolf. And Nina thinks she saw him while he was still in human form."

Logan sat up. "Did she say what he looked like?"

"She only saw him for a moment, and she wasn't sure he was a werecreature, but how many other people could be running around the woods in the middle of the night?" asked Mrs. Jimenez. "I can call her in here to describe him for you. But let me show this to Marco first." She pulled out a small vial half-full of sparkly silvery powder.

"Ma," said Marco. "I can already tell you I hate this plan."

"What is that?" Blue asked.

"Silver dust," she said. "Werecreatures are powerfully allergic to this stuff."

"*Including me*," Marco pointed out.

"But listen," said Mrs. Jimenez. "This will keep you safe. You just turn into a rooster a little before midnight, one of us sprinkles this all over your feathers—"

"NO MOST DEFINITELY NO," said Marco.

"And no werewolf will want to come anywhere near you!" she finished cheerfully. "Safe and sound."

"And sneezing for twelve hours straight!" Marco said. "And covered with hives the next day! No thank you!"

"It's a wonderful plan," she said again, tucking the vial into her purse.

"No means no, Ma!" Marco threw his hands up in the air. "And guess what? *Regular* wolves will still eat me! Also coyotes! Also bears! Why can't I just stay here?"

"Because then your brothers and sisters will want to stay home, too, and your father and I can't supervise you while we're in animal form," she said. "And I don't like poultry indoors."

"Maybe he could come to the Menagerie," Logan suggested. "Isn't there somewhere he could change safely there?"

"YES," said Marco. "THAT IS THE PLAN I AM OKAY WITH."

"I think that would be fine," Zoe said distractedly. "Can we please talk to Nina about the werewolf? I'd like to know what she saw."

"NINA!" Mrs. Jimenez bellowed out the door.

Marco's sister came skipping up onto the porch. "WHAT?" she bellowed back.

"Tell Marco's friends about the boy you saw in the woods." Her mother patted her head.

"Well," Nina said, "he was totally cute. He looked like he was in high school. And he was in a big hurry. And he kept looking around like he didn't want to be seen. And he was carrying something. And he had a scar on his arm and his face."

"Hang on," said Zoe. "That's not a werewolf. Apart from the totally cute part, that sounds like my brother."

Nina shrugged. "That's who I saw." She skipped back down the steps.

"Zoe," Logan said slowly. "Is there any chance . . . ?"

Zoe's eyes widened as she realized what he was suggesting. "No!" she said. "No way!"

"Maybe way," said Blue.

"Matthew is not a werewolf!" she cried. "That's crazy! Someone would have noticed by now!"

"Not if he got bitten this summer," Blue pointed out. "At Tracker camp. Where he got some mysterious scars."

"That was a griffin situation," said Zoe. "He said he made a griffin mad."

"Maybe he made a werewolf mad instead," said Logan. "Zoe, it's possible, right?"

She bit her lip, thinking. "I guess it is possible he took those chains and the tranq gun for himself . . . ," she said slowly. "But why wouldn't he have told someone if he got turned? And if he is—well, there's no way he would have hurt Pelly. That's crazy talk. No, the werewolf has to be somebody else."

"There's one way to find out," said Logan. He turned to Mrs. Jimenez. "Is there any chance we could borrow some of that silver dust?"

THIRTEEN

"Can't I just put a tiny bit on his hand or something?" Zoe asked Marco.

"No!" he protested. "It has to be a lot of exposure so you can be sure."

Zoe felt the weight of the ziplock bag in her jacket pocket. Was she really about to do this to Matthew?

They all stopped at a red light. Marco had retrieved his bike so they could ride to Zoe's. She was really nervous about bringing home yet another random guy from school, but Mrs. Jimenez wanted him to report back on the werewolf situation, and Zoe's parents had said it was okay for him to come see the Menagerie. They didn't know about her Matthew suspicions yet.

"And we mixed it with glitter because—?" Logan said.

"Glitter bomb!" Marco cried. "Awesome, and then if he gets mad, you can be like, oh, sorry, I was just glitter bombing you, which is obviously hilarious. Glitter bomb is totally the way to go."

Zoe had never heard of glitter bombs, but apparently it was a thing, throwing glitter all over people to protest something. She thought it sounded kind of cool—like, a sparkly way to make a point without violence—but she was pretty sure Matthew wasn't going to be thrilled about it. That's if he *wasn't* a werewolf; if he was, and this exposed him, he'd be even less thrilled.

But why wouldn't he have told his family? There couldn't be anyone in the world more understanding of mythical-creature stuff than the Kahns. Was he worried that being a werewolf meant he couldn't be a Tracker?

Zoe didn't know if that was true. In some ways, having wolf abilities would probably make tracking easier. But there might be some SNAPA rule about it, and being a Tracker had been Matthew's dream his whole life. He wouldn't let anything get in the way of that.

But if he's a werewolf, we really need to know so we can help him, she thought. She pictured him alone in the woods, wrapping himself in chains and shooting himself with a tranq gun. Poor Matthew! There had to be a better way to deal with it.

Then again, when Mrs. Jimenez saw the wolf, there were no chains and it wasn't tranq'd. So what happened?

Maybe it wasn't Matthew after all.

"Keiko!" she blurted suddenly. "If Matthew were a were-wolf, Keiko would have smelled it."

"But would she have told us?" Blue pointed out. "She didn't tell us about Marco. It's more likely she'd keep that in her back pocket to blackmail him with whenever she wanted something."

"True," Zoe said with a sigh.

"Keiko with the long braids who plays soccer?" Marco asked hopefully. "She's a werecreature, too?"

The light changed and they set off again.

"No," said Blue. "Different kind of shape-shifter, sorry."

"Still," said Marco. "That practically makes us soul mates, right?"

"Oh my gosh, Marco," Zoe said. "You are so barking up the wrong tree."

"Or crowing," said Logan. "Crowing up the wrong tree."

"Ha-ha!" Marco chortled.

"I'm confused about something," Logan said. "How much do you remember when you're a werecreature? And how much can you control what you're doing?"

"It depends on which kind you are," said Marco. "With us, because it's genetic, we've been practicing since we were born, so we're still pretty much ourselves and can remember most stuff. But newly bitten werewolves have much less control."

Poor Matthew, Zoe thought again. *But I still can't imagine him hurting Pelly.*

They rounded the corner into the Kahns' driveway and Zoe saw a strange car parked in front of the house, behind the sleek black one that the SNAPA agents drove everywhere. As they got closer, she saw that it was a rental car.

"Who's that?" she said to Blue, nodding at the car as they rolled their bikes into the garage next to the old blue van. "Do you think SNAPA sent more investigators?"

"Maybe," he said.

Marco stayed on his bike, glancing at the cars. "Um," he said. "You know, actually, maybe I should stay off this SNAP-PER's radar for now."

"SNAPA," Zoe corrected him. "They're not all so bad . . . well, Agent Dantes can be nice . . . but they are pretty strict about rules."

Marco made a face. "I think I'll go home. Call me when you know about the werewolf thing?" He nodded at Logan. "I put my number in your phone when I borrowed it before."

Logan looked surprised and pleased in a way that made Zoe want to hug him. It was as if people being friendly startled him every time.

Marco rode off, and Zoe took a deep breath, steeling herself for the serious grown-up frowns that might be waiting inside the house.

But the new visitor was much, much worse than more SNAPA investigators.

Zoe heard her voice as soon as she opened the door to the kitchen.

"—shouldn't be surprised this place fell apart without me. Dad, *what* are these? Are these *nonorganic* strawberries? I only eat organic strawberries now. And you'll have to hide those cookies. I don't eat carbs anymore, but you can't expect me to have any willpower when so many stressful things are happening. ZOE!"

Her sister came barreling through the kitchen and flung her arms around Zoe, picking her up as if Zoe were still five years old.

"*Ruby?*" Zoe wriggled free. "What are you doing here? What about college?"

"Oh, Hampshire can survive without me for a few days," Ruby said, waving her hands airily. Her ruby nose stud twinkled in the light, matching her deep red fingernails. "As long as I'm back by the time rehearsals start for *Ontological Uncertainties*. But I had to come when I heard about all the disasters happening here. Nobody told me your *hair* was one of them, though. Are you doing something different? It looks awful. And I'm pretty sure we've talked about the utter wrongness of this shirt before."

Zoe touched her hair self-consciously and avoided looking at Logan. The only thing she'd done differently that morning was forget to brush it, and the truth was, that probably happened more often than it didn't.

"Poor, poor Scratch," Ruby went on, fluffing Zoe's hair and making hopeless dismayed faces at it. "Of course I simply had to fly back to help."

"Using the emergency credit card," said Zoe's dad from the corner where he was studying a folder full of spreadsheets. "Again."

"One of our dragons being tried for murder is *clearly* an emergency," said Ruby. "And I am *clearly* the right person to defend him. After all, I am pre-law."

"More like pre-pre-pre-law," said Matthew as he closed the fridge door and twisted open a juice bottle. "You're barely halfway through your first semester of college."

"And I thought you wanted to be an actress," said Zoe.

"Yes, but my Diction and Dialect class is superb," said Ruby. "It's the perfect preparation for playing a lawyer. I'll be marvelous, wait and see. And luckily I got here in time for the voir dire tomorrow." She patted her blond pixie cut and stared daggers at Logan. "*Who* is *that*? Zoe, didn't we talk about this?" She gave the secret stash of kraken ink a meaningful look.

"Ruby, this is Logan," Zoe said. She braced herself for an embarrassing lecture about bringing boys home, but like a miracle, the dragon alarm suddenly went off and drowned Ruby out.

"INTRUDER! INTRUDER! INTRUDER!" It sounded like Clawdius was on duty today. Ruby closed her mouth and settled for frowning at Logan instead.

Zoe's dad rubbed his forehead and pulled out his walkie-talkie. "Holly, can you please go up and check on the dragons? They might have forgotten that Logan is allowed to be here. Or perhaps they don't recognize Ruby now that she only eats *organic* strawberries."

"Sure thing," Mom's voice crackled back.

"Couldn't have made all this noise two nights ago instead," Zoe's dad muttered grumpily. He swiped one hand through his hair, accidentally making it stand up in tufts, and slapped the folder shut. "I have to go talk to Melissa," he said to the kitchen at large before vanishing in the direction of Blue's mom's office. Zoe realized Agent Runcible and Agent Dantes were sitting at the dining room table, working on their tablet computers.

"Poor Dad is *so* stressed," said Ruby, perching on a kitchen stool and helping herself to a white-chocolate-chip cookie from the plate on the table. "It's a good thing I'm here to help him calm down."

Matthew rolled his eyes expressively at Zoe.

"Well," he said into the silence as the dragon alarm cut off. "I'm going out. You two play nice." He started toward the garage door.

Blue poked Zoe, and Logan made a wide-eyed face at her. Zoe jumped in her brother's way.

"Uh, where are you going?" she stammered.

"None of your beeswax," he said. He turned back to the pass-through to grab his keys off the counter.

Zoe panicked. She knew it was terrible timing with the SNAPA agents and Ruby right there, but she also knew that if Matthew left, she might not see him until the next day, and she needed to know if he was really a werewolf now, tonight, before he went out and ate another sheep and maybe hurt somebody because he hadn't learned control yet.

"SHAZAM!" she shouted, flinging the contents of the ziplock bag in his face.

Glitter flew *everywhere*. Silver sparkles went up Matthew's nose (and Zoe's as well), coated his hair, drifted across his shoulders, scattered all over the floor and the pass-through and the living room beyond, and basically covered everything within fifteen feet of Matthew. It sure hadn't looked like that much glitter when it was in the bag.

There followed an extremely shocked pause. Zoe felt like a basilisk had just stared her in the face. Logan had his hands over his eyes as if he couldn't bear to see what would happen next. Ruby's mouth hung open like a hungry salamander's.

Matthew blinked several times and held his glitter-covered arms out from his sides. A shower of more glitter hit the kitchen floor as he tipped his head down to glare at Zoe.

"What. The. Hellhound," Matthew said, articulating slowly. "Zoe. Have you lost your mind? *Did you just glitter bomb me?*"

So apparently *he'd* heard of glitter bombing, anyhow.

"Um," said Zoe. "Yes? Because it's . . . hilarious?"

"I am going to murder you," he said. "Slowly. Wendigos will probably be involved."

But there was good news. Zoe studied his face and neck and arms. No sneezing. No hives. The silver dust was having no effect on him. Matthew wasn't a werewolf after all.

"Sorry," she mumbled.

"'Shazam'?" said Blue. "Really, Zoe?"

"ZOE!" Matthew yelled, stomping toward the garage in a cloud of silvery dust. "I'm going on a date tonight! And now I'm going to show up *covered in glitter!*"

"I didn't know that!" she cried. "You could have said something!"

"AAACHOO!"

Zoe whirled around.

"AACHOO! AACHOO! AAAAACHOOOOOO!"

Some of the silver dust had floated through the pass-through and landed on the SNAPA agents on the other side.

And now one of them was sneezing like he'd inhaled an entire tree full of pollen.

"Agent Runcible!" Zoe gasped. "You're a werewolf!"

FOURTEEN

"Of course he's a werewolf," Dantes said. Agent Runcible was sneezing too hard to reply. He doubled over as everyone piled into the living room to stare at him. Glitter exploded from him with each violent sneeze.

His partner took his arm and led him to one of the couches, nearly stepping on Captain Fuzzbutt as they went by. The snoozing mammoth snorted and rolled over to flop against one of the pumpkin-colored floor pillows.

"Agent Runcible has been registered as a werewolf ever since he was bitten on an assignment four years ago," Dantes said, trying to brush glitter off his arms. "He's closely monitored by SNAMHP, especially during full moons, and is a model of werecreature comportment. Edmund, are you all right? Can you breathe?"

"AAACHOO!" Agent Runcible answered.

"I'll get him some water," Logan said, hurrying back to the kitchen. Although he didn't have the warmest feelings about the agent who'd come looking for his mom in Chicago, he still felt bad for Runcible. The agent's eyes were streaming and small bumps were appearing along his hands and neck.

"I had no idea that would happen," Zoe said, wringing her hands. "I'm so sorry, Agent Runcible."

This isn't going to improve SNAPA's attitude toward the Menagerie or the Kahns, Logan thought regretfully. He handed the agent a large glass of water and Runcible drank the whole thing in one gulp.

"What is going on out here?" Blue's mom came out of her office with Zoe's dad right behind her.

"Your daughter," gasped Agent Runcible. "Attacked me. Silver dust."

"Zoe!" Mr. Kahn clutched his hair. "Why would you do that to a harmless werewolf?"

"I didn't know he was one!" she protested. "I thought— well, we were just—"

"You thought *I* was a werewolf," Matthew said, piecing it together. "Good grief, Zoe."

Logan reached over and squeezed Zoe's hand, trying to get the tragic look on her face to disappear. "It wasn't her idea," he said. "The rest of us thought maybe . . . well, there was a werewolf in the woods last night, and we thought perhaps he'd come here the night before and eaten Pelly."

"Agent Runcible was in the woods last night," Dantes said, pulling out a device with a small screen on it. "But as you can see, he is carefully monitored while in wolf form—by me, in fact—and this map can tell you exactly where he was at all times on Saturday night." The map on the screen had a green trail on it that ran in large circles through Roosevelt Park. They could all see clearly that the trail had not left the park, and certainly it had gone nowhere near the Menagerie.

Melissa Merevy leaned toward the screen, frowning. "I haven't memorized all the SNAMHP regulations, but a relatively new werewolf running free in the woods—even monitored—doesn't sound like a good idea. What if he encountered and attacked a human?"

"Who would be out in the woods in the middle of the night?" Agent Dantes scoffed.

"Us," Blue offered casually. "We—" He saw the look on his mom's face and stopped. "Oops."

"My office, now," said Melissa, pointing. Blue slunk through the door and she followed him, closing it with an ominous *click*.

Logan glanced at Mr. Kahn, but he seemed too worried about Runcible to notice Blue's slip. Zoe's dad hurried into the kitchen and came back with several wet washcloths. Agent

Runcible leaned back and Dantes draped the wet cloths over his face and neck. His breathing became less wheezy and his sneezing slowed down.

The device with the map on it was still flashing on the corner of the couch. Logan peered at it, then edged a bit closer. If Runcible had stayed on this track inside the park . . .

"Then who ate the sheep?" he wondered before realizing he'd said it out loud. Zoe and the agents turned to look at him.

"Sheep?" Runcible muttered. "Disgusting."

"A sheep was attacked Saturday night, kind of around here," Logan said, pointing to the map. The green trail flashed, a fair distance away from where his finger was. "Dad said there have been a bunch of sheep attacks recently. We thought it was a werewolf—we figured the same one who came after Pelly. But if the werewolf in the woods was Runcible, and he didn't eat the sheep, then who did?"

"Never eat sheep," Runcible muttered from under the layers of wet fabric on his face. "Too woolly. Sticks in my teeth."

"Probably an ordinary coyote," said Dantes.

Zoe met Logan's eyes and tilted her head at the Menagerie on the other side of the sliding glass doors before turning to the SNAPA agents and her dad.

"We should have thought of that. Again, I'm so sorry, Agent Runcible." Zoe's voice was still regretful, but she was edging toward the Menagerie. "Can Logan help me feed the griffins?" she asked her dad.

"Yes," he said, "but we'll be talking about this later tonight, Zoe." He went into the kitchen to get more washcloths.

"And it'll be going in my report," Runcible growled, and Logan's heart sank. *The report about why to shut down this Menagerie,* he thought. *We can't let that happen.*

"You are in *so much trouble,*" Ruby proclaimed as Zoe grabbed Logan's wrist. "I can't believe you did that. This is exactly why I came back, to make sure crazy things like this don't—"

Zoe yanked Logan out the door and slid it shut again to block out the sound of Ruby's voice. Logan shook his head—although Marco's family had seemed like fun, meeting Ruby definitely made him glad he didn't have any siblings. Especially older-sister-type siblings. He didn't know how Zoe could stand it.

She took off running down the hill toward the lake and he had to sprint to keep up.

"I forgot to bring something for Squorp today," he panted.

"We're not going to the griffins," she said. "We're going to see Scratch while the agents are distracted. I bet *he's* the one who ate the sheep—I just don't know how he got past the electric fence."

She stopped at the Reptile House, opened a metal box attached to the outside wall, and took out a small black stick that looked like a wand, with a green light at one end. Then she took off running up the cliff-side path to the dragons.

"Um," Logan called. "Fireproof suits?"

"There's no time," she called back. "They're just a precaution anyway. I'm sure we'll be fine."

Logan was not even a little bit sure of that, but he wasn't going to let her go up there alone.

"Don't worry," she added as he caught up to her. "We don't always wear them. That was mostly for the SNAPA agents." Zoe ducked behind a boulder and pulled him down next to her. "Do you see Firebella?" She peeked over the top of the rock. "I think she's in her cave. Hopefully sleeping. She's the one most likely to accidentally set us on fire."

Logan snatched a glimpse of the caves, but all he could see was Clawdius, standing guard and sniffing the air in a decidedly bored kind of way. "I don't see her," he said.

"Good. Then let's run," said Zoe. She sprinted up the hill and right past the two main dragon caves. As he ran by, Logan saw Clawdius lower his head to stare at them, and a shiver traveled down his spine. But Firebella remained out of sight, and a moment later, Zoe and Logan stood outside Scratch's cave.

The accused dragon was the very picture of woe. His wings slumped under the weight of all the chains wrapped around him, and smoke puffed gloomily from his snout where it rested on the rocky ground. He rolled his eyes toward Zoe in a miserable way and didn't even bother to raise his head.

"Hey, Scratch," Zoe said. She shoved her hands in her

pockets and crouched beside his head. "How are you feeling?"

"Tragic is life of Scratch," said the dragon mournfully. "Mother exterminated. Sister exterminated. Now-soon Scratch to be no more."

"We're not going to let that happen," said Logan.

"Inevitable is fate," sighed the dragon. He gave Logan a curious look, like he was weighing Logan's good and bad qualities.

"But you didn't kill Pelly, did you?" Zoe asked. "Even though you wanted to?"

Logan raised his eyebrows. "He wanted to?"

"Pelly gave Clawdius and Firebella each one of her golden eggs for their treasure hoards," said Zoe. "But she said Scratch wasn't worthy of one. They kind of hated each other." She ran her hands through her hair. "Don't tell the SNAPA agents that."

"Dreadful was the honk-bird," said the dragon. "But not eaten by Scratch was the honk-bird. *Deserved* to be eaten by Scratch was the honk-bird. But most restrained was Scratch. Downright noble was Scratch. Vile the honk-bird grief-causing for Scratch, dead and pre-dead and post-dead."

"Hmmm," Zoe said. She got up and went to look at his claws. The earlier anklet had been taken away—as evidence, Logan guessed. New, thicker anklets had replaced it on all four of Scratch's legs. "Scratch, how did you unlock your restraints?"

"Unlocked it never," protested Scratch. His scaly tail twitched with a *clank*. "Touched it never, even sniffed it never. Broke itself did the anklet. Boom in the foreweek down and off."

"It just fell off?" Zoe puzzled out. "Sometime in the last week? That's . . . worrying. They're really, really not supposed to do that."

"Maybe someone messed with it," Logan suggested.

"Free was Scratch," said the dragon with a dramatic sigh, "but so-ever good was Scratch."

"Really?" said Logan. "You didn't, say, fly out of the Menagerie and eat some sheep?"

Scratch squinted at him thoughtfully. "*Mostly* so-ever good was Scratch."

"Oh, *no*," Zoe said. "Scratch! You really ate those sheep?"

He clawed at the ground and looked pathetic. "Came back to cave, did not Scratch? Fat the empty-head of fluff on legs overtaking planet. Asking to be eaten was the fluff on legs. Hardly to miss among the horde. Plus also and plus hungry was Scratch."

"We feed you plenty," Zoe said, putting her hands on her hips. "I guess that's why you haven't been eating your dinner this last week—you've been full of sheep."

"But not full of honk-bird," said Logan. "I mean, goose. Right, Scratch? It doesn't make sense—even if he didn't like Pelly, why bother climbing into the Aviary to eat her and risk getting caught when he had a steady supply of sheep outside the walls?"

"And that's why you didn't set off the intruder alarm," said Zoe. "You weren't even here."

Scratch hunched his shoulders and made a snuffling noise. "Abject failure as alarm system is Scratch. Remorseful is Scratch the day long."

"The sheep eating also explains the blood on his teeth," Logan pointed out.

Zoe flicked a switch on the black wand and waved it over Scratch's neck. "And your chip isn't working, either. So no electric fence. How did that happen?"

The dragon shrugged. "Technology of mankind puny. Out went the zap. Surprised and flying and glamour-unseen was Scratch of a sudden pow."

Logan flashed back to his first morning in the Menagerie, on Saturday—walking from the griffin enclosure to the lake in the quiet predawn, when he'd felt something like a shadow pass overhead, along with a breath of hot wind. That must have been Scratch returning from his nocturnal wanderings, invisible and full of sheep.

"But it was working a week ago," Zoe said, frustrated. "I know the SNAPA agents checked everything—your anklet, the electric fence chips. How could both of those things break in the same week?"

"Somebody must have broken them," Logan said. "On

purpose. Knowing that SNAPA was coming back, and try-ing to get you in trouble."

Zoe stared at him openmouthed.

"Aha," said Scratch, the first glimmer of hope appearing in his dark eyes. "Perhaps not the fault of Scratch is all things. Perhaps *set up* was Scratch. Perhaps all innocent and noble still is Scratch and plus also not for extermination might be Scratch."

"Don't get too excited, fire-breath. The SNAPA agents will say you could have eaten the sheep *and* Pelly," Zoe pointed out. "This doesn't prove your innocence, I'm afraid."

"But it might help us find the real killer," said Logan. "And this isn't the first suspicious thing. I've been thinking about how the griffins got out of the Menagerie. There was that mysterious hole in the river grate. I think someone cut that hole, probably hoping the griffin cubs would escape that way."

"Stop," Zoe said, putting her hands over her ears. "Why would anyone do that to us? That's—that's sabotage. Like they *want* us to get shut down."

"Exactly," said Logan. "And most likely that same some-one killed Pelly. So now the question is . . . who hates you that much?"

FIFTEEN

Logan was a little distracted during dinner with Dad Monday night. It was hard to focus on pork chops and corn cakes when he really wanted to get back to the Menagerie and keep looking for clues.

"So," Logan's dad said. "Tell me about your day."

Hmm, Logan thought. *I met a family of werecreatures? I had a nice chat with a dragon? I saved my school librarian from getting her memory wiped? We glitter bombed a werewolf?*

He settled for, "I ate lunch with Blue."

"And Zoe?" his dad asked, a little too quickly.

Logan raised his eyebrows at him. "And Zoe."

"Have you, uh—have you met her parents?" Dad asked, poking his pork chop with his fork as if he didn't really care about the answer, but Logan got the feeling he did.

What do you know, Dad?

"Yeah," he answered.

"So they've . . . met you."

"That's generally how it works." There was a pause. *And they recognized me, and Zoe told me everything,* Logan thought. *Is that what you're wondering? Just ask me, Dad.* Finally he added, "They're really nice."

"Hmm," Dad said, with a hint of skepticism in his voice.

"I bet Mom would like them," Logan said boldly. He knew for a fact that his mom had liked them; according to Zoe's stories about Logan's mom, she'd been a regular visitor to the Menagerie, bringing them new mythical creatures at least once or twice a year. *So if you know that, Dad, maybe now would be a good time to come clean. Why else are we in Xanadu? Mom must have told you about this Menagerie. But you haven't gone to talk to the Kahns, or Zoe would have mentioned it.*

"Your mom is usually a pretty good judge of character," Dad said noncommittally.

He doesn't trust the Kahns, Logan realized suddenly. *Maybe he thinks they know what happened to Mom.*

Either that, or he doesn't know anything and I'm being paranoid.

"Do they have any interesting collections?" Dad blurted. "Like silver? Maybe a silver door or silver knives or—" He trailed off. "Never mind."

"Dad, what on *earth* are you talking about?" Logan asked. Silver? Was his dad worried about werewolves? Did he think werewolves had taken Mom?

"Nothing," said Logan's dad. "Just something someone said about the Kahns. Maybe I heard him wrong."

Logan felt like they were each having a totally different conversation inside their heads than the one happening out loud. It made him want to throw corn cakes at his dad until the truth tumbled out of his mouth.

Maybe if I just ask the right question.

"Hey, what was Mom doing on her last trip?" he asked. "Do you know?"

Dad looked up and studied him with serious dark eyes. "Her normal business stuff," he said after a minute. "Why?"

"Normal business stuff like what?"

"Logan," Dad said, putting down his knife and fork. "Listen. I understand."

Logan held his breath. *Do you? Is this it? Time for the truth?*

"I miss her, too." Dad reached across the table and patted Logan's hand. "For now we have to carry on just the two of us, okay? Maybe one day we'll find out more about where she went and what she's doing now. I feel like we will."

Logan looked down at his plate, feeling a rush of

disappointment. "I hope so," he said. "I'm going to go finish my homework." He got up, leaving most of his dinner uneaten, and went to his room.

Later that night, he lay in bed, exhausted but unable to sleep. He couldn't stop thinking about Mom. Purrsimmon landed on his chest and swished her tail in his face as she sauntered down to settle between his feet. Her eyes slid shut and in that irritating, semimagical way cats have, she was out almost immediately. Logan, on the other hand, couldn't seem to quiet his brain.

Mom, where are you?

An hour later, the only part of him that had fallen asleep was his foot. He tried to inch it out from under the cat.

"Mrreow!" Purrsimmon protested. She sat up and glared at him.

"Sorry, Purrs," he said. The curtains at his window shifted in the breeze, and he pulled the blankets higher. Soon he'd have to start shutting the window at night, which would give Purrsimmon a whole new thing to be mad about.

Is Mom thinking about me right now? Is she okay?

She'd gone looking for a Chinese dragon for the Kahns' Menagerie.

She'd sent Logan and Dad a postcard saying good-bye. A postcard postmarked from Cheyenne, Wyoming.

And then she'd disappeared, along with the dragon.

Or actually, it was the other way around, wasn't it? She'd

disappeared, and *then* she'd sent the postcard.

So she couldn't be dead. Dead people don't send postcards.

Maybe someone made her send it.

Logan hesitated, then reached over and grabbed his cell phone from the nightstand. He ducked under the covers and dialed Zoe's number. He didn't think she'd be awake, but maybe hearing her voice on her voice mail message would help him think about something else.

"Hey," Zoe answered sleepily.

"Oh, sorry," he said. "I thought your phone would be off."

"It's okay," she said. "I'm just lying here worrying about why someone would sabotage the Menagerie."

"I can't sleep, either," he said. He listened to her breathing for a moment. "Zoe. What if the same person also took my mom? What if kidnapping her and the Chinese dragon was part of the same plan to shut you guys down?"

Silence.

"Zoe?"

"I had the same thought," she said. "But I didn't want to freak you out."

"Always tell me everything," he said. "Any thought you have about where she might be or what might have happened. You can't freak me out more than I already am."

"All right, I promise," she said. "As soon as this trial is over, we'll focus on finding her, okay?"

Logan had no idea how they would begin to do that.

"I'd better go," Zoe whispered. "Keiko is making extra-grumpy noises in her sleep."

"Okay," Logan whispered back. "See you tomorrow."

Tuesday at lunch, Logan was the first one to get to the courtyard, and he sat at the stone table for a few minutes by himself, worrying, even though he knew he was being stupid, that Zoe and Blue had decided to sit somewhere else. So it was almost funny when Blue, then Zoe, then Marco, and then, almost immediately, Jasmin descended on the table like a bunch of dragons coming in to land.

Jasmin gave Marco a half smile and squished herself next to Blue, wrapping her hands in her autumn-leaf-colored scarf and rubbing them together. "It's so cold out here! Blue, are you sure you don't want to sit inside with me?"

"I'm all right," Blue said in the nicest possible way. "I don't get cold. But thanks."

"Suit yourself," Jasmin said with a shrug. "Question for you, though. Why is there a sixth grader going around telling people that she's coming to my Halloween party on Friday?"

"Oh, Keiko," said Blue. "Sorry, I forgot to check with you." He shot Logan a wicked grin. "Logan really wanted me to invite her."

"What?" Logan nearly sprayed turkey sandwich all over the table.

"Aww, cute," Jasmin said, looking straight at Logan for

the first time. She gave him a sympathetic smile. "Okay, then I'll allow it. The other thing is that I finished *The Hunger Games* and we are *so* going as Katniss and Peeta! I definitely have a bow and arrow somewhere. I'll figure out your part of it, don't worry."

"Um," said Blue.

"Brrr! I'm going inside. See you guys later." Jasmin touched Blue's shoulder again, and this time she graced Marco and Logan with a smile before she hurried away.

"Blue!" Logan exploded as soon as she was gone.

"What?" Blue said, feigning innocence. "What's that I hear? Oh, it's the beautiful sound of retribution. That's right. Snap."

"But *I'm* Keiko's soul mate," Marco said. He stood up, started rolling up his sleeves, and pointed at Logan. "We're doing this right now."

"Doing what?" Logan asked, confused.

"You'd better bring your arms of fury, because I will be battling with the strength of a hundred roosters, and that's— stop laughing," he said to Blue. "Roosters are stronger than you think. Well, they have claws and beaks. Hey, I bet *you* wouldn't want to fight one."

"I'm not going to fight you!" Logan said.

"I'm not going to fight you, either," said Marco. "I'm going to arm wrestle you, and I'm going to crush you, and then I'm going to dance in a circle like a World Wrestling champ, and then you are going to bow out like a gentleman and leave Keiko to me."

"Oh, brother," Zoe said, tucking her hair behind her ears. "Marco, you are in so, so, so much trouble if you think that approach is going to work with her."

"Blue was *joking*," Logan said with a fierce look at his friend, who was laughing so hard he'd nearly fallen off the bench. "I am not *at all* interested in Keiko. Frankly, she is terrifying."

"Great!" Marco said, thumping Logan cheerfully on the back. "That is great, great news. Now you can stay my friend instead of becoming my arch nemesis."

"Except now the *entire school* will think I like Keiko," Logan said. "Thanks a lot, Blue."

"They say let the punishment fit the crime," Blue observed.

"The good news is that now Jasmin will be nicer to you," Zoe pointed out. "Because you've become gossip-worthy, and therefore interesting. Especially since it means you're not, um . . . not with me." They had run into Jasmin while they were together on Saturday, trying to smuggle a griffin cub out of the toy store, and Logan had let her think he was dating Zoe so they could get away faster.

"Man, she is going to have the weirdest impression of me," he said.

"So what happened with the glitter bomb?" Marco asked. The others told him about Matthew's reaction and Agent Runcible and the three weeks of roc nest cleaning and hellhound walking and mapinguari baths that Zoe would have to do as punishment.

"I'm not sure I ever want to meet this mapinguari," Logan said to Zoe.

"You don't," she agreed. "He's a big kind of sloth thing who smells awful. Like basilisk-level awful. And baths don't help him at all; I'm not sure why my mom insists on them." She shot a glare at Blue. "Of course Prince Blue over here didn't get in *any* trouble, even though his mom now knows we snuck out into the woods Sunday night."

"I got a very stern talking-to," Blue said calmly.

"Injustice," Zoe said. "I live with it every day. Oh, and the worst part? Keiko totally knew it was Agent Runcible all along. She was hoping I'd get in trouble somehow for snooping around after him, although naturally I exceeded her wildest expectations. When I got up to our room last night, she was as smug as a fox who's eaten *all* the chickens."

"HEY!" Marco objected. "I'm sitting right here!"

"Sorry." Zoe rubbed her temples. "And Mom and Dad said no crazy investigating today. I have to go right home for the voir dire."

"The what?" Marco asked.

"Jury selection." Zoe stabbed her fork into her salad and sent a cherry tomato rolling onto the ground. "It's supposed to be six of Scratch's 'peers,' meaning other creatures who can talk. Blue, can you round up a few merfolk who might be sympathetic to Scratch? Our other choices include the unicorns, the other two dragons, the phoenix, the griffins . . ."

"Whoa," said Marco. "I'm in."

"I thought you wanted to avoid SNAPA," Logan reminded him.

"Yeah, but unicorns and dragons and griffins? This I gotta see. Besides, one of the agents is a werewolf, so it's like we're practically kindred spirits, right?"

"You haven't met many other werecreatures, have you?" Zoe said to him.

"Just my family," said Marco. "But hey, they can't all be that bad. Ha-ha-ha!"

"The agents will probably be too busy to pay much attention to him," Blue offered.

"True," Zoe said. "All right. We'll all go watch the voir dire after school. I'll tell Dad to prepare Firebella and Clawdius so they don't sound the alarm."

"Awesome," Marco said. He leaned across the table and punched Logan's shoulder lightly. "Dibs on sitting next to Keiko."

* * *

"All right, everyone, settle down!" Mrs. Kahn raised her voice to carry over the hubbub in front of Mooncrusher's hut.

The yeti lived in a kind of sturdy tentlike structure—a yurt, Zoe called it—that Logan guessed he'd built himself. It was made of wood and covered in woven white fur that seemed to be his own. It sat on a little island of ice, and outside the yurt was a glittering garden of ice sculptures, most of them mini-yetis. Some of them even wore giant sunglasses like Mooncrusher's.

The ice ended at a low concrete wall, and on the other side was a grassy area, currently full of milling creatures and people. Captain Fuzzbutt was sprawled on the ice in front of the yurt's door, peeking over the wall at the tables the SNAPA agents were setting up with Mr. and Mrs. Kahn. Beside the mammoth, the yeti stood with his arms folded, glaring at anyone who came too close to his territory.

As Logan, Zoe, and Marco came up from the lake path, one of the griffins—Riff, the one with black feathers—accidentally stepped on Clawdius's tail. The silver dragon roared indignantly, huffing out a small burst of flame that nearly set the top of Mooncrusher's yurt on fire.

"BLAAAAARGH!" Mooncrusher shouted, waving his furry fists.

"Not destined for long life is he who dares to *blaargh* Clawdius," growled the dragon.

"Calm down, both of you," Mrs. Kahn ordered. She glanced at the wand in her hand, as if double-checking that the chips were working on both Clawdius and Firebella. Zoe said the range had been extended to allow them to leave the mountain caves, so the voir dire could take place out of Scratch's hearing, but the Kahns held electric shock wands and were keeping the two dragons on a short leash.

Marco grabbed Logan's arm and shook it. "DRAGONS!" he whispered loudly. "Actual dragons!"

"I know," Logan whispered back with a grin.

Agent Runcible and Agent Dantes stepped back from the tables and nodded at Mrs. Kahn, who raised her hands to get everyone's attention.

Just as it started to get quiet, the roc let out a piercing shriek from inside the Aviary. The two unicorns bolted out of the crowd and started galloping in a panicked circle.

"She's going to eat us!" bellowed Charlemagne.

"Who will protect us?" cried Cleopatra. "Not these worthless serfs who allow beautiful creatures to be eaten under their very noses! Alack the day!"

"Unicorns," Zoe muttered under her breath. She leaned toward Logan and Marco. "Rocs *used* to eat unicorns, but of course Aliya hasn't had anything like a unicorn in centuries. Those two are totally acting up to get SNAPA sympathy. I could strangle them."

"*Unicorns,*" Marco hissed to Logan. "*Actual unicorns.*"

"I know," Logan said, trying not to laugh. He understood exactly how Marco felt.

Still shouting with alarm, Cleopatra vaulted over the concrete wall, slipped on the ice, and skidded into Mooncrusher's meticulously maintained ice sculpture garden. Her hoof struck one of Mooncrusher's mini-yetis and splintered the ice.

"BLAAAARRRRRRRGH!!!" Mooncrusher howled, flying across the enclosure. He roared at Cleopatra until she jumped back over the wall and trotted away with her nose in the air. Then he crouched and patted at the sculpture with his large, furry paws as though it was his own child.

Oh, thought Logan. If he'd thought it was lonely sitting at lunch with no friends for two months, he could only imagine what life was like for the only yeti in Wyoming.

"There he is!" Zoe exclaimed, pointing as Blue came running up from the lake. He was followed by three merpeople: two adults and the teenage mermaid who Logan had met when he first found out about Blue. Her name was something like Sapphire, he thought. She was wearing barely enough clothes to be considered dressed—a skimpy green tank top, short navy shorts, and gold flip-flops—but she didn't seem at all affected by the cold. The mermaid tossed her long blond hair, smirked at Zoe, and sauntered over to the crowd of mythical creatures.

"Really, Blue? That's the best you could do?" Zoe asked.

"I tried," Blue said, giving her a helpless shrug. "Nobody else would even consider coming ashore for jury duty. There's a rumor going around that if the Menagerie gets shut down, Dad and the rest of us will be relocated to the Hawaiian refuge. It's hard to motivate merfolk when tropical waters are on the table."

"But that's not even true!" Zoe shook her head in dismay. "We have no idea where you guys might end up!"

"I know, but once they get an idea in their heads . . ." Blue trailed off as though uncomfortable criticizing merpeople.

Zoe rolled her eyes. "Well, thank you for trying."

"What about Nero?" Logan asked. "He'd qualify for the jury, wouldn't he? Has anyone been able to ask him about the night of Pelly's murder yet?"

"Oh, we've had lots of great conversations with piles of ashes," Zoe said with a sigh. "That bird needs serious anti-anxiety meds. Matthew went to see if he could get Nero to stay nonflammable long enough for the voir dire, but I'm not holding my breath. He'll probably set himself on fire again at the very idea of serving on a jury."

Mrs. Kahn clapped her hands, but between the unicorns complaining loudly, the griffins and dragons growling at each other, and the yeti still blaaaarghing grumpily in the background, the noise level was too high for anyone to pay attention to her.

Agent Runcible stood and blew a short, sharp whistle. The crowd fell silent as he stalked up to join Mrs. Kahn at the front.

Runcible surveyed them, looking displeased. "All prospective jurors need to line up, single file, along the wall. We'll call you forward one at a time. Predators at the front."

"Quickly, please!" Ruby called, bustling up to join him. "Dragons first!"

"She's really going to defend Scratch?" Logan asked Zoe.

"Well, she thinks she is." Zoe frowned at her sister's tailored red suit and the clipboard Ruby was waving at everyone. Ruby caught her expression and sent an equally disapproving look at Logan. "Excuse me."

Zoe went to help escort Riff and Nira into place. The two griffins turned to nudge her affectionately with their beaks. Logan had visited the cubs before coming over here and had gotten an earful about how unfair it was that they couldn't be on the jury and why didn't anyone care about *their* opinions and did juries get snacks? Or treasure? And they would be *great* jurors and hey while Mom and Dad are gone let's have a contest to see who can eat the most pears hooray bye Logan!

Logan smiled, thinking about them, but his smile faded as he glanced over at the SNAPA agents. If this trial went badly . . . not only would it mean Scratch's extermination, but most likely the whole Menagerie would be shut down, with all the animals sent elsewhere, or worse.

Finally the potential jurors were arranged, more or less, in a line. Mr. Kahn led Clawdius forward to a spot in front of the tables, while the agents, Mrs. Kahn, and Ruby took their seats.

Agent Runcible studied the silver dragon. "What are your feelings about Scratch?" he asked carefully.

"Neither wise in years nor stars is Scratch the young." Clawdius inspected his talons and gave the mountain caves a faraway, pensive look. "To leap before time is to break one's wings."

Ruby cleared her throat loudly, then paused to flip a page on her clipboard and jot something down. Finally, she looked up at Clawdius. "Do you think Scratch could have committed this terrible crime? Would he kill Pelly if given the chance? Could he, perhaps, have been acting on natural instinct?"

Logan was no expert, but it seemed counterproductive to ask that many questions at once. Particularly of a dragon, whose speech was a little convoluted to begin with.

"Of little consequence is loss of fat the honk-bird," Clawdius observed. Behind Logan, Melissa snorted. "Evermore after-dragon meets not the honk-birds." His silver scales caught the afternoon sunlight as the dragon cocked his head before continuing. "Caring not about honk-bird or eating of honk-bird is Clawdius. Only hopeful is Clawdius for delicious the meal and trouble the worthwhile for Scratch."

"I see. Very clear," said Agent Runcible. "We respectfully dismiss this juror."

Ruby frowned, but the other SNAPA agent was already waving Firebella forward. Agent Dantes looked up at the female dragon, then quickly down at her notes with a deep breath.

While Clawdius reflected light, Firebella seemed to absorb it. Her scales were velvety black with an occasional flash of purple. Logan did not want to encounter her in the dark of night. Well, he didn't particularly want to encounter her anytime without a fireproof, bite-proof, claw-proof suit and lots of backup.

The graceful dragon stopped in front of the yurt and blinked her yellow eyes at Runcible and Ruby.

"Could you be impartial in this trial?" Runcible asked her.

"Sssssssssssssssssssssssssssssssssss," hissed Firebella, flicking her tongue at him.

Runcible glanced at the electric shock wand in Mrs. Kahn's hand, perhaps wishing they were all wearing fireproof suits. "If we promise not to wake you with any more inspections?" he offered.

"Rrrrrrrrrll," growled Firebella.

"Wait," said Mrs. Kahn as Runcible reached for the wand. "Firebella, we just want to know—do you think Scratch is guilty or not?"

"No," said Firebella. And then, with equal force, "Yes. Guilty. Not guilty. No scales off my tail to both. Prefer to be sssssleeping would be Firebella."

Ruby stepped forward, but with a wary glance at Firebella's narrowing eyes, she didn't waste any time. "How do you feel about Pelly's death?"

"Long the march of time is on and on. Moonrise to sunset and ever the star-time, but all things to death in close of brief years. Briefer for man-things. Briefer also but less brief for golden honk-birds."

"I'll take that as a not bad," Ruby muttered. She turned to Runcible. "The defense has no objections."

"Nor the prosecution. Firebella, you will be on the jury."

The dragon narrowed her yellow eyes still more and breathed a long plume of white smoke. "So-ever and ever delighted is Firebella."

"Yes, well," said Dantes, clearing her throat. "Both dragons should return to their caves now."

"I'll take them," Matthew said from the back. Logan and Zoe twisted to look at him and Zoe mouthed "Nero?" Matthew made a face and waved his hands like a puff of smoke. He took the wand from Mrs. Kahn and led the dragons back to the mountain path.

Logan hoped he'd be fearless like that by high school. Maybe he could go to Tracker camp, too, like Matthew, and become a Tracker like Mom one day.

He glanced at the griffins. Then again, he wouldn't mind staying in one place, either, and taking care of mythical creatures instead of chasing them around the world.

Riff was next, flapping his wings and strutting importantly. It quickly became clear that his only opinions about dragons were that they had entirely too much treasure and that he'd be a better guardian of the Menagerie than they were.

Griffins have been noble guardians of precious things for thousands of years, he declared with another wing flap. **No geese would ever have been eaten on our watch. Ahem.** He shot an arch look at Mr. and Mrs. Kahn.

"And how did you feel about Pelly?" Ruby asked.

The giant griffin clacked his beak. **Nasty bundle of feathers, always snapping at my cubs. But I certainly don't approve of anyone getting eaten around here.**

"He's okay by me," Ruby said to Runcible, who nodded.

"Griffins!" Marco whispered to Logan.

"*Actual griffins,*" Logan whispered back, and Marco grinned.

Nira looked less smug but more powerful as she stalked up in front of the agents. She sat down purposefully and ruffled her neck feathers once before settling.

"Nira, what are your preconceptions of Scratch?" Ruby asked.

The white griffin yawned. **That scrawny dragon? No match for me or my family. My cubs could take him down with their wings tied behind their backs.**

Logan had seen enough of the six griffin cubs playing with their mother to believe she was probably right.

"Do you think he's guilty?" asked Agent Runcible.

Nira shrugged. **I haven't seen the evidence yet, have I?**

Ruby and Runcible consulted for a minute, then passed Nira through to the jury. The two griffins paced off to the side and sat down with their tails curled around their paws, watching the rest of the crowd with their sharp gaze.

The merpeople went next. The first mermaid was named Coral; she had long dark hair and blue fingernails, and she snorted with disgust when she found out there would be no pay for jurors. She shot Blue a disgruntled look before turning back to Runcible and Ruby. "Why would I waste my time then?" she asked.

"Because one of the Menagerie's charges is dead and another is suspected of killing her. We need a jury of Scratch's peers to evaluate the evidence and decide if he's guilty," Mrs. Kahn explained patiently.

"I would *hardly* call mermaids and dragons *peers*," Coral said haughtily. "And he's definitely guilty. But I don't know how much of a crime it really was. That goose was obnoxious—always demanding the best fish from the lake. As if she were the only one—"

"I think we've heard enough. Coral, you may be excused," Ruby interjected.

The mermaid tossed her hair and flounced back to the lake without waiting for the other merfolk. The next one, a stocky merman named Baleen, was placid and agreeable and had no opinion on the case; he was passed straight through to the jury. Then came Sapphire, who kept winking at Blue and flirting with Runcible, but managed not to say anything terribly awful, so she ended up on the jury as well.

While Runcible was interviewing Charlemagne, Mrs. Kahn leaned over and whispered something to the other SNAPA agent. Dantes nodded and slid a box out from under her chair, then passed it down the table to Zoe's mom and Ruby.

Logan noticed that Zoe was watching the box with fierce concentration. "What is that?" he whispered.

"The evidence," she whispered back. "SNAPA said we could look through it today in order to prepare for Thursday."

"Looks like they're wrapping up," Marco said as Runcible and Ruby compared notes, then waved Charlemagne through to the jury. "Can we get closer to the unicorns?"

"Let's introduce you to the griffins instead," said Logan. "They're a bit less . . . megalomaniacal."

"Oooo, spelling bee word," Marco said.

"Who'd they pick?" Blue asked. "I stopped paying attention."

"Looks like the jury is Firebella, Riff, Nira, Baleen, Sapphire"—Zoe made a face—"and Charlemagne." She grabbed Blue's shoulder. "Quick, while they're finishing up, let's see if we can look at the evidence first."

She sidled up behind her mom and gave her a nudge. Mrs. Kahn was listening to Ruby argue with the agents and distractedly slid the box toward Zoe.

Logan shivered as Zoe pulled out a sealed clear plastic bag with one bloodstained feather inside. Underneath it were a set of photos of the crime scene—blood and feathers everywhere—followed by a picture of Scratch's bloodstained teeth.

"Oh, no," Zoe said. "They just have to show these to the jury and the trial will be over. Who wouldn't convict him?" She glanced up at the mountains. "Poor Scratch."

"We have two more days," Logan said, although the pictures made him feel pretty discouraged, too. "We'll find the real killer."

"Yikes," Marco said, peering over Zoe's shoulder at the photos. "Oh, man, I am totally having nightmares tonight. Remind me not to hang out with any dragons while I'm a rooster." He took the bag from her and held it up so the afternoon sun shone through the feather. "Wow, and she was super-old, too. Imagine making it all the way to four hundred and then getting eaten just like that."

Zoe turned slowly to stare at him. "What are you talking about?"

Marco fluttered the plastic bag with the feather in it. "Four hundred and twelve? Four hundred and sixteen? Somewhere in there, I think."

"Pelly was a hundred and three years old," Zoe said.

"Oh," said Marco. He lifted a few more thin bags of feathers out of the box and studied them for a moment, then looked up at Zoe, Logan, and Blue. "Then these feathers came from some other goose."

SIXTEEN

Pelly could be alive.

Zoe felt weird tingles up and down her arms. If Pelly was alive—if they could get her back—

She glanced down the table, but her mom and the agents hadn't heard Marco. Ruby was arguing loudly for a later court date, so no one was paying attention to Zoe or the others. Except for Captain Fuzzbutt, whose big brown eyes were watching her curiously from the island of ice.

"In here," Zoe whispered to the others, pointing at the yurt. She dropped the photos and feather bags back into the evidence box, climbed over the low concrete wall, and slid across the ice to Mooncrusher. Behind her she could hear

Logan and Marco and Blue wobbling and crunching carefully between the ice sculptures.

"Blaaaaaargh," the yeti observed, looking down at her with his arms folded.

"I know," Zoe said. "I wouldn't want a crowd like this outside my room, either. Can we use your yurt for a minute?"

Mooncrusher lifted his sunglasses and squinted at her.

"It's for a good reason," she promised.

"Blaargh blaargh," he said, waving one paw at his front door. Captain Fuzzbutt scrambled to his feet and edged out of the way. Zoe kissed the tip of his trunk as he went by, and he patted her on the head with it.

Zoe lifted aside the thick red wool curtain and beckoned to the others. As they ducked inside, Logan and Marco both made strangled "gaack" noises.

Which wasn't entirely fair. Zoe knew that Mooncrusher kept his yurt as neat as possible. He swept it every day, made the bed in the corner, cleaned up the scraps around his weaving loom, and only watched the small TV at night, when all his groundskeeper duties were done. It wasn't his fault that he shed like a normal yeti—which is to say, all over the place all the time. Or that he hated to take baths, also like a normal yeti, so the whole yurt smelled like a herd of damp yaks.

Blue sat down on Mooncrusher's weaving stool. Logan and Marco eyed the furry futon and the furry recliner and opted to stay standing. Zoe peeked through the curtain, making sure her parents and the agents were still occupied and out of earshot, then turned back to Marco.

"Okay," she said. "Explain. Those aren't Pelly's feathers?"

He shrugged. "Those feathers come from an old goose, at least four hundred years old. I can't really explain how I know. It's sort of a wererooster thing."

"I'm sure *that's* going to stand up in court," Logan said. "This is our feather expert, who is twelve and an unregistered werecreature, but he's going to crack this case wide open."

"I wonder if there's a way to verify it," Zoe said. "Like DNA testing or something."

"On goose feathers?" Marco said. "Sure, I bet the FBI will get right on that."

"But they aren't ordinary goose feathers," Logan said. "They're huge and kind of sparkly, like Pelly's. You can't just pick up feathers like that on your average farm, right? Nor do average geese live to be a hundred, let alone four hundred."

"So they must have come from another goose who lays golden eggs," Zoe said. Seeing Logan's surprised look, she added, "There are about ten or twelve of them, I forget exactly. Not like Nero, who is the only phoenix in the world."

"So someone got those feathers from another golden goose and brought them here," said Blue.

"The blood probably isn't hers, either," Logan said. "Which means whoever it is wants us to *think* Pelly's dead, but they actually stole her."

"For her golden eggs," Blue guessed.

Logan and Zoe exchanged glances. *Or because they knew that without those golden eggs, the Menagerie would financially collapse,* Zoe thought. *Because they hate us, although I have no idea why.*

"So all we have to do is track down the thief, rescue Pelly, and clear Scratch, and then we save the Menagerie!" Zoe said.

"No problem," Blue said. He shot her a wry smile. "At least it's better than going after a werewolf on a full moon."

"And now we know where to start," Zoe pointed out. "We find out where the thief could have gotten the fake feathers—which other menageries have golden geese, and if any of them are that old."

"How would we check that?" Logan asked. "Do you have some kind of database?"

"Sort of, but ours is way out of date," Zoe admitted. "The best way to check would be on one of the agents' tablet computers."

"So we tell them—" Blue started.

"No!" Zoe said quickly. "We shouldn't tell anyone yet—they won't believe us until we find Pelly, and they'll just have lots of questions for Marco. We need to focus on getting her back before the trial."

"And then they can't exterminate Scratch," Logan said. "Right? He won't be in trouble for the sheep?"

"Some trouble, but not extermination-level trouble," Zoe said. "The fact that he came back to the Menagerie instead of escaping after eating the sheep will help." She went to the door and peeked out at the agents. Mrs. Kahn was sorting through the evidence with Ruby; Runcible stood next to them with an impatient expression on his face. The strap of his computer bag crisscrossed his chest, and he held on to it with one hand as he waited. Zoe couldn't imagine getting his computer away from him.

But Delia . . .

The other agent slipped her tablet into a case and put the whole thing inside her purse, which was brown leather with brass buckles and hung from one shoulder. She unclipped her long dark hair, shook it back, and clipped it up again. Her gray gaze drifted to the dragon mountain caves and Zoe thought she looked a little sad. She'd always seemed so nice—asking them to call her Delia, saying reassuring things about the Menagerie. Maybe she wouldn't even mind if they asked to look at her computer . . . but just in case, it was safer not to ask.

"We'll need a distraction," Zoe said.

"Can we download the database somehow?" Logan asked.

"Not on one of those computers," Marco said. "Not in a hurry without a particular attachment. Victor has a tablet like that, which, by the way, is totally unfair, because it's not like he really needs it for high school and I'm pretty sure he just uses it for video games and watching YouTube videos about eating mice."

"Gross!" Logan yelped.

"Owls eating mice," Marco pointed out. "Not people. Obviously."

"Slightly less gross," Logan amended.

"So you'll have to get the computer," Blue said to Zoe. "You know all the menageries. You'll understand the database better than any of us."

Zoe rubbed her arms, trying to chase away her goose bumps. "So you guys will be the distraction."

"I have an idea," Logan said. He pointed to Riff and Nira, who were stretching their wings and clacking their beaks at each other. "If you can get Agent Dantes to take them back to their den, I'll put Squorp in charge of being distracting. It's one of his particular skills." He grinned.

"Okay," Zoe agreed. Logan pushed through the curtain, maneuvered carefully through the ice garden, and took off running toward the griffin enclosure on the far side of the lake. As soon as he was out of sight, Zoe climbed on the wall beside Nira and whispered in her ear.

Hmmmm, Nira rumbled. Will this get us thrown off the jury? Because I'm quite looking forward to participating in the judicial process.

Zoe raised her eyebrows. "Really?"

Of course. I'm especially looking forward to the part where someone else watches my cubs for a few hours while I get to use my brain and have adult conversations.

"Oh," Zoe said, remembering that she still hadn't had a talk with Riff about being more helpful with the cubs. *After the trial. I'll put it on my to-do list.* "Sure, okay. Well, don't worry, you'll still be on the jury. But we need your help to get this evidence. I promise you'll see why during the trial."

All right, said Nira. **But if I get thrown off the jury, you're babysitting them all day Saturday.**

"Deal," said Zoe.

What are we doing? Riff asked. **Something terribly noble?**

Yes, dear, said Nira. **Just follow my lead.** She flapped her wings and paced over to the SNAPA agent. Delia looked up from packing her purse and jumped at the sight of the massive griffin peering down her beak at her.

Escort us home, suggested the griffin in a way that didn't sound remotely optional. **I wish to discuss my cubs' eating habits.**

"Oh, um," said Delia, glancing at Runcible. "That's not really SNAPA's—"

Two of them will eat anything, Nira continued

implacably. **But the other four are being extremely difficult.**

I'm terribly worried, Riff jumped in, clacking his beak. **Sage has eaten nothing but pickles for the last two days and Clonk has been demanding chocolate coins instead of lovely fish and Clink is trying to organize a hierarchical system where she gets all the best food first but of course Yump won't stand for that and then Flurp keeps pooping rainbow-colored poop. RAINBOW POOP, SNAPA AGENT! Pink! And lime green! And fluorescent orange! What sort of dreadful disease is this?!**

Delia blinked.

Whoops, Zoe thought. She hadn't had a chance to warn the griffin parents about the crayons Flurp had eaten while she was hiding in the town library.

Nira smiled an inscrutable griffin smile and put one wing around Delia's shoulders, steering her toward the lake. **We would very much like to hear your opinions.**

"I—I don't really have any opinion about, uh . . . rainbow poop," Delia tried, but the griffins weren't letting her slip away. They ushered her along the path, both talking at the same time. Once the SNAPA agent was at the griffin enclosure, the next step would be up to Logan. Zoe turned to Blue.

"Go get a bucket of fish, so it looks like we have a reason to be there," she said. "Hurry."

Blue and Marco ran down to the lake while Zoe followed the griffins and Delia. Riff hopped along on Delia's other side, swishing his lion tail dramatically and expounding on the various eating dilemmas of his six children.

Squorp and Yump are such good cubs, he declared proudly. **They'll eat anything, really anything, and they're constantly hungry, but then I worry, are we overfeeding them? Or perhaps they're hungry because we're not feeding them enough? What do you think? Is twelve hamburgers a day enough? Should we be giving them more broccoli? I never ate broccoli a day in my life and I turned out fine but Zoe had this cookbook that said—**

He probably thinks this really is what they need to talk to her about, Zoe thought fondly. Riff was a goof, but no one could say he didn't love his cubs.

Zoe hung back as they reached the griffin pen, waiting for Blue to catch up with the fish from the lake. She watched as the agent unlatched the gate and swung it open—and three griffin cubs exploded out the door, squawking at the top of their lungs.

Delia shrieked and dropped her purse.

"Quick, catch them!" Logan yelled, running out of the

enclosure and chasing Squorp down the hill. Flurp butted Delia's legs and galloped away. Clonk chased after her, waving his wings like he was hoping if he ran fast enough he'd end up airborne.

My cubs! Riff bellowed frantically. My beautiful cubs! He charged after Squorp, nearly running Delia over.

You let them out, Nira said calmly to Delia. You can get them back.

The agent let out a cry of dismay as Flurp shot past her once more. Delia grabbed for the cub's tail, missed, and ran after her around the wall of the griffin enclosure.

Zoe bolted toward Delia's purse, pulled out the computer, and ducked behind Nira's outspread wings. Out of the corner of her eyes she noticed Blue and Marco joining the chase. The happy yowls of griffin cubs filled the air as Flurp, Clonk, and Squorp charged in circles through the grass, yipping with glee. Nira sat down and examined one of her front paws.

The computer made a little *ping* noise as the screen lit up. The background was a photo of a smiling couple with a little girl. Zoe guessed it must be Agent Dantes at about age eight or nine, with her parents. She had the same hairstyle and the same wistful expression. Zoe wondered how she'd been recruited to be a SNAPA agent.

She scanned the icons on the home screen until she found one that said "Creature Index." When she tapped on it, a spreadsheet popped up that listed creatures by name, location, species, and previous homes, with a section for notes on each one. Zoe touched one of the tabs to rearrange it by species, then scrolled down to "Golden Geese."

There were eleven listed besides Pelly; Pelly's line was in red, with a note saying "DECEASED; SUSPECTED DRAGON ATTACK" next to it.

Zoe read down the list, trying to memorize it and look for anything surprising. *Too bad it doesn't list their ages, too*, she thought. There was one goose at the New England Menagerie with a note that said "DECREASED EGG PRODUCTION. STRESS? PROXIMITY TO DRAGONS?" Another had been relocated to Vancouver from a tiny menagerie in Parkville, Missouri; the note said "MENAGERIE CLOSED DUE TO EXPOSURE; KRAKEN INK ADMINISTERED TOWN-WIDE."

Zoe shuddered. That could have been them if the griffin cubs had been spotted by someone in Xanadu. *Shoot.* Someone *had* seen them—Miss Sameera. Zoe still needed to deal with that.

Come back, my beautiful cubs! Riff bellowed, careening past with his feathers flying. **I promise to give you more love and affection!**

Zoe focused on the list again. One goose had been sent to the Costa Rica Conservatory after the Amazon menagerie was shut down because of a dragon attack. Five of the geese were in Europe and one was in Mongolia, at the site of the original Kublai Khan menagerie.

And one was at Camp Underpaw in Colorado.

Zoe gasped.

That was Matthew's Tracker camp.

SEVENTEEN

The late-afternoon sun filtered through the pear trees inside the griffin enclosure. Logan sat on one of the boulders, tossing a baseball for the cubs. He'd tried tennis balls first, but they hadn't held up well in the sharp little beaks, and now neon-green fuzz was scattered across the grass. There was also quite a bit of fuzz stuck to Clink's feathers, as the largest griffin cub had apparently decided the tennis balls were a threat to her treasure and disemboweled them all.

Now the black cub was perched beside him, glaring intently at her brothers and sisters as they galloped after the baseball.

"It's just a game," Logan reassured her. He'd promised

to stay and play with the cubs if they helped distract Agent Dantes, which they had done with great enthusiasm. It had taken about twenty minutes to round up the three escapees, and finally Dantes had staggered off to the main house without noticing that her computer had been briefly borrowed.

Nefarious ball is unpredictable, growled the black griffin cub. **Nefarious ball threat must be squashed and defeated.** She clacked her beak sharply.

The only other cub not playing was Yump, the plump red griffin. He'd planted himself firmly on Blue's foot and was keeping his eagle eyes on the bucket of fish Blue was holding out of reach.

"Can I see my mom's bracelet for a minute?" Logan asked Clink. She dipped one wing toward him and slid the gold "treasure" he'd given her into his hands.

He turned it over and studied the twelve charms. What he'd thought were an elephant, a fox, and a lizard suddenly looked totally different to him: a mammoth, a kitsune, and a basilisk stared back in stamped gold form.

These are the creatures she tracked, he thought. *A new charm each time she found one; that's why she always added one to the bracelet after each trip.* But she never took the bracelet with her. She always left it with Logan. Maybe she'd been planning to explain it all to him one day—her job, where she went all the time, the minor fact that unicorns and dragons existed.

I wonder if Dad would tell me anything if I asked him about this bracelet.

Squorp came galloping back with the baseball in his beak and the other cubs close on his tail.

Squorp triumphant! he bellowed inside Logan's head.

"Can I try?" Marco asked Logan.

"Sure," Logan said. "Squorp, give the ball to Marco." The golden griffin cub dropped the baseball in Marco's hands. As Marco stood up to throw it, the other three cubs all tackled him at once, knocking him to the ground.

"Aaaaaaaaaaaaaaaaaaaaah!" Marco yelled. "Help! I'm drowning in griffins!"

Squorp to the rescue! shouted Squorp with glee. He leaped into the fray, wrapped his front paws around Flurp's shoulders, and started rolling vigorously around on top of Marco.

"Aaaah! Less help, less help!" Marco cried.

Logan laughed and glanced across at Nira, who was fast asleep on a boulder outside her cave. He was glad to give her a break from the craziness of playing with her cubs all day long.

"Zoe!" Blue called. "Stop pacing and come talk to us."

Zoe had been walking in circles around the inside of the fence, rubbing her wrist anxiously, ever since Dantes had left.

She shoved her hair back and climbed up to sit next to Logan.

"There's a golden goose at Camp Underpaw," she said to Blue. "But that doesn't mean Matthew did this. Right? I mean, why? Why would he take Pelly and ruin the Menagerie like this? Why would he let Scratch take the blame?" She shook her head. "Does he need money for something? He *has* been acting weird since camp."

Sage, the smallest griffin cub, jumped off Marco and scrambled up the boulder to curl in Zoe's lap like a cat. Zoe stroked her long head feathers and scratched between her wings, and Sage made a contented purrlike noise.

"Where were the other geese?" Logan asked.

Zoe rattled off a list that didn't mean much to him.

"What about the SNAPA agents?" Blue said. "They go from menagerie to menagerie all the time. It'd be easy for Agent Dantes or Agent Runcible to collect extra goose feathers from somewhere."

"Yeah, but we know where they were Saturday night when Pelly was taken," Zoe pointed out. "Runcible was a werewolf, with a tracking device, no less, and Delia was monitoring him so he wouldn't eat anybody." She ruffled Sage's fur with her fingers.

"So we should at least check out Matthew," said Logan. "Where is he now?"

Zoe nudged Sage off her lap and jumped off the boulder. "Let's go find out."

Blue hung the bucket of fish from a high branch of the tree for Nira and Riff to hand out later, prompting tremendous caterwauling from Yump.

Not FAIR! Why TORTURING YUMP WHY?

"It'll be dinnertime soon," Logan promised him. He glanced at his watch, realizing that meant he needed to head home before long. His father had texted that he'd be home for a late dinner, if Logan was up for it. Another uncomfortable dinner with Dad didn't exactly sound awesome, but it was unavoidable. Logan's plan this time was to talk about football and nothing else. That seemed like the best way to save both of them from telling any more lies.

Mommy's turn to throw the baseball! Squorp announced as Logan went out the gate.

Hooray! chimed the other griffin cubs, racing over to their sleeping mother.

There was no sign of Matthew back at the house. The only person in the living room was Keiko, sprawled across one of the couches with a magazine.

"Hi, Keiko!" Marco blurted loudly.

She glanced up, narrowed her eyes at him, and went back to reading.

"That doesn't look like homework," said Zoe.

"It's more important than homework," Keiko said. "I'm choosing a costume for the Halloween party."

"Jasmin's party?" Marco said with a little too much

enthusiasm. "I'm going to that, too! On Friday! In costume! I'll totally be there!"

"As what?" Keiko said, flipping a page without looking up. "A chicken?"

"HA-HA-HA!" Marco said. "Uh, you know there's a difference between a chicken and a rooster, right? Roosters are much tougher."

"Right," Keiko said, yawning. "And they're a little saltier, too. Still delicious, though."

Marco opened and closed his mouth a few times, looking equal parts horrified and fascinated. Logan took his elbow and dragged him up the stairs behind Zoe.

Matthew's room was at the end of the hallway, beyond Blue's room and opposite the bathroom. The door was always closed, as far as Logan had seen, and it was covered with sketches of stern-looking griffins and fierce dragons and a few creatures he couldn't even name. The drawings were pretty great, actually; Logan wished he could draw like that.

Zoe hesitated outside the door, then knocked.

"Go away!" Matthew's voice yelled, making them all jump.

"Guess we're not sneaking in there," Blue whispered.

"Matthew," Zoe called. "Logan wanted to ask you a question about Tracker camp." She signaled to Blue that he should take Marco into his room and the two of them ducked out of sight.

The door creaked open and Matthew looked out at Zoe

and Logan, frowning. He had dark rings under his eyes and smelled like coffee and damp leaves.

"I'm not speaking to either of you," he said. "I've showered twice and I'm still finding glitter in my ears and armpits and between my toes. Even my sneezes are sparkly. It is NOT. COOL."

"Please?" Zoe said. "Isn't there a deadline for applying?"

Matthew raised his eyebrows. "You want to apply to Tracker camp?" he said to Logan.

"Uh, yes," Logan said, although he hadn't thought about it seriously. "I mean, I think so. Did you like it?"

"Yeah," said Matthew, not very convincingly.

"Matthew was the star of Tracker camp," Zoe said.

"False," Matthew said. "Now go away."

"Oh, please," Zoe said. "The first couple of weeks, it was like we got an email every day from the counselors talking about how you're so great with the animals and you're working so hard and you've inherited the Kahn touch and all that."

"Yeah, well," said Matthew. "After a while they figured out they were wrong." He started to close the door and Zoe stuck her foot in the way. "Zoe, stop annoying me."

"Can you just show Logan your application?" she asked. "Please? I'll do your Reptile House chores tomorrow."

Matthew pointed at her. "And take my turn cleaning out the unicorn stable."

"All right," she said with a grimace.

"Fine." He gestured into his room. "Come in, but don't touch anything."

Logan's first impression was that Matthew's room was a huge mess. Clothes were scattered across the dark green rug, on top of the desk, over the rolling desk chair, and basically everywhere except in the laundry hamper. Pine-green sheets were tangled with a white-and-green-striped comforter on the bed; no sign of a pillow anywhere. Giant corkboards covered two of the walls, and about a million sketches of mythical creatures were pinned to them, plus a map of Xanadu with several red X marks all over the surrounding woods. The only clear spot in the room was on the desk, where a box of colored pencils sat neatly on a blank sketch pad.

Zoe looked around in surprise. "Where's your Tracker dreamboard?" she asked.

"It was stupid," Matthew said.

"No, it was cool," Zoe protested. She turned to Logan. "When Matthew was ten, he made this awesome dreamboard about how he was going to be a Tracker when he grew up, and he put it on the wall to keep himself focused."

"Lame," said Matthew, tossing clothes off his desk chair.

"Is it in the closet?" Zoe asked, opening the closet door.

"Don't go in there!" Matthew yelled.

Zoe blinked at the piles of clothes and shoes on the closet floor, then tilted her head at Matthew. "Why are you acting weird? There's nothing in here. Except this." She reached up and gently touched a set of tiny wind chimes that were hanging from the otherwise empty bar. The small jade tablets of the chimes tinkled, sending strange ripples along Logan's skin. Matthew shivered as well, frowning, but Zoe didn't seem to feel it.

"I mean, it's a little crazy to have wind chimes in your closet, but I won't call any authorities on you, don't worry," she joked. "Oh, here it is." She pulled a large white foam square from the back of the closet and propped it on the bed for Logan to look at.

In the center of the board was a photo of Logan's mom with her arm around a ten-year-old Matthew. Her warm brown eyes crinkled over her huge smile, and Logan felt his own eyes prickle alarmingly. He was so not going to cry in front of Matthew.

"Oh, so you *do* know your mom's a Tracker," Matthew said curiously from behind him.

"Only because I told him," Zoe said. "These are some of the other Trackers who have brought us animals." She pointed to a few other photos on the board; in each one, Matthew stood beaming beside a grown-up, most of whom looked like they'd just leaped off a safari truck, rolled through the mud, wrestled a hippo, and dragged it all the way home with their bare hands.

There were also words cut from magazines pasted all over the board, like BRAVE and ADVENTURE and CARING and CLEVER and AMBUSH and FAST. Each one made Logan think of his mom. There were also more animal sketches and an ancient-looking map of the world with HERE BE DRAGONS written in the oceans.

"Anyway," Zoe said. "I thought you'd like to see that. Matthew, did you find your application?"

Matthew unearthed a file folder from the mess under his desk and tossed it to Logan. "It's not as fun as it sounds," he said. "You learn a lot, but it's hard work." He crossed to a table Logan hadn't noticed before and lifted a towel off a giant glass cage that looked like an ant farm.

"Because of all the animals there, right?" said Zoe. "You have to help take care of them in between training. I heard Camp Underpaw has a manticore."

"No way," said Matthew, looking at her like she was crazy. "Those are really dangerous." He pointed to a sketch on the wall beside him of a red lion creature with a creepy man's face, sharp teeth, and nasty-looking spines poking out of its tail. "SNAPA never puts them anywhere near minors, and Camp Underpaw is for ages thirteen and up."

Maybe I could go next summer, Logan thought. *If we can find Mom by then. I bet she could talk Dad into it.* He opened the folder and saw a brochure with a bunch of grinning, dirty teenagers in the woods, looking exhausted and happy. There were no photos of the mythical creatures—that was against SNAPA's rules—but Logan could still get an idea of the place from the photos of kids studying tracks with a magnifying glass, climbing a rocky mountainside, and pointing at the sky. It looked like more fun than tennis camp, that was for sure.

"So what animals do they have?" Zoe asked casually, perching on the edge of Matthew's bed.

"Some of the same things we do," Matthew said. "Griffins, unicorns, halcyons." He picked up a small jam jar that seemed to be seething with movement inside. Logan squinted at it and realized it was full of ants. "Plus a pegasus, a chimera, a bunch of selkies and yawkyawks, a hippocamp, stuff like that." He shook a few ants into the top of the ant farm and sighed. "And a bonnacon."

"What's a bonnacon?" Logan asked, watching the ants curiously. Why were they in a jar instead of in the farm?

"That," Matthew said, pointing to another sketch. The dark blue creature looked like a bull, but with a horse's mane, fierce red eyes, and two sharp, curving horns that pointed in toward each other. "It smells awful and it hates everyone in the world. But the worst part is that it poops fire. I mean, not just fire—giant poop that's *on fire*. It is *the worst*."

"Oh, that's the thing that caused the accident this summer," Zoe said. "Right? It burned down some fences or something?"

Matthew flushed and glared at his ant farm. "That's right," he muttered.

A sudden movement inside the cage caught Logan's eye. Something was tunneling rapidly up through the sand—something bigger than your average ant.

An insect as long as Logan's pointer finger erupted from the sand below the ants and gobbled them all in ten seconds flat. It licked its lips and gave the glass, and Matthew beyond the glass, a golden-eyed *Is that it?* look.

"Whoa," Logan said. He crouched and peered in at the insect. It had the body of an ant—but the head of a tiny lion. The lion's face snarled at him, shaking its mane. "What on earth is that?"

"It's an ant-lion," Matthew said. "Obviously."

"Obviously," Logan echoed.

"There are two more in here somewhere." Matthew bent down to look inside the glass as well.

"Hey, didn't something escape during the fire?" Zoe asked. "Dad told us something got loose. It wasn't a golden goose, by any chance, was it?"

Matthew turned slowly and gave her a sharp look. "Zoe," he said. "Now you're asking weird questions. And your weird questions often lead to weird behavior, like throwing glitter up my nose. So what are you up to?"

Zoe fidgeted with his comforter for a moment before blurting, "We think Pelly's still alive."

"How—" Matthew started.

"Those aren't her feathers at the crime scene," Zoe said. She told him about Marco and checking the SNAPA agent's computer. Logan watched the ant-lion stamping around inside the farm, roaring hungrily. Another lion face poked through the sand and growled at it, and the first ant-lion growled back, and they stood there growling at each other and wriggling their ant butts fiercely for a while.

"So we thought maybe you had access to the camp goose's feathers . . ." Zoe trailed off.

Matthew sat down heavily in his desk chair. "Zoe, what is up with you suspecting me of crazy things? First I'm a were-wolf, now I'm a goose-napper?"

"Well, obviously I don't think you're much of a suspect, since I'm telling you about it," Zoe pointed out.

"I didn't kidnap Pelly," Matthew said. "Camp Underpaw's goose is only about sixty years old."

"So why are you acting so weird?" Zoe cried. "You've been different ever since you got back from camp, all moody and secretive." She pointed to the scar on his arm. "I don't believe a griffin gave you that. You are awesome with grif-fins. And you keep disappearing so even Mom and Dad don't know where you are. What's going on?"

Logan shoved his hands in his pockets and studied the pictures on the wall, wondering if he should slip out of the room. There was a long pause as Matthew ran his hands through his hair and stared at the floor.

"Fine," Matthew said finally. He got up, unpinned a sketch from the corkboard with the Xanadu map, and handed it to Zoe.

She blinked at it. "A qilin? A qilin didn't give you that scar. They're really gentle." She passed the sketch to Logan. The slender creature Matthew had drawn was shaped a bit like a deer, but with horse hooves, blue fish scales all along its back, and one long horn pointing backward from its head instead of forward like a unicorn horn.

"A qilin is what escaped from Camp Underpaw," Matthew said. "Because of me."

He opened his computer and pulled up an email with a video attachment. The email was from a Geoff Landers with the subject line "The Great Matthew Kahn rides the Bonnacon Rodeo." The message just said: "Worst cowboy ever. Watch whenever you need a laugh." Logan noticed that it had been sent to a whole camp list.

"Who's Geoff Landers?" Zoe asked, leaning over his shoulder.

"A huge jerk," said Matthew. "Him and Bryson Polo. Every time I screwed up, they'd be there laughing at me. I felt like an idiot all summer. Turns out I was an idiot, because when they dared me to ride the bonnacon, I said yes." He hunched his shoulders. "I didn't want them to think I was a coward as well as a terrible Tracker." He clicked on the video, which expanded to fill the screen.

The video was blurry and jumpy, as if it had been taken by a camera phone at night. The primary sound was two guys laughing their heads off, but in the background there was also a bellowing ox-like noise, crashing, and the high-pitched shrieks of other animals. A large shape bolted across the screen, pooping fireballs in a long trail behind it. If he squinted, Logan could recognize Matthew in the figure clinging to the bonnacon's twisted horns.

"Whoa," Zoe said.

"Yeah." Matthew exhaled slowly. "See that fence it's running toward? The qilin lived on the other side of it." As he spoke, one of the bonnacon's fiery poops went tumbling toward the fence and instantly set it ablaze.

In the video, Matthew twisted around, saw the fence on fire, and threw himself off the bonnacon. Logan couldn't tell whether he'd hurt himself getting on the animal in the first place, or if he was slashed by the horns on the way off, but Matthew got up with blood streaming down his face and one arm. He staggered over to the fence and started beating at the flames with his jacket, yelling for help.

"Geoff!" he called. "Bryson! Come on, we have to put this out!"

"Loser," snickered a male voice.

"Let's get out of here," said the other. The video ducked toward the ground, catching a shot of shoes running, and then abruptly stopped.

"The fence burned down and the qilin escaped," Matthew said.

"Have the counselors seen this?" Zoe demanded. "Or

Mom and Dad? I can't believe Geoff and Bryson just left you like that! Plus, taking a video of a mythical creature could get them barred from working for SNAPA for the rest of their lives."

"No, they only sent this to the other campers," Matthew said gloomily. "But everyone knows this was all my fault, even though Ashley kept me out of the official report because she's friends with Dad. Zoe, the only way I'll ever get to go back to camp—the only way I'll have a chance of becoming a Tracker—is if I find that qilin and bring her back myself."

He got up, went to the closet, and pulled out the wind chimes, letting them dangle from one of his fingers. "That's why I took this. It's like a mystical homing device that calls to this particular qilin. So she has to be nearby—she must have followed these chimes when I brought them back to Xanadu—but I haven't even come close to catching her yet."

Zoe sat up suddenly. "A qilin!" she said. "Aren't those the ones—"

"That can sense guilt," Matthew finished. "Right. That's the other thing. If I can find the qilin by Thursday, we can bring her to court, and she can prove that Scratch is innocent."

Roaring suddenly erupted from the ant farm. Logan whirled and saw the two ant-lions grappling, each trying to bite the other one's head off. Without paws and claws, all they had for fighting was their teeth, which they were using to viciously rip at ears and noses and manes. It looked like they were seriously about to hurt each other.

Logan jumped forward, grabbed the jar of ants, and shook a handful into the farm right on top of the battling ant-lions. The fierce little creatures jumped apart and attacked the ants instead, ravenously chasing them down and eating them all.

Logan looked up and found Matthew staring at him.

"You've never seen an ant-lion before?" Matthew asked. Logan shook his head. "So you just knew that was the way to stop them from fighting? Somehow, with your magic powers?"

"It was only a guess," Logan said uncomfortably. He hadn't even stopped to think about it. It just seemed logically like the right thing to do.

"You know he has some kind of instinct for this stuff," Zoe said. "So be smart and use him."

"All right," Matthew said with a long sigh. He held out his fist to Logan. "Tomorrow, you and me, tracking a qilin. Deal?"

Logan bumped his fist, trying not to look too thrilled. "Deal."

EIGHTEEN

Wednesday was too drizzly and wet and cold to eat lunch in the courtyard. Logan and Blue wolfed down their food in the hallway and met Zoe outside the library.

She put a finger to her lips and pointed through the door's window at Miss Sameera. Nobody else was around, and the librarian was fast asleep with her head on her desk. Her hair had escaped its ponytail and was running wild across her keyboard. There were little Band-Aids all over both of her hands, and her ruby-red blouse was missing a few silver bells.

Logan caught Zoe staring at Miss Sameera's cup of chai tea, steaming quietly on the desk. Zoe's hand went to the pocket of her backpack where he knew she kept a vial of kraken ink.

"Don't do it," he whispered. "We still have no idea what she knows."

"We know she knows too much," Zoe muttered.

"I agree with Logan," said Blue. "No messing with people's heads if we can avoid it."

"Fine," Zoe said, blowing her hair out of her face. "But if she starts telling people that she's seen griffin cubs and anyone believes her, don't blame me if we have to end up dosing the whole town."

"SNAPA can do that?" Logan asked.

"They did it in Parkville, Missouri, when the menagerie there was exposed. I saw a note about it on Delia's tablet next to one of the golden geese." Zoe's expression grew mournful. "They shipped her away—along with all the other creatures."

"That's not going to happen here," Logan told her firmly. "We won't let it."

Zoe shot him a grateful look, then turned and led the way into the library.

The school library was a lot smaller than the main library in town, with dark blue walls, sky-blue carpets, tall bookshelves, cheerful displays of new books that changed each month, and reading nooks in every corner with beanbags or armchairs. Whenever he walked in the door, Logan felt as if all the books were flinging themselves against a glass wall at him, like puppies in a pet store desperately wanting to be taken home.

Logan followed Zoe to a back corner, where she pushed open one of the big windows that faced the back parking lot. Matthew popped out of the Menagerie's van and ran over. He clambered through the window, scattering raindrops on the rug.

"Shhh," Zoe scolded him as one of his boots thumped against the radiator. Logan glanced at the other end of the room, but Miss Sameera didn't wake up.

"Why are we sneaking Matthew in the window?" he asked, keeping his voice low even though Miss Sameera was pretty far away. When Zoe had suggested a meeting in the library, he'd imagined Matthew would saunter through the front door like everyone else.

"So he doesn't have to sign in at the front office and give a reason for being here," Zoe said. "Which might tip Mom and Dad off to the fact that he's not in school, where he's supposed to be."

"Plus it's the cool stealth Tracker thing to do," Matthew said, shaking water off his hat. "We're—*they're* like ninjas meets spies meets Indiana Jones."

"Ninjas climb in school library windows all the time, didn't you know," Blue said to Logan, deadpan.

"Wearing everything in their closets, apparently," Zoe said. She looked Matthew up and down. He had on at least two sweaters under his jacket, plus a green scarf and a fuzzy brown hat with enormous furry earflaps. "Are you hunting a qilin or trekking to the North Pole?"

"It's *cold* out there," Matthew said. "Believe me, I've been searching the woods every day for two months. It gets *really freaking cold* after the first, like, hour."

Logan winced. He had a feeling Matthew wasn't going to be too happy once he heard Logan's theory.

He'd spent the night reading about qilins in the books Zoe had loaned him, instead of doing his English homework. But Matthew had been training to be a Tracker his whole life. Surely he had thought of everything Logan had. Wouldn't he hate Logan coming in with a bunch of suggestions, implying Matthew had done it all wrong?

Zoe plunked herself down on a beanbag and looked up at Logan. "I can tell you have an idea," she prompted him. "Just say it. We need that qilin before the trial tomorrow."

"Unless we can find Pelly," Blue pointed out.

"That's why I think we should split up," Zoe said. "After school, you and Logan and Matthew look for the qilin, and I'll take Marco to look for Pelly."

"How is Marco going to help?" Matthew asked, looking ruffled. "He's not a Tracker."

"By bringing along his werebear brother with the amazing sense of smell," Zoe said. "We just need one feather that is really Pelly's, and I'll see if Carlos can follow her scent out of the Menagerie." She exhaled. "If he can be helpful, maybe we'll never need to bribe Keiko again."

"The feather outside the Aviary!" Logan said. He pulled out his camera phone and showed Zoe the photo he'd taken of the feather on the grass. "I bet that one's really hers. I've been wondering why it was around the front of the Aviary if her kidnapper or murderer or whatever went in and out through the back door. I bet somebody made it look like they used the door by the roc so we'd think it was a big predator, but really they drugged Pelly and took her out the front. So maybe you can use that feather, if it's still there."

"Good idea," she said, nodding.

Matthew rubbed his hands together and breathed on them to warm them up. "I'd better get back to the woods."

"Wait," Zoe said. "Logan, where would you start looking?"

"Um," Logan said awkwardly. "Actually, I think—I think she's probably not in the woods."

Matthew stopped stamping his feet and stared at Logan. "Are you serious? Do you know how much time I've spent tramping around out there?"

"I know, sorry," Logan said. He pulled out a map of Xanadu that he'd printed off the internet. Zoe and Blue leaned forward to look at it.

"The one thing all the books say about qilins is that they won't harm any living things," Logan said. "They even walk across grass without crushing it."

"Right," Matthew said. "That's one reason they're impossible to track—they literally don't leave any tracks. Of course I'd accidentally release the one creature that can't be found."

"Also, they won't eat living things," Logan said. "They'll only eat plants if they're already dead." He pointed to the woods on the map. "Right now there are plenty of leaves that have fallen off the trees in the forest, but it wouldn't have been like that when she got here in August. So I don't think she would have gone to the woods then—she'd have found somewhere with food she could eat. Right?"

Matthew smacked his own forehead. "Obvious. I'm an idiot."

"No, no," Logan said. "I just thought, maybe if she found a place to hide, with food, she'd probably stay there. Right? Especially if it's indoors, since it's getting colder."

"Tell me about it," Matthew muttered. He took the map from Logan and studied it. "Hey, this is from the Wild Wild Xanadu website."

"Is that what it's called?" Logan asked. He'd found the map on a website advertising some kind of Wild West tourist attraction nearby—a whole reconstructed town from the outlaw days, like Deadwood, although Logan hadn't found anything about it anywhere else. The site hadn't been updated in a while, but it was the best overall map of Xanadu he'd seen.

"It was Mr. Sterling's big idea to make Xanadu famous, back before he was running for mayor," Matthew said. "People call it Wild Wild Xanadu as a joke. It opened for like a week and was a huge failure." He turned the map sideways. "So we're looking for somewhere with a lot of dead plants that a qilin could eat."

Blue tilted his head curiously at the map. "Like the dump or something?"

"No, qilins like clean spaces," Matthew said. "Anything elegant."

"Maybe something that reminds her of her original home in China?" Logan asked. "And the plants don't have to be rotting or anything. I figure it can mean plants that aren't growing anymore—like flowers that have been picked."

"A florist!" Zoe said.

"Or fruits and vegetables," said Matthew, starting to pace.

"A supermarket!" said Blue.

"A vegetarian restaurant!" said Zoe. "Okay, really any restaurant."

"That's it!" Matthew cried. Across the library, Miss Sameera stirred, and he lowered his voice in a hurry. "Veggie Monster Café. The best vegetarian Chinese restaurant in Wyoming."

"Possibly the only vegetarian Chinese restaurant in Wyoming," Zoe said wryly. "Dad and I love that place."

"There's a garden out back with several spots where a qilin could hide," Matthew said. "And the whole place is decorated with Chinese art and Buddhas and looks kind of like her enclosure at Camp Underpaw. I can't believe I didn't think of that sooner." He punched Logan's shoulder lightly. "All right, fine. I'll write you a reference for the camp application."

Logan tried not to let his grin cover his whole face. "Thanks," he said.

"I'll go check it out now," said Matthew. "But if I don't find her, I'll pick you up here after school."

"Sounds great," Logan said. He was relieved that Matthew wasn't mad at him—plus now hopefully he'd get to see a trained almost-Tracker in action.

"This is weird," Matthew said, leaning against the van in the restaurant parking lot. Light rain misted down over him and Logan and Blue. "Tracking is an outdoor thing. Like jungles and waterfalls and arctic landscapes and deserts. Not supermarkets and florists and Chinese food."

"Well, now that there are probably more supermarkets than jungles, the animals have to go somewhere, right?" Logan said.

"But wouldn't someone have seen her in the last two months?" Blue asked.

"Qilins can choose who sees them, more or less," Matthew

said. "Like, they're only supposed to appear to good-hearted people, but the problem is that qilins tend to think almost everyone is good-hearted. But I bet she's been extra-cautious because of what happened at camp." He sighed. "I hope I haven't ruined her faith in people forever."

He strode over to peer through the windows of the Veggie Monster Café. None of the front lights were on, and the door was locked when Logan tried it.

Logan held his hands up to the glass to get a better view. The walls inside were red and covered with Chinese scrolls; paper lanterns in shades of gold and orange hung from the ceiling. The wooden tables floating throughout the room didn't leave much space for a qilin.

"There's a light on in the kitchen," Blue said. "Maybe someone's setting up in there."

Matthew, Blue, and Logan circled round to the back entrance, where the kitchen door was propped open, looking out on a spacious garden courtyard where tables would be set up for outdoor eating in the summer. The plants were starting to take over, and Matthew was right. There were plenty of places where a qilin might hide. Logan and Matthew and Blue poked a few of the bushes, but nothing happened.

"Any chance we could use those chimes to lure the qilin out?" Logan asked.

"It's worth a shot," Matthew said, pulling the jade wind chimes from his messenger bag. They tinkled softly from the movement, and Logan felt that shivery sensation again as Matthew swung them gently.

"We'd be able to see her, right?" Blue asked.

"Well, if she really wanted to slip past us, she could, but I've brought a pocketful of shredded kale, which is her favorite. Or it used to be." Matthew looked glum.

Logan felt a surge of triumph as he heard something in the kitchen approach, but it was quickly dashed as a woman's voice rang out.

"Bobby, is that you?" The door creaked open further and a slender, long-haired woman in an apron stepped out.

Matthew quickly stuffed the chimes back into his bag.

"Oh, sorry, I thought you were my husband. He was supposed to be back from the farmer's market by now. Can I help you?"

Logan and the others exchanged glances.

"Did you say farmer's market?" Matthew asked.

Sounds like a perfect buffet for a qilin, Logan thought.

"Yes, we get our produce from them whenever we can." She smiled at them. "Fresh veggies always taste better, don't you think?"

"They sure do," Blue said enthusiastically. "Could you give us directions to get there?"

She laughed. "Sure, but you don't have to go far. It's just at the end of the street, in the church parking lot." She pointed up the road.

"Thanks very much," Logan said. Matthew was already sprinting toward the spire they could see over the tops of the trees.

The parking lot of the church was lined with aisles of open-air booths and busy with people. A bluegrass band of old, bearded men played cheerfully in one corner. Logan could smell hot cider and competing fruit pies as they made their way through the stalls.

"Let's spread out," Matthew suggested. "Whistle if you spot anything odd."

"Like a deer with a backward horn and scales?" Blue said.

"Or, you know, someone eating seaweed," Logan teased.

Blue perked up. "You think they sell seaweed?"

"Focus, Blue." Matthew pointed to the farthest aisle. "I'll start over there and we can meet in the middle."

Logan and Blue headed in the other direction, but the first few booths sold mostly baked goods and jars of home-made preserves. They snagged some cheese samples from a woman who was knitting in a camping chair and turned to scan the aisle ahead of them.

"Do you see any booths with lettuces or kale or any-thing?" Logan asked Blue.

"Not yet."

Logan and Blue kept walking, pausing to peer so intently at a stall of beans and carrots that the middle-aged man in charge of it frowned at them and they had to sidle away.

Finally, as they rounded the corner, Logan spotted a booth on the edge of the next aisle that overflowed with greens: crates and crates of giant lettuce heads, alfalfa, asparagus, and leeks. He elbowed Blue and nodded toward the chalkboard outside the booth, which proudly proclaimed: "The best organic kale in all of Wyoming."

Two women were chatting in front of some kind of vegetable Logan didn't even know the name of. Logan and Blue circled the booth slowly. Logan kept his gaze fixed on the vegetables, thinking he might spot a clue even if the qilin was invisible.

Sure enough, after a few minutes, he saw a bundle of kale on the edge of the pile suddenly tip over and fall to the ground. It rolled a few feet away, disappearing behind the farm's truck.

"Kale overboard," Logan whispered to Blue, pointing. Blue nodded and headed for the back of the truck while Logan edged slowly past the hood, holding his breath and thinking pure, noncarnivorous thoughts.

The kale lay on the ground, jumping and shivering in a weird possessed-vegetable kind of way. Small bits of it were disappearing into thin air.

Logan crouched and held out both hands, palms up. "Qilin?" he said softly. "Don't worry. I'm a friend."

There was a pause, and then something that felt like velvet brushed across his fingers. A moment later, the air shimmered and a small, tawny head appeared, followed by the rest of the qilin, inches away, staring at Logan with deep brown eyes. It felt like Logan had just stepped into a ray of bright sunshine. The qilin's gentle aura wrapped around him.

"Matthew has been really worried about you," Logan murmured.

The qilin cocked her head and sent Logan a wave of confidence, as though he shouldn't have doubted her.

Blue poked his head out from behind the truck. "Are you—is it—?"

"She's right here," Logan said. "It's okay, Blue is a friend, too. You're safe with us."

The qilin arched her neck to consider the newcomer, then made a quiet nickering sound and lowered her head back to the kale. Logan saw a faint shimmer in the air again, and this time he could see that it was around her horn.

"Oh, wow," Blue gasped.

"She's beautiful," Logan said. The qilin's yellow-brown hair gave way to luminous turquoise and cobalt scales along her back, and her legs tapered gracefully to the ground. He easily believed she could move lightly enough not to crush the grass beneath her. Logan reached forward and hesitantly patted the qilin's neck.

"I'll text Matthew," Blue said, pulling out his phone.

Moments later, Matthew joined them. Logan could tell from his reaction that the qilin was already visible to him.

Maybe she'd decided back at camp that Matthew counted as good-hearted and so she'd always be willing to let him see her.

"Thank goodness you're okay, Kiri." Matthew's voice rang with relief as he crouched beside her. The wind chimes he'd tied to his bag tinkled and Logan sensed a wave of comfort from the qilin in response.

Matthew reached forward and gently stroked her head. The qilin nuzzled closer, and Logan got a powerful feeling of gratitude—images of fire and danger, and Matthew trying to save her, and his kind hands untying her from a burning fence, and fleeing for safety, and appreciation. He hoped Matthew could feel it that strongly, too. From the look on Matthew's face, he thought probably.

Matthew scooped the kale from the ground and held it for her with his other hand. "Let's get you back to the Menagerie."

As they moved out from behind the truck, Logan glanced at the people nearby, but no one seemed to notice the unusual creature next to him. She stepped daintily through the market, stealing nibbles from the kale in Matthew's hand as they walked.

They were almost out of the fair when someone called out Matthew's name. Logan glanced over his shoulder and saw Jasmin's brother, Jonathan, jogging after them.

Matthew let out an exasperated breath. "You guys go ahead. Get Kiri loaded in the van. I'll be there as soon as I can." He broke off to intercept Jonathan.

Blue slipped into Matthew's place at the qilin's side and they picked up their pace. Logan's heart didn't slow down until they'd managed to lift the qilin into the back of the van.

"Nice," said Blue. "We kind of rock."

"Yeah." Logan grinned. Maybe he had inherited his mom's talent after all. Maybe if they found Mom, he wouldn't even have to go to Tracker camp. She could train him herself and they could go on missions together. He'd get to see all sorts of amazing magical creatures and bring them back to the Menagerie.

If the Kahns still *had* a Menagerie after tomorrow.

He really hoped the qilin could clear Scratch.

NINETEEN

" This is the worst idea in the history of ideas," Marco pointed out as Zoe led them into the Menagerie. His younger brother strutted along behind him, sniffing the air and goggling at the unicorns drinking down by the lake. The rain had stopped, but the sky was still gray and overcast.

"Why?" Zoe asked. "Because he might be dangerous in bear form?" She spotted Captain Fuzzbutt grazing near the griffin enclosure and waved. He lifted his trunk and waved back.

"Where are the dragons?" Carlos demanded. He'd agreed to help only after being bribed with dragons. Zoe wasn't sure that made him much of an improvement on Keiko.

"Because he'll be even more annoying in brother form," Marco said. "He's already a little too pleased with himself for being the biggest predator in the family. Now he's going to think he can be *useful* and that cool older kids will want to *hang out* with him."

"That's not a problem," Zoe said. "I'm not cool at all."

Two of the hellhounds came bounding across the grass toward them. Marco tensed and Carlos bared his teeth, which wasn't terribly impressive when he wasn't a bear.

Zoe crouched and scratched the hellhounds behind their ears. Sheldon immediately flopped over for a belly rub. Jaws sat down beside him, watching Marco and Carlos with his glowing red eyes. Their breath smelled like sulfur and granola bars. Zoe's hands were instantly covered in thick black fur.

"Wow," Carlos murmured, apparently distracted from dragons.

"Hmm," Marco said, edging away from the giant dogs. "You seem pretty cool to me."

Zoe shrugged. "Well, maybe if the kids at school could see me gathering ink from a kraken they'd be a little more impressed." She rumpled Sheldon's neck fur and stood up again. "That's the Aviary over there." As she started walking again, she heard the thump-thump of mammoth feet galloping up to join them. Captain Fuzzbutt gave Marco a friendly nudge as he came up beside them, and the wererooster boy jumped a mile.

The brothers and the mammoth followed her to the spot by the lake where Logan had seen the feather. Zoe was surprised to find it still there—the agents must have missed it when they were collecting evidence. It was soggy from the rain and lay plastered to the grass.

"What do you think?" Zoe asked Marco. "Is this actually Pelly's feather?"

"Without having met the lady, I can't be sure," Marco said, studying it without touching it. "But it's certainly from a goose about the right age."

"Good enough," Zoe said. "Can you follow her scent?" She turned to Carlos and found him already half-undressed. "Ack!" she yelped, covering her eyes.

"Carlos doesn't care who sees him naked," Marco assured her.

"Well, I do!" she said. She kept her hands over her eyes until Marco said, "All clear," in an amused voice.

Carlos's clothes were piled in a heap; Zoe gathered them up so they wouldn't get wet. The black bear cub snuffled around the feather, making thoughtful grunting noises. The mammoth hovered curiously behind him, poking his trunk everywhere the cub's nose had just been, imitating his grunts and snuffles. Carlos swiped at the Captain's trunk with one paw, and the mammoth jumped back, then hustled forward again, delighted with this wonderful new game.

With a small growl, the bear turned his back on the

mammoth and began trotting purposefully toward the outer wall of the Menagerie. Captain Fuzzbutt followed close on his heels—almost close enough to step on him—which earned him a few grumpy looks and a snap of Carlos's jaws that the mammoth clearly found very entertaining.

Beyond the wall Zoe could see the tops of the pine trees that surrounded the Kahns' territory. The cub padded across the paved trail and paced in the grass for a while. Finally he stood up on his hind legs and batted at the stone with his paws. Thrilled, the mammoth thumped the same part of the wall with his trunk and nearly knocked the cub sideways by accident.

"The goose scent stops here, at least on this side," Marco said. He tilted his head back to look at the top of the wall. One long branch reached from outside into the Menagerie right above them. "If someone hung a pulley from that branch, they could probably get a tranquilized goose over the wall, even without help."

Zoe looked around, wondering if Mooncrusher could bring them a ladder, and her eyes met the Captain's. He gave her a wide mammoth smile and flapped his trunk at his back, which was only a few feet below the top of the wall.

"Give me a boost," Zoe said to Marco, setting Carlos's clothes on the ground. He cupped his hands and helped her climb onto the Captain's back. She grabbed handfuls of the mammoth's long brown fur to pull herself up, hoping it wouldn't hurt him. At last she reached the top of his broad, shaggy back and cautiously stood up with her arms out for balance. Captain Fuzzbutt shuffled a little closer to the wall and she reached up to grab the top of it.

It took some maneuvering and kicking and a lot more arm strength than Zoe would have given herself credit for, but finally she made it to the top of the wall, and from there it was easy to climb onto the tree branch.

There was a spot on the branch above the Menagerie side where the bark was worn down, as if something had been attached to it. Zoe leaned to look down on the far side and thought she saw two divots in the muddy earth, where a ladder might have rested against the wall.

"Meet me outside," she called to Marco and Carlos. "Thanks, Captain! See you later!"

The mammoth saluted with his trunk and gave the cub a friendly pat on the back that sent the bear rolling down the hill toward the Aviary. With an *oops* expression, Captain Fuzzbutt trotted off toward Mooncrusher's yurt.

Zoe clambered along the branch and slid down the tree, wincing as splinters dug into her hands. Carlos and Marco caught up to her soon after, and the bear cub started vigorously nosing around in the pine needles.

He made a whuffling noise and trotted off, nose to the

ground, leading them through the trees until they reached the road. Tire treads in the dirt showed that something bigger than a car had been parked here recently.

The bear sniffed the air, sat down, and started turning back into a boy.

Zoe grabbed his clothes from Marco and flung them at the cub, then covered her eyes.

"Why is he turning back?" she asked Marco. "We haven't found Pelly yet."

"The scent trail ends here," Carlos answered for himself. "I can't smell goose anymore—only truck. And this truck soon gets mixed up in all the other car smells on the road so I can't follow it. Sorry." She heard him scrambling into his clothes.

"That's it?" Zoe said. "You can't tell me any more than that?" She'd been so sure this would lead them straight to the missing goose. Now what were they going to do?

"She was definitely drugged," Carlos said in a superior, detective sort of voice. "I could smell something sleepy about her."

"You *smelled* something sleepy?" Marco echoed skeptically. "That's not very scientific. You mean you could smell chloroform or something?"

"*I* don't know what it was," his brother said, brushing himself off. "Sleepy, chemical, weird, whatever. Can we go back inside and meet some dragons now?"

Zoe sighed and pulled out her phone to take a picture of the tire tracks. There was a message she'd missed from Logan.

"Oh!" she said happily, scanning the text. "They found the qilin! They're on their way!" *That gives us some breathing room. We can use the qilin to prove Scratch's innocence before the trial tomorrow, and then concentrate on finding Pelly after that.*

They waited in the garage with Carlos hopping impatiently from foot to foot. To set a good example, and because it seemed entirely possible that Carlos could annoy a dragon into breathing flames at him, Zoe put on her own fireproof suit and made him and Marco wear them as well. For some reason, Carlos found this excessively thrilling.

"We could get set ON FIRE!" he yelled at his brother.

"AWESOME!" Marco shouted back.

"Or maybe we'll get EATEN!" Carlos hollered, bouncing off the walls.

"Your brother has a strange idea of fun," Zoe said.

"You're telling me," Marco agreed.

The family van came chugging up the driveway, rumble-coughing, and rolled into the garage. Logan and Blue hopped out of the back and held the doors open as a delicate creature jumped daintily to the ground and peered around the concrete room. Her eyes met Zoe's and Zoe felt instantly calmer.

"Whoa," said Marco.

"Isn't she gorgeous?" Logan said, stroking her neck.

"DRAGONS!" Carlos shouted. "Dragons dragons dragons!"

"Quit being embarrassing or you're going home right now," Marco ordered.

"You're not the boss of me," said Carlos. "You're just a bird. A *farmyard* bird."

The qilin stepped forward and gently touched each brother's hand with her nose. They both went quiet, looking at her.

"The dragon is in one of the mountain caves," Matthew said to the qilin. She nodded and stepped to the door, waited for Zoe to open it for her, and then set off across the Menagerie. The others all followed, although Blue stopped to put on a fireproof suit and had to run to catch up.

Zoe felt her excitement growing as they climbed the mountain path. They'd fixed Matthew's problem and now they were going to save Scratch.

"Are we sure this is going to work?" Blue asked, his voice distorted by the fireproof helmet. "I mean, Kiri doesn't talk, so how does she indicate if someone is innocent or guilty?"

"Their horns change color," Zoe said, pointing. "Yellow if the person is innocent, blue if they're guilty."

They climbed past the first set of caves, where Firebella was sitting with her tail coiled around her claws, glaring down at the Menagerie.

"Hey," Zoe said, pausing as the others scrambled quickly past. "Firebella, how come you didn't set off the intruder alarm for Carlos?" She pointed at Marco's brother, who had stopped to stare in slack-jawed awe.

The black dragon narrowed her eyes at the werebear. "Worth not my voice nor energy is intruder so puny."

"Hmm," Zoe said. "Okay."

"She called me puny!" Carlos whispered in delight as Zoe dragged him behind her to Scratch's cave. "She noticed me!"

Scratch lifted his head mournfully as the qilin stopped in front of him. He didn't look like he'd gone inside during the rain; his scales still glistened damply and his waterlogged wings drooped. He also looked skinnier, and Zoe guessed he was too miserable to eat. She knew that feeling.

"It's okay, Scratch," Logan said. "We've brought Kiri to help."

"What do you think?" Matthew asked, crouching beside her. "You can see that he's innocent, right?"

The qilin gazed at Scratch for a long moment. Slowly a weird feeling started creeping over Zoe—a sick feeling, coated with violence, as if she was remembering something awful she'd done and didn't want anyone to know about.

The qilin's horn began to glow faintly blue, then stronger and stronger. The color of guilt.

"Doomed," Scratch pronounced with a long, smoky sigh.

"That's impossible!" Zoe cried. "He didn't eat Pelly! We know she's still alive!" She turned to Matthew in alarm. "Why is she wrong?"

"I have no idea," Matthew said, looking ill. "Kiri, try again. We're sure he's innocent."

Kiri stamped her foot once. Her horn stayed blue.

"I think—" Logan said in a choked voice. "Perhaps—well, the stuff I read last night wasn't totally clear. But my guess would be that the qilin reads someone's own feelings of guilt and innocence along with their memories. They don't answer specific 'did he do this or that?' questions . . . they just sense whether they're guilty of *something*. So she's probably sensing how ashamed he feels about the sheep he ate."

"Also failure as alarm system," Scratch put in gloomily. "Deep-full of regret for always is poor doomed Scratch."

"But this makes things worse than ever!" Zoe said.

Matthew ran his hands over his head, looking frazzled. "Maybe we could hide her again until after—"

"INTRUDER! INTRUDER! INTRUDER!"

Zoe had never been up the mountain, this close to the dragons, during an intruder alarm. Firebella's bellowing sounded loud enough to blow out her eardrums. Zoe clapped her hands to her ears, but the suit's helmet got in the way. The others had all buckled to the ground, trying to block out the noise as well.

"Make it stop!" Carlos yelled.

"Good-bye, ears!" Marco shouted. "I will miss you!"

Zoe could barely hear them over the blaring voice of the dragon. She staggered back to the path and climbed down as best she could with her mind reeling from the clamor.

Firebella paused, mercifully, and glowered at Zoe.

"Please stop!" Zoe called. "You said Carlos wasn't worth warning us about."

"Not the intruder is small human of bear smell. New these intruders are. Coming this way are these intruders." She cocked her head. "Excellent job required by Firebella for these intruders." Without any more warning than that, she began bellowing again. "INTRUDER! INTRUDER! INTRUDER!"

Zoe's head was pounding with the noise. What did Firebella mean? New intruders—multiple intruders—were coming this way?

She turned to look down the mountain and saw a group of adults climbing toward them: the two SNAPA agents, her parents, and two strangers.

She ran back up the mountain and waved her hands wildly at Matthew. They had to hide the qilin. Not to mention both Matthew and Logan, who were not in fireproof suits. The Menagerie had enough trouble without further protocol violations, particularly when it came to the dragons.

Matthew blinked at her in confusion, but Logan jumped forward right away. He pointed into Scratch's cave and she nodded.

Except the qilin wouldn't go.

Kiri planted her hooves and shook her head at Matthew

as he tried to coax her into the cave. Zoe wasn't sure if it was the smell of dragon, or whether she was determined to have her guilty verdict noticed, but she wasn't budging.

Zoe leaned over one of the boulders and saw the heads of the SNAPA agents passing Firebella. Mr. Kahn signaled to the black dragon, and she went silent with a haughty sniff.

Logan saw the look on Zoe's face and grabbed Matthew. They bolted into Scratch's cave, disappearing into the dark moments before the adults arrived.

Mrs. Kahn saw the qilin first. She stopped with a gasp.

"Zoe!" she said. "Where did this come from?" She hurried forward and circled the qilin, who blinked serenely at all the newcomers.

"That's the qilin from Camp Underpaw!" Delia cried. "The one who's been missing for the last two months!"

"Matthew found her," Zoe said quickly. She wanted to make sure he got credit for that—it was his one shot at getting back on the path to being a Tracker one day. "He's been looking for the qilin ever since she ran away, and he just found her today, so we brought her here . . ." Her voice faltered. She knew they were all staring at that blue horn.

"Proof," said Runcible in a steely voice. "Right there for all to see."

"Now hold on," said Zoe's dad, a little desperately. "You know as well as I do that qilin judgments are known for being unspecific. A qilin's horn is not sufficient proof in a court of law, especially in cases with capital punishment." He glanced at one of the newcomers, and Zoe took a good look at them for the first time.

One of the strangers matched the other SNAPA agents— he wore a suit and looked like someone had pinched his face into a severe expression it could never fall out of. He was long and skinny with a long nose; a long, skinny neck, and even skinnier legs; and his skin was slightly sunburned, so he looked a little like a disapproving flamingo.

But there was nothing funny about the other stranger. He was tall, almost a foot taller than everyone else, and he wore black from head to toe, including a hooded black coat and black leather gloves. His face was entirely covered with a mask, showing only his dark eyes. He was like a shadow come to life. The only light anywhere around him was the glitter of the sun reflecting off a thin silver chain around his neck, holding an X-shaped key that fell at about the middle of his chest.

Zoe knew immediately who this must be.

The Exterminator. The one who was here to execute Scratch.

"Oh, we'll still have the trial," said Runcible, stepping forward and patting the qilin triumphantly on the head. "We'll let the jury look at the qilin tomorrow and decide. Tell your brother thank you for saving us the trouble of flying in a caladrius bird. This will do quite nicely. Quite nicely indeed."

Zoe sank onto one of the boulders, wishing her mammoth were there, wishing she could run back to her room and cry, wishing she could start this whole day—this whole week—over again. The Exterminator stood there, glowering with dark purpose.

The qilin had only made things worse. And there was no way to track Pelly.

Tomorrow, Scratch was going to die.

TWENTY

"Good morning!" Jasmin sang out right behind them. Logan saw Blue nearly jump into his locker, but he got ahold of himself and turned around with his usual easy smile.

"Hey, Jasmin," he said.

"Are you excited for tomorrow?" she asked him, hugging her textbooks close. Her long dark hair was held back with a sunny yellow velvet headband, which matched the thin stripes on her gray wool dress and the tall yellow rain boots below that. Logan wondered, not for the first time, how long it took her to get dressed in the morning, and how many clothes she had, because it seemed like she wore something different every day.

"For tomorrow?" Blue echoed.

Logan couldn't even think about tomorrow. It felt like the world was going to end today, Thursday—the day of the trial. The qilin had failed them, and they hadn't found Pelly. If they didn't come up with something in the next few hours, by tomorrow Scratch would be exterminated for a crime he didn't commit.

The only thing he could think of was tracing the fake goose feathers. If they could figure out where those came from, surely that would point them to who had scattered them around the crime scene. But how were they going to do that?

"My party!" Jasmin's smile wavered a little. "Oh, like you forgot." She laughed, but Logan thought she sounded nervous, and he felt bad for her all over again.

"Right," Blue said. "Right, no, I'm excited. Almost Friday. Already. Time for a party."

"Okay, new plan," she said. "Wouldn't it be funny if we went as cowboys? But, like, ironic cowboys. You'd be Wild Bill Hickok and I'd be Calamity Jane, and we'd do the whole hats-and-spurs silliness. My dad still has loads of costumes left over from his Wild West park. What do you think?"

"Wasn't there a plan somewhere along the way where I just wore brown and carried a bow and arrow?" Blue asked.

"That one sounded okay to me."

"You're right," Jasmin said, twisting her hair around her fingers. "It's almost too ironic. I'll keep thinking. Maybe we go back to a knight and warrior princess after all."

Someone bumped into her from behind and Jasmin nearly fell, but Blue reached out and caught her arms. She whirled around, frowning.

"Who—oh, hi, Miss Sameera." Jasmin's frown melted into a smile for the school librarian.

"Sorry, sorry, dear," Miss Sameera said, trying to smooth down her bird's nest of hair. She looked even worse than she had the day before—completely exhausted and more disheveled. Her bright colors were muted; today she wore a black skirt with several unraveling gold threads coming out of the seahorse pattern, and her tunic shirt was a plain grape purple, apart from a stain that looked like hot chocolate on most of one sleeve.

Mumbling something that sounded like "Not even sure there's any caviar in the state," the librarian hurried off in the direction of the library.

"Wow," Jasmin said. "I'm all for colorful fashion choices, but does she even look in the mirror before she leaves the house? Maybe nobody cared in Missouri, but in Wyoming at least some of us are paying attention."

"Missouri?" Logan interjected. Something was pinging at the back of his brain like a phone buzzing far away.

"Somewhere like that," Jasmin said with a dismissive wave. "It's on her key chain—Parkville, Missouri, or Mississippi, or one of those."

"Excuse me," Logan said, shutting his locker door in a hurry. He abandoned Blue with Jasmin—despite the evil eye Blue was giving him—and ran into homeroom. Zoe was sitting at her desk with her head in her hands, staring hopelessly at a coded page of her "things to do" notebook.

"Parkville, Missouri," Logan said. He slid into his seat in the desk next to hers. "Wasn't there a golden goose there?"

"Yeah," said Zoe, tilting her head at him.

"Miss Sameera was there," Logan whispered. "She came from Parkville."

Zoe's eyes widened. "That menagerie was shut down. Maybe because of her! Maybe sabotaging menageries is what she does!"

Logan still found it hard to imagine the nice school librarian as some kind of sinister mythical-creature hunter. But then, he would never have guessed what his mom did for a living, either, so maybe he wasn't a great judge of these things.

"Today at lunch," he whispered. "It's time to find out what Miss Sameera knows."

The first problem was luring the librarian out of the library.

Logan and Zoe peeked through the open doorway. Miss Sameera was tapping on her keyboard with a giant pile of books beside her. She yawned hugely and rubbed her face. As usual at lunchtime, there was no one else in the library.

They ducked back behind the next corner, where Marco and Blue were waiting.

"If she knows about the Menagerie, she knows about you," Logan pointed out to Zoe. "And maybe about Blue. And she might have noticed us together."

"We send in Marco," Zoe decided.

"Yes!" Marco said, pounding the air. "I am the king of undercover missions! I'll tell her—uh—I'll tell her—um, okay, I'll think of something. Like a book emergency! Oh, there's a book stuck in a tree that needs rescuing! That would work, right? Or I need help with my locker, like there's a book stuck in it? Hmm. I might need some help with my cover story, guys."

"I meant as a rooster," Zoe admitted.

"Oh, *no*," Marco said. He clutched his hair.

"Any self-respecting librarian will chase a rooster out of her library," she pointed out. "Make her chase you all around the school and keep her away as long as possible."

"This is a terrible plan," he said. "My parents will kill me for shifting during school. What if I get caught?"

"Don't get caught," Blue suggested.

"We'll rescue you if that happens," Logan reassured him.

"And just think of Pelly," Zoe said. "This could be her only chance! Bird solidarity, right?"

"Actually, roosters and geese are historical enemies," Marco said. "They find our plumage 'ostentatious,' if you can believe that, and we find them very shallow. You should hear the way geese gossip. It makes seventh-grade girls seem totally interesting and mature."

"Oh, come on," Blue said, dragging him into the boys' bathroom across the hall.

A few minutes later, Blue came back out carrying Marco's clothes and shoes. He held the door open as a rooster strutted slowly out of the bathroom behind him, eyeing Logan and Zoe with fierce dignity.

"Thank you, Marco," Zoe said.

"*BAWK*," he grumbled. He paced around the corner and made a beeline for the library entrance. The red crest on his head wobbled and his sharp little claws *tip-tapp*ed on the dirty tile floor.

They watched him stalk into the library and then ducked out of sight.

A moment later, there was a shriek that was much louder than Logan had expected.

"ABSOLUTELY NOT!" shouted Miss Sameera. "I'm not cleaning up ANY MORE FEATHERS and if you peck ONE THING I will clobber you with this—OH NO YOU DIDN'T."

The rooster burst out of the library, BAWKing and flapping its wings frantically, and charged down the hallway with

Miss Sameera in hot pursuit. She was waving a stapler, which made Logan wince in sympathy. He really hoped she had terrible aim, for Marco's sake.

Zoe and Blue and Logan ran into the library and hurried to her desk. Logan pointed to Miss Sameera's cup of tea.

"See, if you'd dosed her earlier this week, she might have forgotten where she stashed Pelly," he said.

"Yeah, but if someone had dosed her in Parkville as they were supposed to, she would have left our Menagerie alone," Zoe said. "Blue, guard the door."

Blue picked up a book from one of the carts and leaned casually in the door frame.

"I feel like I've become such a criminal since I started hanging out with you guys," Logan said as Zoe went behind the desk. "Sneaking into Jasmin's house, sneaking *out* of my house, kidnapping innocent roosters, borrowing a federal agent's computer, and now snooping in a librarian's stuff. Is this, like, normal life for you?"

"There's never been a librarian involved before," Blue said, deadpan.

"I don't see her cell phone," Zoe said, sifting through the piles of paper. "Or anything about mythical creatures. This all looks school related." She moved the mouse and peered at the computer screen. "Overdue books. She doesn't even have email open."

"Can you search her computer for . . . I don't know,

griffins or something?" Logan asked, leaning over to look at the screen.

"Or the name of the guy she was talking to on the phone," Blue suggested. "Mr. Claverhill."

"Whoa," said Logan. "How did you remember that?"

"He's annoying that way," Zoe said. "But useful, too." She typed "Claverhill" into the "Search programs and files" box.

One file popped up—a Word document. Zoe clicked it open.

"It's a letter," she whispered.

Logan jumped up and came around to read over Zoe's shoulder.

> *Dear Mr. Claverhill,*
>
> *This is my fourth formal request for additional Free Ranger resources to be assigned to Xanadu. I'm not sure why you persist in ignoring my letters. I admit that I was wrong about Newton and Grantham, and the whole situation in Parkville was very confusing and unfortunate, but this time I am one hundred percent certain that there is a government facility imprisoning the creatures we're looking for here in town. Think of all the good we could do!*
>
> *And this letter is different, because now I have proof. If you would just send two more Free Rangers to verify the situation, you'll see that I've gotten my hands on the most marvelous*

That was where the letter ended.

Logan wasn't sure whether to be relieved or horrified.

"It's her," Zoe said, looking up and meeting Logan's eyes. "She says she has proof. You know what that means?"

Logan nodded. "Miss Sameera has Pelly."

TWENTY-ONE

Miss Sameera's house was small, like Logan's, all on one level, and painted a pale orange with a dark red roof. Cheerful yellow and pink chrysanthemums sat in planters beside the door and along the path from the street, clashing merrily with the house.

"You're sure she won't come straight home?" Logan said to Blue. His stomach was churning nervously. He almost wished her address hadn't been so easy to find online. This was worse than hiding out in the library past closing time, although perhaps not as awful as sneaking around the Sterlings' house with a griffin cub while they were right on the other side of the secret passageways.

"She always stays late to monitor the kids in detention," Blue said. "At least, that's what Marco said."

Marco's mom had appeared in the classroom door at the end of the day like a wrathful griffin, giving Marco the full steely glare. She'd heard from someone at the supermarket that there had been a rooster loose at the middle school that day. Marco had been marched sheepishly out to the parking lot without even getting to say good-bye to the others.

"Poor Marco," said Zoe. "I hope he forgives us."

They left their bikes around the side of the house and tried to peek in the windows, but all the bright pink and sequin-covered purple curtains were closed.

"I don't think she'd keep Pelly here," Zoe said. "I mean, if she went to the trouble of getting goose feathers from Parkville and staging a whole crime scene, wouldn't she also have prepared some kind of secret location to hide her in?"

"I don't know," Logan said. His instinct was still telling him that the librarian wasn't a plan-ahead kind of person, despite the elaborate crime scene, which didn't fit at all with his image of her. "I think this is worth checking out, though."

The front door was locked, so they walked around the house, poking at all the closed windows, until they reached the tall wooden fence that enclosed her garden. The gate just had a latch, which they easily lifted to slip inside, into a tiny garden riotous with wildflowers.

"Maybe there's a back door we can—" Zoe started, then stopped, her mouth dropping open.

Sunning herself on the little stone patio was an enormous goose.

Pelly opened her eyes and spotted them.

"NOOOOO!" she shrieked. "I'm not going back! You can't make me!" She lurched upright and bolted for the house, but Blue and Logan were faster, throwing themselves between her and the sliding glass patio door.

Pelly hissed and snapped her beak at them. Logan remembered the Band-Aids all over Miss Sameera's hands and winced.

"Out of my way," she ordered in her drawly quack of a voice. "You and your Menagerie people had your chance and now I've moved on. Oh, I know everyone takes me for granted and sees me as merely a *lowly goose* who happens to be blessed with perfect feathers and golden eggs and a wonderful personality, but I have *feelings, too,* you know. I have *never* complained about all the *neglectful treatment* I suffered for so long, but now I have *finally found* a loving caretaker who worships the ground I squawk on and who *appreciates* my many fine qualities, and so I have decided I am never leaving her, never never never." The goose flung her wings about petulantly.

"But Pelly, we're here to rescue you," Zoe said.

"No," Pelly said. "I decline. Go away."

Zoe was already pulling out her phone to call her parents. "I'm sorry, but you don't have a choice. You have to be under SNAPA supervision. You can't just be some random person's pet."

Uh-oh, Logan thought.

Pelly drew herself up with an incredulous *HONK*. "PET?" she cried. "PET?! I shall never be anyone's pet! I am Sameera's beloved guest. No one has ever loved me the way she does. *You* never fed me grapes from your own hands. *You* never stayed up all night rearranging my blankets, buying me a new heater, using a hair dryer on my cold feet, and singing me show tunes. *You* never bought me *Once Upon a Time* on DVD so I could watch the special features on my favorite episodes. *You* never brought me peppermint cocoa every morning at sunrise! I am only the most important animal in the whole Menagerie, but no one would ever guess it from the *bare modicum* of appreciation I have ever gotten from you people. Sameera adores me, as I deserve. She understands how unique and adorable I am and would never, say, make me share my space with a hundred other twittering nitwits. Hrrmph." She pointed her beak in the air and fluffed her feathers.

"I don't have time to argue with you," Zoe said, dialing. "We have to get you home before the trial is over and Scratch is exterminated and the Menagerie is shut down."

"Ooooo," said Pelly. "You didn't tell me they might exterminate Scratch."

"It's true," said Logan. "He's been accused of your murder. He could be dead by the end of today if we don't show SNAPA you're alive."

"Even more reason to stay here," Pelly said, plunking herself down on her makeshift nest of blankets and spangled denim cushions. "Oh, I'm sure nobody missed me. I'm sure my death was met with yawns or cheers. I'm sure you haven't even had a touching memorial service for me, no, no, why bother, it's only Pelly, the entire reason our organization is financially solvent. Would anyone cry for such a paragon of feathered beauty? But if that dragon is taken out of the world because of it, then all my tremendous suffering becomes worthwhile."

Suddenly the sliding glass door behind Logan began to move. With a yelp of fright, he jumped away, then froze as Miss Sameera stepped out onto the patio.

They stared at the librarian. She stared at them.

We are in so much trouble, Logan thought.

"Sameera!" Pelly cried. She waddled over and butted Miss Sameera's hands imperiously with her head until the librarian began scratching the goose's neck. "You're just in time to save me again. Behold, my horrible captors have arrived to drag me away!"

Miss Sameera's head shot up. She looked at Zoe with a glimmer of something in her eyes—desperation? Or . . . was that *hope*?

"You want her back?" she said.

"In the fuzziest sense of the word *want*," Blue answered.

Zoe held out her phone. "My brother is listening to this whole conversation," she warned. "So you'd better hand over that goose and let us go."

"I told them you would never part with me," Pelly declared, flinging her wings around Miss Sameera's waist. "I told them how we have bonded for life and this is my home now and you will fight them to the death before you'll let me go."

"Right," Miss Sameera said. "Of course. But look, there are three of them. I'm quite outnumbered. It's a terrible shame, but I'm afraid you'll have to go with them."

"But these three are PUNY!" Pelly barked. "Together we can defeat them! We can run off into the sunset together and find even better peppermint cocoa somewhere far away! We don't need anyone else! I'll be with you till the day you die!"

Miss Sameera got a despairing, haunted look in her eyes.

"Pelly," Logan interjected. "You'll never be safe out in the world. Miss Sameera may treat you kindly, but there are lots of people who wouldn't, and if you fall into their hands, you'll have much worse problems than wanting another yeti-fur blanket. The Menagerie can protect you. That's their whole purpose."

The goose made a huffy sniffing noise. "Oh, I *see*. Leave my only friend in the world and go back to a place where I am not appreciated and that arsonist phoenix threatens my nest every day. Of course, that does make brilliant sense.

Why didn't I think of it myself? I mean, I do so love conversing with hummingbirds and being fed only four times a day."

"You only feed her four times a day?" Miss Sameera asked Zoe. "Not eight?" She turned to Pelly. "You told me you *had* to be fed eight times a day or you would literally die."

"Did I?" Pelly said, giving Zoe a shifty look. She shuffled closer to Miss Sameera and started absentmindedly nibbling one of the gold threads on her skirt. "Oh, I may have *implied* as much . . ."

"What about requiring the most expensive swordfish in the supermarket?" the librarian demanded. "Was that a lie, too? The lavender salts and daffodil petals for your bathwater? The hours of dancing kittens you had to watch on YouTube?" Miss Sameera yanked her skirt out of Pelly's beak and stepped back. "You made all that up! I thought you were a delicate mythical creature with unusual magical needs!"

"Nope," said Zoe. "She's really just a giant goose with an even more giant ego."

"See how nobody loves me!" Pelly squawked. "Oh, everyone wishes I were dead!" She flung herself down on her back with her wings outstretched and flapped around on the stone. Then she sat up abruptly and gave Miss Sameera a beady glare. "What about the Dreadful Experiments they were doing on me? You promised to save me from those!"

Miss Sameera hesitated.

"There are no dreadful experiments, Miss Sameera," Zoe promised.

"But you're the government," Miss Sameera said, tugging at her sleeves. "In all the books, supernatural things must be kept out of the hands of the government. Or else there will be top-secret facilities and dreadful experiments! That's what they're really doing at Roswell, you know."

Blue smothered a laugh.

"What they're doing at Roswell is breeding dragons," Zoe said. "It's difficult and messy and hard to keep quiet, but it's not sinister. The dragons are very happy there. And our creatures are happy at our Menagerie, too."

"Oh, if you ignore my misery, I suppose," Pelly said. "As everyone always does."

"We have to take her back," Logan said to the librarian. "There's a dragon's life on the line. Everyone thinks he killed her, and if we don't get her home quickly, he'll be executed for it."

Now Miss Sameera looked horrified. "Why didn't you say so?" she demanded. "Take her and go! Now! Hurry!" She spun around, patting her skirt although it clearly had no pockets. "I'll drive you. Quick!"

"On your Vespa?" Blue asked curiously.

"Oh, right," she said. "I'll call you a taxi!"

"Good lord, no," said Zoe. "My brother will be here in a minute with our van."

"NOOOOOOOOOOOOOOOOOOOOOOOOOOOOOOO OOOOOO!" Pelly wailed.

Blue covered his ears. "Haven't your neighbors wondered about all the noise?" he asked Miss Sameera.

"They think my demanding, partly senile great-aunt is visiting," she admitted.

"OH NOW I AM BEING MOCKED AS WELL AS TORTURED," Pelly howled.

"Do you have any extra tranquilizer darts?" Zoe asked the librarian. "It'll be easier to get her home that way."

Miss Sameera looked puzzled. "I don't have anything like that," she said.

"Then how did you get her here?" Zoe asked. A frantic car horn started beeping outside. "Never mind, we'll ask you later." Logan knew Zoe was picturing a conversation over a nice cup of kraken ink tea. "Blue, go get a dart from the van."

"I WON'T GO!" Pelly squawked. "You can't make me! I know nobody cares and nobody has ever cared but I *am* the most important goose in the whole world and I—"

Matthew fired a dart into her neck from the garden gate, and the goose immediately slumped over, her beak still wide open as if she intended to keep complaining even while unconscious.

"People on the street are giving this house weird looks," Matthew said. He jumped up onto the patio, flung a blanket over Pelly, and neatly wrapped her into a bundle. Logan hurried to pick up one end, and together they carried her out and stowed her in the van.

Miss Sameera followed them out to her driveway, wringing her hands as they all lifted their bikes in. "Am I doing the right thing?" she said. "I don't think the other Free Rangers would approve, but they haven't had to deal with *her* for three long, awful days—"

"Three days?" Zoe said, pausing with her hand on the van door handle. "Don't you mean five? Since Saturday night?"

"No," Miss Sameera said, shaking her head. "I liberated her on Monday afternoon from your cabin in the woods."

"Our what?" Zoe said. "We don't have a cabin in the woods."

"Yes, you do," Miss Sameera insisted. "I followed your partner there."

Logan and Zoe exchanged glances.

Miss Sameera was never inside the Menagerie, Logan realized. *She rescued Pelly by accident from someone else. Pelly's real kidnapper.*

"Wait, who did you follow?" Zoe asked. "What did they look like? Was it someone you know?"

Miss Sameera raised her eyebrows, started to say something, then stopped with a mischievous, canny expression.

"I'll tell you everything I know," she said, "if you take me to meet a unicorn."

TWENTY-TWO

Matthew pulled into the garage with a squeal of tires. His phone buzzed as he turned off the engine.

"Uh-oh," he said, checking the screen. "Mom says they've started closing arguments."

"Already?" Zoe cried. She pulled out her phone and saw the same message. She'd expected them to take the whole afternoon on the trial, but it was barely past four. Neither of her parents were answering their phones, which was why she'd called Matthew from Miss Sameera's house instead.

"Does it matter?" Logan asked. "We have Pelly—so he's obviously innocent, no matter how the trial turns out."

"I don't trust that Exterminator, though," Zoe said, her

skin prickling. "He looks like he's itching to execute a dragon as soon as possible." She jumped out of the van and pulled open the back doors.

"Exterminator?" Miss Sameera said in a wobbly voice.

"Only in extreme circumstances," Blue said, patting her shoulder.

Logan and Zoe wrestled the blanket-wrapped Pelly out of the van, through the door to the Menagerie, and onto a golf cart that was waiting for them. With Matthew behind the steering wheel, there was room for only two more people.

"You two go," Blue said. "I'll take Miss Sameera into the main house."

The librarian was staring around the Menagerie with her mouth open. "This place is huge!" she said. "How has nobody noticed it before? Don't airplanes fly overhead and spot you?"

"We have a thing," Zoe said, fighting the mental drag that always came with mentioning the deflector. "We don't talk about the thing."

"INTRUDER! INTRUDER! INTRUDER!" the dragon alarm bellowed.

"Oh, brother," Matthew said, unclipping a walkie-talkie from the front bar of the golf cart. "Mooncrusher, tell Clawdius we know!" he yelled into it. "We brought her in!"

"BLAAAAARGH!" agreed the walkie-talkie, and a few moments later the bellowing stopped.

Zoe held on tight to the side rail as the golf cart zipped

down the hill, around the lake, and up to the yeti's area. The crowd around the trial seemed bigger than she would have expected, and she realized several of the merpeople had decided to come watch the proceedings. King Cobalt stood in the middle of them, towering and majestic-looking as usual, spinning a trident slowly between his hands.

"Blue's dad thought he should get to judge the trial," Zoe whispered to Logan. "Since he's 'the most royal personage on the continent,' apparently. He wasn't too pleased when SNAPA said no."

The flamingo-looking judge sat behind a card table, facing the lawyers. His long neck twisted as he followed the ping-pong argument Ruby and Runcible were having from their separate tables. Off to the side, the jury sat with expressions ranging from bored (Firebella) to extremely bored (Sapphire). And on the other side was Scratch, laden with chains and drooping gloomily. Zoe's dad stood beside him, holding an electric shock wand and wearing most of a fireproof suit, apart from the helmet.

And standing ominously next to the prosecution's table was a masked figure, all in black, with the hood of his coat pulled up. Even seeing him from a distance made Zoe shiver.

"You don't need more time!" Runcible shouted at Ruby. "You have no witnesses! You have no evidence!" He pointed to the qilin, standing peacefully beside the judge with her horn glowing softly blue. "The qilin knows he's guilty, so give up!"

"We've presented our theory regarding his guilt over the sheep; the qilin cannot distinguish what he is guilty of," Ruby yelled back. "And we might have a witness if he would stop setting himself on fire every time we go anywhere near him. We need to force the phoenix to testify before we can close this case."

"He was probably a pile of ashes during the murder, too," Runcible growled. "He won't know anything, and he's unreliable even if he claims he does." Zoe noticed that the agent's eyebrows seemed bushier than usual—and were his teeth getting a bit longer and sharper? She couldn't exactly blame him. Talking to Ruby usually made her mad enough to turn into a wolf, too, if she could have.

Delia put a calming hand on Runcible's shoulder, but he shook her off.

"We don't know that for sure," Ruby pointed out. "And we want those feathers tested. We have reason to believe they're not Pelly's at all—"

"A reason you've declined to share with the court!" Runcible said, flinging up his hands and giving the jury a *can you believe this?* glare.

"Judge Martindale, all we're asking for is a three-day extension—" she began.

"Wait!" Matthew called. "Stop the trial!"

Everyone turned around, and Zoe suddenly felt like she was in one of those dreams where she had to give a speech to a million people but she'd overslept, run onstage in her pajamas, and forgotten what the speech was supposed to be about.

Matthew lifted the bundle from the back of the golf cart and hauled it over to set it down in front of the judge. Logan and Zoe stood on either side of him as he unwrapped the blanket with a flourish to reveal the slumbering form of the golden goose.

Muffled gasps came from the audience and the jury.

"Pelly's dead body!" Sapphire shrieked.

"No, no, she's alive!" Zoe shouted over the uproar that ensued. "She's just drugged! She was kidnapped!"

"Scratch was set up!" Logan added. "He's innocent!"

Zoe glanced over at the dragon, whose whole body was alive with hope now. Scratch's eyes glowed and he clawed at the ground.

The SNAPA agents nearly overturned their table in their haste to get up and examine Pelly. Delia brushed her hair behind her ears, looking pale as she felt for Pelly's pulse. Zoe wondered how it must feel to have nearly condemned an innocent dragon to death—especially when your whole mission in life was to keep them safe.

"They're right," Delia said, then, clearing her throat, she said it again louder. "They're right. Judge Martindale, this goose is alive." She turned to Zoe. "So what about the blood on the dragon's teeth?"

"Just from the sheep he ate," Zoe said, shaking her head.

"You're sure?" Delia said anxiously. "He didn't attack any people while he was loose?"

"Xanadu's a small town," Matthew said. "We'd know if anyone had been attacked by a dragon this past week. I promise."

The SNAPA agent breathed a sigh of relief. "Very well. We withdraw our case against the accused, for now."

Runcible let out a small growl and stalked back to the table, where he started slamming papers and books around.

Delia's hands brushed through the goose's feathers, checking for injuries. "And she seems okay," she said. "Did she tell you what happened to her or where she's been?"

"Not yet," Zoe said. "We found her at our librarian's house, but we think someone else took her from here, and then Miss Sameera rescued her by accident."

Delia tilted her head. "Did you say Sameera?"

"Yes," said Zoe. "Sameera Lahiri, our school librarian."

The agent sighed. "Oh, lord. The craziest Free Ranger of them all."

"What's a Free Ranger?" Logan asked. Zoe had never heard of them, either, before seeing Miss Sameera's letter.

"A misguided movement to find and free all our mythical creatures," Delia said. "They're like SNAPA's worst nightmare. They have no real proof that these animals even exist, but they're so convinced and so determined that we can't seem to shake them. It turns out kraken ink doesn't work on memories of completely made-up supernatural encounters."

"Oh," Logan said. "Like people who say they've been abducted by UFOs."

"Right," said Delia, "except those people usually have had a real run-in with a will-o'-the-wisp or a tooth fairy." She stroked Pelly's head. "Sameera Lahiri has been trouble before. She exposed a menagerie in Missouri and we had to dose the whole town. I thought we got to her, too, but maybe our dosage wasn't high enough. Some people have stronger resistance to kraken ink than others."

"Well, we brought her back here to answer some questions," Zoe said. She made a mental note that they'd have to give Miss Sameera extra kraken ink—maybe a lot extra. She hoped that would work; she'd never heard of anyone resisting it before. "So we'll see what we can find out, and where she found Pelly, which might lead us to the real kidnapper."

"Good idea," Delia said. "Runcible and I will interrogate her as soon as we've packed up here."

A movement behind the agent caught Zoe's eye, and she turned to watch as her dad unclipped most of the chains from around Scratch. The dragon stretched his wings, beaming happily.

Runcible came storming back and stood over the goose, fuming. "You still have to answer for that dragon escaping," he said. "I can see plenty of reasons to shut down this whole place."

Zoe's heart sank. After all that, hadn't they saved the Menagerie?

"Oh, I think not," said a voice behind Runcible. He stepped aside with a frown as Melissa Merevy strolled up with a clipboard full of forms. She tipped it so he could see the top page, where several lines were highlighted. "According to the SNAMHP rule book, anyone who's been a werewolf less than seven years is not allowed to run free in wolf form within fifty miles of human habitation, regardless of whether he's tracked and monitored. Moreover, with children out in the woods Sunday night, you could both be facing serious endangerment charges." She paused, letting that sink in as Runcible turned purple and Delia stared blankly. "Unless, of course, we can reach some kind of mutual agreement about the longevity of this Menagerie's prospects . . ."

"What?" Logan whispered to Zoe.

"I think she's blackmailing them into letting us stay open," Zoe whispered back.

"Oh," he said. "Awesome."

He grinned, looking relieved. She wished she felt that way, too, but she couldn't shake the feeling that their problems were far from over. She kept thinking about those goose feathers—the ones that weren't Pelly's—and wondering where they came from and who would have had access to them.

She felt someone's gaze on her and turned to see the Exterminator watching, dark eyes glittering through his mask.

They'd returned Pelly and saved Scratch, but they hadn't figured out who was trying to sabotage the Menagerie.

And Zoe was sure whoever it was wouldn't be giving up that easily.

TWENTY-THREE

" That's not much of a costume."

Logan jumped and turned around. His father leaned in the doorway, looking amused.

"Aren't you going to a Halloween party?" Mr. Wilde asked. "What are you, a grim reaper?"

Logan looked down at the black sweater and black jeans he'd been instructed to wear. "No, Blue is picking my costume," he said. To his dad's raised eyebrows, he added, "I kind of lost a bet."

"Ah," said his dad. "Unfortunate."

"Yeah, so I'm meeting up with him to get dressed and then we'll go over to the party together." Logan wiped his hands on his jeans, wondering whether to admit that a party at Jasmin Sterling's house terrified him. Probably even more than grumpy dragons or basilisks.

"I'd rather you weren't riding around on your bike after dark," said his dad, flipping his car keys over one finger. "I'll drive you and you can call me for a ride back."

"You don't have to do that," Logan said.

"Sure I do. I'm your dad. Ready to go?"

Logan reluctantly trailed his dad out to the car. His dad had been acting a little weird all week, calling him a lot and asking more questions than normal, especially about Zoe Kahn. Logan was almost certain that his dad knew everything about the Menagerie and the Kahn family, but he was still waiting for Dad to come clean about Mom. After he did that, Logan was willing to tell him everything.

But if his dad did know something, this drop-off was going to be a bit awkward.

Sure enough, as they came to the bottom of Zoe's driveway, Logan's dad leaned forward, frowning up at the tall walls of the Menagerie.

"I can walk from here," Logan offered.

"Isn't this the Kahns' place?" Dad asked.

"Yeah," Logan said, squirming internally. "Blue and his mom live here, too. Like, in an apartment in a separate part of the house. So that's where I'll be. With Blue."

"I hope so," his dad said, stopping the car and turning to face Logan. "Listen, buddy, I'm not sure hanging out with Zoe Kahn is such a good idea."

Here it comes. Logan held his breath. *Maybe now Dad is ready to talk.* "Why?" he asked.

"That whole family is trouble," said Dad. "I've heard it from enough people to be worried. I'd rather you made some different friends instead."

"Oh, sure," Logan said. "No problem. 'Cause making friends is so easy here. I just spent two months all by myself because I figured it would be character building."

"Logan, I'm serious," said his dad.

"Me, too," said Logan. "I've finally met people who want to be friends with me—people who are kind of awesome—and you want me to stay away from them based on what? Town rumors? That doesn't sound like the kind of friend you've always told me to be."

"I'm just saying—"

You're just saying a pack of lies instead of finally telling me the truth, Logan thought furiously. He knew he was madder than he should be, but he couldn't help it.

"I'm not giving up my only friends without a really good reason," Logan said, climbing out of the car. "Thanks for the ride." He closed the door and headed up the driveway before his dad could respond.

"Stop fussing." Zoe lightly slapped Logan's hand away. "You'll mess it up."

"I cannot believe you talked me into this," Logan grumbled around the fake fangs in his mouth. He shot a look at Blue, who was standing in the doorway to the bathroom looking much less like an idiot than Logan did.

Zoe smoothed the last patch of fake fur onto Logan's cheek and stepped back to inspect her work. He peered at the mirror. A hairy wig perched on his head, dark brown to match the sideburns. Ruby had chipped in with her eyeliner and helpful suggestions on how to create crags around Logan's eyes and on his forehead and cheeks. Somehow, they'd also managed to make his eyebrows look ridiculously bushy.

"Why do I have to be a werewolf?" Logan asked, reaching up to scratch at the wig.

"Because," Blue said, "now you'll be itchy and uncomfortable all night. Just like me."

Zoe sighed. "Be nice. You're lucky Jasmin wants you there." She plucked a piece of lint out of Logan's fur.

"What exactly are you supposed to be?" Logan asked Blue.

Blue looked down at the torn blue pants and open-chested white shirt Jasmin had sent over. "I have no idea. Jasmin said it would make sense when I saw her. I'm thinking zombie, though—what do you think?"

"I am a hundred percent sure Jasmin does not want you to be a zombie," Zoe said.

"Zombies are totally in," Blue informed her. "They are the new vampires."

"No, no, no," Zoe said. "Nothing that wants to eat your brain will ever be attractive, and I guarantee Jasmin wants to show you off tonight."

Blue shivered. He grabbed the makeup on the counter and began coating on a pale shade.

"Well, maybe if I'm something gross and spooky, she'll stop liking me." A minute later, he snapped his head toward Zoe. "Yargh! I'm going to eat your brain!" His lips were slightly green and he'd circled his eyes with a dark gray eye shadow.

"Terrifying," Zoe said. "Especially the part where Jasmin might kill you for ruining her plan."

"I'm going to grab my shoes. Meet you downstairs, Logan." Blue patted Zoe on the shoulder as he headed out.

"Are you sure you won't come with us?" Logan asked once Blue was gone. He knew it would be weird for her to show up at Jasmin's party, but maybe there would be enough people there that Jasmin wouldn't even notice her. Or maybe Jasmin would forgive her and they could at least talk to each other again.

Right. Or not.

"Nah," Zoe said with a shrug. "Way too awkward. But you'll have to tell me everything. I want to know what her mysterious costume finally is. Plus you have to make sure Blue is nice to Jasmin."

"I'm on it," he promised. He hesitated. "Have you—has anyone heard anything from the SNAPA agents?"

"No." Zoe sat down on the edge of the bathtub, frowning. "They took Miss Sameera away before we could even introduce her to the unicorns, like we promised. And they took Pelly, too, to run some scans and make sure nothing bad got into her system. Mom and Dad said not to worry, we'll get a chance to talk to both of them once SNAPA is done, but we have to follow official protocol or something like that. It's frustrating. I feel like there's someone out there, planning the next awful thing to do to us, but we have no idea who it is and our best chance of finding out is locked up in a secret SNAPA facility."

"They'll find out what she knows, though, right?" said Logan. "Maybe they'll show up tomorrow, give back Pelly, and hand over the answers to all our questions."

"Hmm," Zoe said. Logan didn't really believe it, either. But surely SNAPA couldn't just make Miss Sameera disappear forever. They'd get a chance to talk to her sooner or later—and perhaps Pelly would be able to identify her kidnapper, too.

Downstairs, they found the Kahns and Blue in the kitchen with Keiko, who was glaring at them all defiantly. She was dressed in a sleek sci-fi outfit, but there were furry blue ears perched on her head and a carefully groomed bushy tail emerging from the back of her suit. Logan blinked a few times to make sure he was seeing it right. Yup. Keiko was a blue spacesuit-wearing fox.

"Keiko, this is a little . . . reckless, don't you think?" Mrs. Kahn was saying.

"I don't see why." Keiko practically stomped her foot. "It's not like anyone will know by looking at my costume that I really am a fox."

"But that's your actual tail!" Ruby exclaimed. "You dyed it blue!"

"It'll wash out," Keiko snapped.

"What if someone asks to try on your tail? Aren't they going to be a little curious that you can't take it off?" Ruby put her hands on her hips.

Zoe rolled her eyes at Logan.

"No one would dare," Keiko said. "I'll be fine."

Mr. Kahn sighed. "It's okay, Ruby. Logan and Blue will be there to make sure she doesn't get into any trouble. Although I don't see why you have to go as a fox, Keiko."

"I'm not just any fox, I'm Krystal from the Star Fox saga. You're the ones who are always telling me it's good to connect with my cultural roots. Star Fox was a totally popular Japanese video game, according to this old magazine of Matthew's I found. God."

"She's got you there, Dad," Matthew said, a smile hovering

on his lips. Zoe's brother lounged against the counter, a bag of potato chips in his hand. He looked ten million times happier now that the qilin had been found.

"Okay, okay." Mr. Kahn raised his hands in a placating gesture. "Just be careful."

Keiko smiled smugly and sauntered toward the front door. "I bet I have the best costume at the party."

Logan caught the wistful expression on Zoe's face before she could hide it. "Don't worry," he said. "You won't miss anything. We promise not to have any fun."

She laughed. "Oh, good."

As they went down the driveway, Logan looked back over his shoulder and saw her standing in the doorway, leaning against Captain Fuzzbutt's furry leg. The mammoth had his trunk wrapped around her waist, making her look smaller than usual.

At least she's not alone, he thought. *The saboteur is still out there, but we saved the Menagerie, for now. And I'm going to my first Xanadu party. Maybe it's okay to relax just for tonight.*

Jasmin's house loomed out of the darkness, light shining from the windows and illuminating the curved paved driveway. Giant spiderwebs with giant spiders in them hung from the trees and a trail of jack-o'-lanterns carved like various spooky creatures lit the way to the front door. Logan reminded himself to act like he'd never seen the place once they got inside—even though he'd been in her house just last weekend with Zoe and Blue, trying to track down the last missing griffin cub.

"Act normal," Blue said to Logan.

"Me?" Logan said as they climbed the front steps. Blue was practically humming with nervous energy. "You're the one who looks like he might steal one of their cars and make a run for the border."

"Ha-ha," Blue said, his eyes darting toward the garage as if that sounded like a fine plan to him.

"This is going to be so cool!" Keiko bounced in place on the front step as they rang the doorbell. Logan had never seen her so excited. It was actually kind of cute, in a younger-sister kind of way.

Keiko spun to face them before the door opened. "Okay, ground rules. Do not come near me once we're inside. I don't want you two losers dragging me down. When it's time to go, I'll find you."

Logan rolled his eyes at Blue. So much for sisterly affection.

"Oh, hello," Jasmin purred, pulling open the front door.

Blue would have fallen off the steps if Logan hadn't grabbed his arm to steady him.

Her hair was clipped back from her face with little pink seashell clips. She wore a pink-seashell bikini top, her midriff was bare, and from the waist down she was encased in a sparkly green-scaled tail.

Jasmin was dressed as a mermaid.

"Hi, Keiko," she said. "Wow, you're a . . . blue fox . . . in a spacesuit."

"Krystal," Keiko said. "You know. From Star Fox."

"Right. Okay," Jasmin said. "Aww, and Logan is a wolf to match, right? Too cute." Jasmin gave Logan a knowing look.

"Thanks for having me," Keiko chirped, pushing past her into the main foyer and vanishing into the party.

Jasmin flipped her hair over her shoulder and smiled at Blue. "Do you get it now? I'm the mermaid and you're the drowning sailor that I saved! Although—" She surveyed his morbid makeup with raised eyebrows. "Hmm. It looks like I got to you too late."

Logan glanced at Blue, but he clearly wasn't going to be capable of speech anytime soon.

"We thought he was supposed to be a zombie," he said.

"Too funny," Jasmin said. "I can work with that. Come on, Blue. Let's spray down your hair so at least you look like I just pulled you from the sea. You know, your classic zombie-mermaid story of true love. Tale as old as time, right?" She laughed, taking Blue's hand.

"Um. Um. Um," Blue stammered. Logan nudged him in the ribs and mouthed "act normal!" behind Jasmin's back. "Is that really—do we have to—maybe I should—" The sound of Blue's voice trailed away as Jasmin tugged him down the hall.

Logan shut the front door behind him. He could hear

people's voices from the den to his left, but Blue and Jasmin had disappeared toward the kitchen at the back.

He took a deep breath, realizing he'd have to go into the party alone. But if he could face dragons and charm a qilin, he could handle walking into a room full of his classmates, right?

The den was packed, although the crowd spilled over into the adjacent dining room. Everyone from their grade was there, except Zoe. Keiko seemed to be the only sixth grader, but she wasn't letting that slow her down. She sashayed— that was the only word for it—over to the couch and settled in beside two girls. They all started talking and giggling like they'd been best friends for years, but Logan knew Keiko had only moved here last year. How did girls do that? Or was that kind of confidence a special kitsune power?

Logan spotted Marco, dressed as a ninja, hanging out by the food in the dining room.

"Oh, hey, Logan." Marco slapped Logan on the back. A tray full of miniature quiches went sailing by, and Marco somehow managed to snag about twelve at once. "Great costume. Just promise not to eat me. Ha-ha!"

Logan laughed.

"Yeah, right," said one of Marco's soccer friends. Logan was pretty sure his name was Aidan. "You're far too stringy to make a good meal."

"True. Plus who would want to deprive the world of my charming personality? I mean, this wouldn't even be a party if

I weren't here. Logan, when I showed up the only decorations in here were sparkly pumpkins. How boring is that? I mixed it up, don't worry."

"EWWW!" a girl cried from the kitchen. "Why are the walls all sticky?"

"Is that a cockroach?" another voice shrieked.

Marco grinned and, with a dramatic flourish, produced a ziplock bag of fake bugs and an empty bottle of goo. Aidan laughed, gave him a high five, and ambled off to the kitchen.

Logan nodded at Marco. "Pretty clever. Better hope Jasmin doesn't realize you're the one who slimed up her walls."

"I can handle her. Hey, so . . . did you come with Blue and Keiko?"

"Yeah, Keiko's in the den and Blue's—"

"Cool. See you later." Marco grabbed a handful of popcorn from the dining room table and headed purposefully toward the den.

Logan made his way into the enormous, gleaming kitchen and found Blue staring gloomily at a can of soda.

"Hey," Blue said.

"You're alive!" Logan said.

"Barely. I think Jasmin just tried to drown me." His hair was plastered to his head and the ends were still dripping slightly. The water formed little rivulets in his makeup as well, making him look like a melting zombie. Blue tugged at the collar of his shirt, lifting it up to wipe his hair. Logan glanced around to make sure they were alone.

"I didn't know merfolk could drown," he joked.

"Hardy-har-har." Blue's expression turned serious. "Do you think she knows?" he whispered. "About me?"

"No way. How could she?"

"I don't know. But why would she pick that costume? I'm kind of freaking out about it." Blue's version of freaking out was so much calmer than Zoe's that it was almost hilarious.

"It's a coincidence," Logan reassured him. "Don't worry. Come on, let's head back to the den and act like regular guys who didn't just spend a week rescuing griffins, hunting a qilin, arguing with a goose, and saving a dragon."

"Check this out," Marco was shouting as they entered the room. "I'm a ninja warrior! Hiya!" Marco whirled in place, kicking out one leg. Unfortunately, his foot snagged in a curtain and he toppled over, landing on Keiko and the other two girls on the couch.

"Aaahh! Get off!" Keiko cried, shoving at Marco's flailing limbs.

Jasmin sauntered in from the dining room, and the whole room seemed to pause for a moment as they all turned their attention to her. She smiled and tossed her hair back. "All right, everyone. Time to play Truth or Dare."

"Ooh! Me, me!" Marco volunteered from the floor, where Keiko had dumped him. "I'll take any dare. I'm not scared of anything!"

"Okay, Marco," Jasmin said. "I dare you to shut up for fifteen minutes. Who's next? Cadence, where are you?" Jasmin scanned her guests and Blue ducked behind a marble statue.

"I hate Truth or Dare," Blue muttered. "I'm going to hide until this whole thing is over."

"Sounds like a plan." Logan followed him out of the room. "I know a great secret passage that's cozy," he joked.

Blue perked up. "Hey, yeah, that would work."

"I was kidding, Blue."

"Mr. Sterling's study, then," Blue said. "No one else will dare go in there, and if it's empty, we can wait out the game."

Logan and Blue inched open one of the huge carved wooden doors and Logan peeked inside. "Coast is clear." He and Blue slipped in and carefully closed the door behind them.

"Check out all this cool travel stuff," Blue said, pointing at an antique globe in the corner.

Logan looked around the room, which he'd been in too much of a panic to fully appreciate on Sunday morning. Two of the walls were lined with bookshelves, and the one behind the ornate desk was floor-to-ceiling clear glass window panes. He could see the sunset painting the sky a bright pink and orange above the trees outside.

Blue flopped into one of the leather chairs and pulled out his phone to check his messages. Logan examined the miniature jade dragon on Mr. Sterling's desk. It was delicately balanced on its hind legs with one claw outstretched and its eyes were glittering rubies.

"They've got a great backyard," Logan said. "They don't have any pets?"

"No." Blue got up and joined him. "Jasmin's allergic. It's too bad. This house could sure use a puppy to cheer it up. It's so cold."

"Yeah," Logan agreed. The place was immaculate and everything in it was expensive and high-quality, but it didn't feel like a home.

"What are you guys doing in here?" a voice demanded from the door.

Logan and Blue whirled around, crashing into each other. Logan tried to right himself, catching the edge of the desk with his hand, but it slipped off, sending papers flying. He found himself sitting on the floor, Blue's leg pinning his knee.

"Ow." Blue held his hand up to his head.

"Oh my gosh, are you all right?" Jasmin rushed over, helping Blue to his feet.

Logan was brushing himself off and starting to rise when something caught his eye. He froze.

One of the papers he'd knocked to the floor was a drawing. He could only see a corner of it—but that corner was clearly marked "Dragon Lair."

He glanced at Jasmin, but all her attention was focused on Blue. Quickly he slid the paper out from under the others and unrolled it.

It was a map, like the kind you might see for a zoo or amusement park. In the center was a familiar-looking lake with an island labeled "Mermaid Retreat." On the left were roads looping through something called "Unicorn Safari." The northern end featured three caves in the side of a cliff, labeled "Dragon Lair," and south of that was what looked like an enormous roller coaster called "Flight of the Griffins." To the right of that was a "Frozen Tundra" with a small drawing of a mammoth in a cage. East of the lake was a large dome-covered building marked "Bird Lodge."

Worst of all, in place of the house, there was a building labeled "Research Laboratory—Medical/Pharmaceutical Experiments."

Logan was holding a map to the Menagerie—or rather, a horrible vision of what might happen to the Menagerie.

The Sterlings knew all about it. They hadn't forgotten anything Jonathan might have told them. In fact, it looked like they had plans of their own for the mythical-creature sanctuary—plans that involved exposing it and then making a pile of money off it.

He had to get back to the Kahns and warn them. This was even worse than whoever was trying to sabotage them.

The Menagerie was in grave danger.

To be continued . . .

CAMP UNDERPAW'S GUIDE TO MYTHICAL CREATURES

A Brief Overview for Trackers in Training

You've made it to Camp Underpaw—your first step on the path to becoming a Tracker!

Now, forget everything you think you know about "mythical" creatures. Being a Tracker is not about riding magical unicorns and cuddling griffin cubs. It is a dangerous career suitable only for the toughest, most committed creature hunters. It takes determination and resourcefulness, guts and brains, and all the skills you'll learn in this intensive, hands-on Tracker camp experience.

And it starts with memorizing this list of the most notable and notorious creatures you're likely to encounter out in the world. Look it over and think carefully . . . is this really the right future for you? Are you ready to face venomous teeth and razor-sharp claws and kraken ink?

If so—welcome to Camp Underpaw!

REMEMBER THESE CREATURES

ALICANTO

Most commonly found in Chile, these birds are easily recognized by their wings, which shimmer and clatter as if they were made of gold and silver. Their primary food source is metal, with a strong preference for gold and silver, but in captivity alicantos are usually fed lesser metals and often survive on a diet of pennies. Search for these birds along waterways and high in the mountains near precious metal mines. You will know you are getting close when you hear a sound like raining coins. Protective earplugs highly recommended.

ANT-LION

A small insect with the body of an ant and the head of a lion. Very aggressive and territorial, but can be mollified with food (other

insects, crumbs, scraps of meat, etc.). Wear thick boots
and be careful where you step when tracking these tiny,
ferocious biters.

BAKU

A big, gentle, nocturnal creature resembling a tapir. Native
to Japan, bakus eat dreams, particularly nightmares. Usually
found near humans and can sometimes be summoned after
especially vivid dreams.

BASILISK

A deadly, venomous giant lizard; its gaze kills anyone
who looks at it. Do not underestimate the threat of these
creatures; bring backup and a mirror if you must track one.

The crow of a rooster will put the basilisk to sleep, but only a weasel can kill it.

BONNACON

A giant, vicious creature shaped like a bull with a mane like a horse, horns that curve backward, and fiery dung. Extremely easy to track by its excretions, but approach with caution. Bring nose plugs and a fire extinguisher.

CALADRIUS

A pure-white bird roughly the size of a gull. It is known for being able to discern whether someone is telling the truth or lying.

CHIMERA

A creature that is part lion, part goat, and part snake (and all dangerous); beware its ability to breathe fire.

CHUPACABRA

The chupacabra has the head of a dog, a spiny back, and scaly skin; its red eyes can hypnotize and it leaves a sulfurous odor in its wake. Tends to feed on goats and other livestock, but has been known to bite people as well.

DRAGON (Chinese)

Related to Western dragons, but without wings or fire-breathing; Chinese dragons can change their size and love the water.

DRAGON (Western)

Enormous fire-breathing creatures with scales, talons, and vast wings. Usually they choose the relative safety of captivity and do not require Tracking.

GOLDEN GOOSE

A larger-than-average goose who can lay golden eggs.

GRIFFIN

A lion-eagle hybrid, with the body, paws, and tail of a lion and the wings and head of an eagle; they are traditionally guardians, mistrust horses, and love treasure. If you can identify what treasure a griffin is protecting, they are easier to track.

HALCYON

A small blue bird with white throat feathers that looks something like a kingfisher and can affect the weather.

HELLHOUND

Oversized black dogs with sulfurous breath and glowing red eyes. Try to avoid their slobber as it can sting if it comes in contact with broken skin.

HIPPOCAMP

A water animal with the head and front legs of a horse but the tail of a fish.

JACKALOPE

Only found in Wyoming, a jackalope looks like a rabbit with antlers. Beware its ability to imitate the human voice, as it may lead you on a merry chase.

KAPPA

Water sprites from Japan with scales, faces like monkeys, and turtle shells on their backs. They love cucumbers but will also happily eat children.

KELPIE

A malevolent kind of water horse who lurks by ponds and rivers to lure people into the water for the purpose of drowning and/or eating them. Basically, if you see a horse standing next to a lake, leave it alone.

KITSUNE

Native to Japan, a kitsune's true shape is a fox, but they can also shift into human form, so they are monitored by the SuperNatural Agency for Mostly Human Protection (SNAMHP). They are very difficult to catch because a full-grown kitsune can often read minds, see the future, fly, possess people, and create illusions that mimic reality. A clever Tracker might spot one by its fox-shaped shadow. Dogs are sometimes useful for tracking them as a dog can sniff out a kitsune's true nature.

KRAKEN

Possibly the largest of all mythical creatures, the kraken is shaped like a giant squid and lives deep in the ocean. Their ink can wipe all supernatural memories from your brain, and more than one promising Tracker's career has been derailed by an unfortunate encounter with it. Only specially trained deep-sea Trackers are qualified to search for creatures like this.

MANTICORE

A fierce and deadly creature with a lion's body and claws, a scorpion's tail, and a face like a man with rows of sharp fangs. Extremely dangerous—do not approach!

MAPINGUARI

A giant sloth-like animal found in the dark jungles of South America. They are slow, but willing to eat people, and fearsomely bad-smelling—bad enough that they can often be tracked by their terrible scent.

MERMAID

Exactly what you think they are: people with fish tails from the waist down who prefer to live underwater. Classed as Mostly Human and therefore monitored by SNAMHP.

PEGASUS

A winged horse. The primary difficulty in tracking them is that no ordinary saddle will fit around their wings.

PHOENIX

A beautiful scarlet-plumed bird who occasionally dies in a burst of flames and is then reborn from an egg found in the ashes. There is only one in the world, currently located in the Wyoming Menagerie.

PYROSALAMANDER

The mythical cousins of a regular salamander, pyrosalamanders are small, bright red, and eat fire. Handle with caution and be sure to feed them regularly!

QILIN

Sometimes confused with unicorns or called a "Chinese unicorn," as they are usually found in China or Japan. A qilin has the slender body of a deer, fish scales along its back, and one horn pointing backwards from its head. They are able to sense the guilt or innocence of others. Extremely difficult to track as a qilin passes over grass without flattening it. Take care when capturing one as it is bad luck to wound a qilin.

ROC

A gigantic bird of prey, usually with white and gold feathers, capable of carrying an elephant in its massive claws. Found in the most uninhabited mountainous regions of the world.

SELKIE

Another Mostly Human sea hybrid; selkies take the form of seals in the water, but can slip off their sealskins and assume human form while on land. Please try not to bring in ordinary seals who are "acting suspicious," as this happens entirely too often and SNAMPH is not amused by it.

TANIWHA

A long serpentine creature from New Zealand with some of the qualities of a dragon, except that they are usually wingless and prefer to live in the ocean. On land, they can be tracked by the tunnels they leave behind as they dig their way through the earth.

UNICORN

A graceful horselike creature, usually a shimmering white, with a horn in the center of its forehead. Warning: can be rather sensitive and temperamental, so be sure to demonstrate respect when dealing with them.

WENDIGO

These shape-shifters are cannibalistic, ruthless hunters with sharp, jagged teeth and skeletal frames. A rare example of a creature whom Trackers are encouraged to kill in the wild, as they do poorly in captivity and seem to be impossible to rehabilitate or tame. Typically found in cold regions, they turn their victims into wendigos as well and can hunt through a victim's dreams. They can be killed if you melt their hearts of ice.

WEREWOLF

Mostly Human; these are humans who have either been bitten by a werewolf or inherited the gene from their parents. At the full moon, they involuntarily transform into wolves from midnight to dawn; at other times, they may choose which shape to present. Werewolves are the most well-known example, but werecreatures exist in all shapes and sizes, from weremice to werewhales. These creatures fall under the purview of SNAMHP, but occasionally you may have to track a rogue werecreature on their behalf.

YAWKYAWK

Water spirits from Australia who often look like mermaids, but can also shape-shift into crocodiles, swordfish, snakes, dragonflies, or humans. They may have the power to create storms, so try not to make them angry.

YETI

Also known as a Bigfoot, a Sasquatch, or an Abominable Snowman, these huge hairy manlike creatures are covered in fur and generally live in cold climates. Somewhat human, but not Mostly Human, so they are covered by SNAPA instead of SNAMHP.

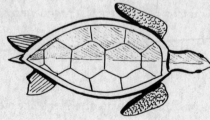

ZARATAN:

A turtle the size of a small island, and yet shockingly difficult to track.

Keep reading for a sneak peek!

ONE

Logan Wilde stared down at the map in his hands. Mr. Sterling's oak-paneled study seemed to be spinning around him.

Dragon Lair.

Flight of the Griffins.

Unicorn Safari.

One week earlier, he had discovered that his little town of Xanadu, Wyoming, contained a secret home for mythical creatures called the Menagerie. Emphasis on *secret.* As in, nobody was supposed to know about it, and anyone who accidentally found out would get their memories wiped with kraken ink. He'd only been allowed in because he could understand the baby griffins and because of his mom's ties to the Kahn family who ran the Menagerie. But he already understood how important it was to protect and hide these endangered magical animals from the world.

The map in his hands represented the exact opposite of all that: a vision of the Menagerie as an amusement park where rich tourists could snap pictures of mermaids, ride a chained-up woolly mammoth, and probably buy yeti-fur blankets and baby pyrosalamanders of their own at the large "GIFT SHOP" marked prominently in the corner.

Logan's heart was hammering in his chest. The Sterlings didn't just know about the Menagerie. They knew all the details—the layout, the animals who lived there. Ruby Kahn's ex-boyfriend Jonathan must have described it to his parents. And either Ruby hadn't given them kraken ink like she was supposed to, or it hadn't worked for some reason.

He slipped his phone out of his pocket and quickly snapped a photo of the map. The Kahns needed to see this right away.

It was awkward working with his hands since they were covered in faux fur and he had fake claws protruding from his fingers for his werewolf costume. Across the hall, he could hear the noise and thumping music of Jasmin Sterling's Halloween party. It was the first party he'd been invited to since moving to Xanadu—and now he needed to find a polite way to bolt out of there two hours early.

"What on earth are you looking at?" Jasmin said from behind him, making him jump. He'd almost forgotten that she and his friend, Blue Merevy, were even in the room. Logan fumbled his phone back into his jacket and tried to roll up the map, but she was already reaching around to take it from him. "There can't possibly be anything interesting in my dad's boring papers about boring real estate and boring politics and—" She stopped, raising her eyebrows at the map. "Oh, *Dad*."

"What?" Blue asked, leaning over her shoulder to look. Jasmin glanced sideways at him with a smile and tilted it so he'd lean closer to her.

"Isn't my dad the cheesiest?" she said. "Remember that Wild West theme park he tried to start a few years ago? The huge enormous failure?"

"Oh yeah," Blue said, looking at her instead of at the map. "We went with Zoe on opening day."

"Right," she said, laughing. "And we all got totally sick on the free root beer, and you fell off a horse that was *barely* moving, and then Zoe nearly locked herself in the old jail cell while I was pretending to be sheriff." She paused, and a wistful expression crossed her face that was almost an exact match for the look Zoe got whenever she talked about Jasmin.

She misses Zoe, too, Logan realized. Zoe had had to stop being friends with Jasmin six months ago, when the whole Sterling family was dosed with kraken ink after Jonathan tried to steal a jackalope. Or *supposedly* dosed, anyway. He tried to shoot PAY ATTENTION, TIME TO FREAK OUT vibes at Blue, but the blond boy was . . . what *was* he doing? Giving Jasmin a rather goofy-looking grin, for one thing.

"Anyway, look," Jasmin said, shaking her hair back. "Dad's got another brilliantly terrible idea. A theme park full of imaginary creatures? Who does he think is going to drive out to the middle of seriously absolutely nowhere for some lame animatronic unicorns? I mean, really, right?" She giggled and waved one hand at her Halloween costume. "Maybe you and I can play a couple of the mermaids."

Logan saw the moment where Blue realized what he was looking at. Even without the terrifying labels, it would have been easy to recognize the Menagerie from the giant lake in the middle of it—the lake where Blue's father, King Cobalt, ruled over the merfolk.

The normally unflappable merboy jumped back as though the map had snarled at him. All the color drained out of his face.

"Blue?" Jasmin said, turning toward him. "Are you all right?"

"We have to go," Logan said quickly. "I was just telling Blue—that's why we're in here, sorry."

"No!" Jasmin cried, genuinely upset. "Blue, you can't leave already. You just got here. We haven't danced or anything. And there's, um—there's red velvet cake! In the shape of a ghost! You *can't* leave before the cake."

Blue shook his head and ran one hand through his hair. "Sorry, Jasmin. It's, uh—"

"My cat," Logan jumped in, right as Blue said, "My mom."

Jasmin glanced between them suspiciously.

"His mom," Logan agreed.

"Got bitten by his cat," Blue blurted.

Logan shot him a look. *You are the worst liar.* Poor Purrsimmon, maligned so unfairly.

"What?" Jasmin said. "Is she all right?"

"Yes," Logan said.

"No," said Blue, and Jasmin's eyes went wide.

"His *mom* is *fine*," Logan said firmly. "He means my *cat*, who is now *missing*, and we have to *find her*, so we need to leave *now*." *Before this lie gets any more absurd.* He pushed Blue toward the door.

"Are you taking your disturbing sixth-grader with you?" Jasmin asked. "Because she just dared Cadence to bite off one of her own fingers, and then got rather outraged when she wouldn't. I'm not sure she completely understands that Truth or Dare is a game. Also, she might be a psychopath."

"Keiko, yes," Blue said distractedly. "We should get Keiko."

"This is going to go over well," Logan muttered. He took out his fake fangs as they left the study. At least he wouldn't have to wear his uncomfortable costume any longer.

They found Keiko perched on the kitchen counter, chatting to three seventh-grade girls, while Marco stood beside her holding two plates of snacks. Keiko took a tiny meatball from one plate and a mini-quiche from the other without looking at him. Her blue fox ears twitched, but no one seemed to notice that they were real.

"Terrible idea," Keiko said to her fascinated audience. "Getting you together would be an utter waste of time. Violet, stop liking him at once. There are much more useful things you can be doing with your brain than thinking about idiots and how to get those idiots to pay attention to you."

"Aidan's not that bad," Marco protested faintly.

"And he's so cute . . . ," Violet said.

"He is twelve, and a boy," Keiko said, as if this were boringly obvious. "He'd require an exhausting amount of training. You wouldn't have any time for soccer." She speared another meatball.

"What kind of training?" Marco asked. "I'm a fast learner. Just in case you were wondering."

Keiko gave him a skeptical look and then spotted Logan and Blue heading toward her. Her expression shifted into a glare full of daggers.

"Absolutely not," she said, pointing her toothpick at them. "Take those pathetic faces elsewhere. I will rip off your eyelashes if you try to make me leave right now."

"It's an emergency, Keiko," Blue said.

"*You're* an emergency," she said.

"Seriously, we have to go right now," Logan said.

"Aw, really? Already?" Marco held up the plates. "Look, she's letting me hold her fancy miniature foods!"

Keiko studied Blue's eyes for a minute, then growled softly. "Help me down," she ordered Marco.

He hurriedly dropped the plates on the counter, scattering crumbs everywhere, and took Keiko's outstretched hand. She jumped lightly to the floor and patted him on the head. "Think about what I told you," she said to the three girls. "See me in school on Monday if you have any questions."

Logan turned toward the exit and nearly ran into a woman wielding a gleaming knife.

"Aah!" he yelped, leaping back.

"It's all right, you're safe from me unless you're a cake," Mrs. Sterling said, smiling. Her gold-rimmed glasses caught the light so it was hard to see her eyes.

"Oh—sorry, Mrs. Sterling," Logan said awkwardly.

"I'll forgive you this time, young man," she said, tipping the knife slightly toward him. Her dark hair was swept back from her face and pinned into a bun. Her orange-and-black dress was made from some kind of shiny material, and she had on what looked like ten pounds of jewelry between the diamonds dangling from her ears, the bracelets sparkling on her narrow wrists, and the giant pearl nestled in a gold-and-silver pendant at her neck. His mom would never have worn anything so fancy. That much jewelry would have gotten in the way of wrestling chimeras or whatever she had to do in her secret Tracker job.

"Jasmin says you're leaving already?" Mrs. Sterling said to Blue. He nodded, and she made a little fake sad face with her mouth. "Oh, what a shame. I hope we get to see you again . . . soon."

As an exhibit in our theme park? Logan wondered. She must know Blue was one of the merfolk, if the Sterlings knew everything else. She probably knew about Keiko being a kitsune, too. He felt a sudden flare of anger. Blue and Keiko weren't specimens; they were his *friends*. Well, Keiko was more like the unpredictably grouchy younger sister of a friend, but still. He'd do anything to protect her, or Blue, or the Menagerie.

"Come on," Logan said, taking Blue's arm and dragging him away. He could feel Mrs. Sterling's eyes on his back as they left the kitchen, as if she were thinking, *I know where you're going. And it will be mine soon.*

TWO

In the main entrance hall, Logan and Blue found Jasmin sitting on the stairs with her chin on her hands and her elbows on her knees, staring sadly into space. Her mermaid tail was a green, glittery waterfall flopping over her feet, and her hair was a dark curtain around her thin shoulders.

Blue hesitated, glanced at Logan, and then went over to sit on the stair beside her. He gently put one hand on Jasmin's back.

"I'm sorry we can't stay," he said. "I'm sure it'll be an awesome party."

"Of course," she said, mustering a smile. "All my parties are awesome. You're so missing out." She looked into his eyes for a minute, then turned away, wrapping her arms around her legs.

Blue tucked a strand of her hair behind her ear, leaned over, and quickly kissed her cheek. "See you Monday," he mumbled, jumping up and practically running for the door.

Keiko was already outside, so Logan was the only one who saw the radiantly hopeful expression spread across Jasmin's face. He waved good-bye to her and followed Blue out.

"Don't say anything," Blue warned him as they walked down the long driveway, past the eerie glowing jack-o'-lanterns. Logan hadn't noticed it on his way in, but now half the carvings made him think of mythical creatures. Was that one an octopus, or a kraken? That one could be an ordinary ghost . . . or the yeti the Sterlings were planning to imprison and exploit. And that one was definitely a dragon. Its orange eyes seemed to be glowering malevolently at him.

"I'm not saying anything," Logan said. "Jasmin seems . . . kind of okay once you get to know her."

"Yeah," Blue said, kicking the gravel. "She's not really like how she acts at school now. It was always great hanging out with her, before . . . everything with Jonathan. I don't get it, Logan. How do the Sterlings know about the Menagerie?"

"Agent Dantes said some people have stronger resistance to kraken ink, didn't she?" Logan pointed out. "Maybe Ruby didn't give them enough."

"Or maybe she didn't give it to them at all," Blue said grimly.

"Wow," Logan said. "And then lied to everyone that she did? That would be *so* unfair to Zoe."

"Tell me about it," Blue said. "Zoe dosed Jasmin and stopped speaking to her, to protect the Menagerie. It was pretty much the worst thing she ever had to do. And if it was for nothing—if Ruby didn't even dose the other Sterlings—"

"Then we should feed her to a . . . a . . . what's the most dangerous mythical creature?" Logan asked.

"Yeah!" Blue said. "We should feed her to a pyrosalamander!"

The tiny fire-eating lizards weren't quite what Logan had had in mind. He'd been thinking of something larger and toothier.

"You're the one doing my math homework for the next month," Keiko informed Blue as they caught up to her at the bottom of the driveway. "As for you—how's your Spanish?" she added to Logan.

"Keiko, when you hear why we had to leave, you'll understand," Blue said. "You're in danger, too."

She tossed her head. "In danger of being *lame*," she muttered. "Leaving a Jasmin Sterling party before nine. My followers are not going to believe this." She growled at a passing group of trick-or-treaters and a tiny pirate shrieked and hid behind his mom.

Soon they turned up the drive to Zoe's house, and Logan breathed a sigh of relief. The sprawling colonial-style house looked just the same as when they'd left it, although Zoe was no longer staring mournfully out the front window. An enormous wall stretched in either direction, abutting the sides of the building and hiding the Menagerie from view. Everything seemed quiet.

"Oh, look at that," Keiko said snidely. "Still standing. I was expecting *at least* a smoldering pile of rubble, given all the *extreme panic-stricken urgency* and everything."

"How do you guys keep people from asking what's inside those walls?" Logan asked Blue. "The Sterlings must drive by this place every day—but they can't be the only people who've ever been curious about all the land hidden back there."

"It's the thing," Blue said vaguely.

"The thing?" Logan asked.

Blue scrunched up his face. "We have a—well, you know."

Logan blinked at him. "No, I don't. How would I know? What are you talking about?"

Blue waved his hands. "The . . . thing."

"Blue! WHAT thing?"

"The whatchamacallit that makes you not think about it so that—hey, your wig is falling off." Blue didn't seem to notice that he'd shifted topics midsentence.

Logan reached up and pulled off his werewolf wig, rubbing his head. If he understood Blue's evasive weirdness right, it sounded like there was some kind of device that could block anyone from noticing it, and its power worked on the whole—

The front door flew open. A vampire in a long, slinky red dress stood framed in the doorway, flashing her fangs at them.

"HAPPY HALLO—oh, it's you," she said.

"Don't let any real vampires see you dressed like that," Blue said, frowning at her. "Those fangs are just insultingly wrong. And why are your arms all sparkly? Are you a vampire or a pixie?"

"I'm not dressed as a *real* vampire." Zoe's sister Ruby sniffed, rearranging her black wig. "I'm dressed as a *Twilight* vampire."

"Oh, much better," Blue said. "Nothing makes a real vampire more likely to bite you than bringing up those books. There's a safety tip for you," he said to Logan.

"Okay, thanks," Logan said, following him into the house as Ruby sashayed off up the stairs.

A furry head with two enormous, flapping ears poked around the corner of the living room.

"EEEEEHHHH-WEEEEIIIHHHH-NUUUU!!!" The woolly mammoth trumpeted in excitement and bounded into the hall.

"Ew, no, get off!" Keiko shrieked as Captain Fuzzbutt tried to pat her with his trunk. "Don't you dare touch me, you overgrown hairy elephant!" She swatted him away and the mammoth turned happily to Logan, stretching out his trunk. Logan stepped forward and gave it the fist bump the mammoth was looking for.

Zoe appeared behind the Captain. "Why are you guys back so early? Is Jasmin all right?" She narrowed her eyes at Blue.

"They made me leave," Keiko said huffily. "Apparently it's the end of the world. Can't you tell? Now I have to go wash mammoth drool out of my hair, so—"

"Wait, Keiko," Blue said. "You should hear this, too. Zoe, where are your parents?"

"In the kitchen," she said, twisting her hands together anxiously. "What's happened?"

Logan pulled out his phone as they went after Blue into the kitchen. Mrs. Kahn was reading from a cookbook while Zoe's dad shaped a mound of lumpy oatmeal dough into giant dog biscuits. Two of the hellhounds sat below them, slavering rivulets of drool all over their paws. The room smelled like pumpkin bread, and cello music played softly on the stereo in the corner. Logan could see Zoe's older brother, Matthew, doing homework at the large table in the next room.

They all looked so peaceful. Logan wished he didn't have to be the one to tell them that their troubles weren't over after all.